the girl
with
no past

the girl with no past

KATHRYN CROFT

bookouture

Published by Bookouture

An imprint of StoryFire Ltd.
23 Sussex Road, Ickenham, UB10 8PN
United Kingdom

www.bookouture.com

ISBN: 978-1-910751-24-4
eBook ISBN: 978-1-910751-23-7

ACKNOWLEDGMENTS

I am hugely indebted to a number of people for supporting me and helping make my third novel come to life.

First of all I'd like to thank my agent, Madeleine Milburn, and the whole team at the agency, who all work tirelessly to support their authors.

A huge thank you to Keshini Naidoo, my fantastic editor, for believing in me and for offering valuable insights that helped make this book as strong as it could be. A special thank you also to the rest of the Bookouture team: Oliver, Claire and Kim, thank you so much for taking me on and welcoming me to the team. I am extremely excited and proud to be a Bookouture author.

I would also like to thank all the authors I have met over the last couple of years who have encouraged and supported me, and understood the journey, particularly A. J. Waines and Mel Sherratt.

And finally, as always, thank you to my husband and the rest of my family and friends for their continued love and support.

DEDICATION

For Grace and Phillip

PROLOGUE
2003

Everything is silent and for a second I think I must be dead. But then I hear a deafening screech and I don't know who or where it's come from, I only know I haven't made the noise because somehow I am okay. I want to turn my head to check what's left of the wreckage, but I can't move because pain is shooting through my neck, warm blood trickling down my face.

There is a strange smell: burnt rubber mixed with petrol and something far, far worse. The scent of death. I don't need to look around to know that I am the only person breathing in this car.

Panic sets in, crushing my chest, worse than the physical injuries I have sustained. This can't be real.

Cracks spread across the windscreen like a gigantic spider's web, and through the maze of lines I can see lights, still and flashing, blue and yellow and red, and faces peering in, their mouths forming circles, trying to make sense of what's happened. The panicky yells and shouts are muffled to me, as if I'm in a bubble, catching only waves of sound. But I know that whoever is out there, they, like I, will remember this moment for the rest of their lives.

The steering wheel digs into my ribs but I can't move. Or perhaps I don't want to because it's safer in here than out there, having to face whatever is next. I know already what I can expect:

some sympathy because accidents happen, but mostly blame and hatred because I am the driver so I must take the responsibility for this.

Someone manages to haul my door open and strong, uniformed arms lift me out and place me onto what must be a stretcher. It's thin and hard but at least I am flat now. I close my eyes and wonder how it's possible I haven't died.

CHAPTER ONE
2014

Walking home that evening, something felt wrong. It was nothing I could identify, because everything appeared normal. I was just one of many people heading home from work, or heading somewhere at least. It was bitterly cold and I'd left my scarf hanging over my banister that morning, but the chill was nothing out of the ordinary. It was to be expected in November.

The feeling I couldn't shake off could only be about tomorrow. I hadn't forgotten what day it was. Perhaps the foreboding was anxiety manifesting as something else? But even that didn't make sense because I had learnt to deal with it. As I did every year, I refused to think about it until the day arrived, descending on me like a hurricane. I had become skilled at closing that door.

Garratt Lane was busy as always, and I blended into the other pedestrians, a part of the London landscape. This was how I always felt walking home, as if I was nothing more than a puppet in a scene, being moved along by someone else. Perhaps I just felt strange because I was later than usual leaving work, and I wasn't good with change to my routine. I needed order and structure, otherwise everything fell apart.

I was only late because I'd stayed to help Maria; I couldn't leave her by herself to deal with the order of books that had come in, even if my day at the library had begun three hours before hers. Besides, what did I have to go home to?

I smiled, remembering Maria recounting details of a new man she'd met, while we unpacked and tagged the books. Maria had only been working at the library for a few months, but in that time I had got to know probably every detail of her life. She was my polar opposite: open and talkative, while I was reserved and kept as much of my life private as possible. I knew that she was single and often had dates, and liked hearing her stories. This new man's name was Dan, and the whole time Maria talked, raving about the smallest thing he might have said, I allowed myself to get lost in her life. This was how it was with us; she talked and I listened. But every now and again I would catch her staring at me, giving me that look. The one that showed how badly she wanted me to let her into my life.

The library was only a short walk from my road so it didn't take long to get home. My flat was small – no, not small: minuscule – the upstairs floor of a converted house, but it was affordable for London, and at least I had my own front door, even if the neighbours' one was practically joined to mine. I also had my own staircase, making the place feel a bit more spacious.

But my decision to rent it was not made on practicalities like price or location. It was the name of the road that convinced me I had to live there. Allfarthing Road. It made me picture a time – way before I was born – that I could only imagine from what I'd read in books. A time when people greeted each other on the street and knew all the neighbours. I knew I was romanticising and I didn't long for anything like that – it just wouldn't suit how I needed to live – but it was comforting to think a time like that had existed once. That times that came before never truly disappeared.

I climbed the five steps leading up to my door and dug in my bag for my keys. It was a ridiculously tiny cross-body bag, but there wasn't much I needed to haul around with me, so it was only a matter of seconds before I realised my keys weren't in it. My purse, mobile phone, some hand sanitiser, but no keys.

Puzzled, I tried to stay calm and consider the possibilities. I definitely had them that morning because the front door needed to be double locked, and I never forgot to do that. I wouldn't have needed them at the library so couldn't recall noticing them, which could mean two things; I'd dropped them on the walk to work or they'd fallen out of my bag at the library and were at that moment gathering dust somewhere in the building.

The first possibility filled me with panic, and after a quick scout of the steps and concrete garden area, I grabbed my mobile and dialled work. Pressing my phone against my ear to try and drown out the hum of traffic, I could only just make out the ring tone. It seemed to purr in my ear forever until Maria finally picked up, trying to get her words out between heavy rasps of breath.

'Maria, it's Leah.'

She seemed relieved I wasn't a customer after some help, and I gave her time to gather her breath. But with every passing second my panic was rising. I was already late home and now I couldn't even get inside. My whole evening was being disrupted by something I had no control over.

'No problem,' Maria said, once I explained my keys were missing. 'I'll go and have a look. Call you back.' And she hung up, eager to get off the phone and help me. All I could do then was wait, with the icy November air biting my skin, desperate to be in my only slightly warmer flat, shutting the door on another day of existing.

It was too cold to stand still so I paced up and down the steps, ignoring the bemused looks I received from a couple of passersby. Minutes ticked by and nearly half an hour passed before Maria finally called back. I held my breath and waited for her to tell me she couldn't find them.

'I've got them,' she said, jingling them to prove it.

Relief flooded through me. 'Where were they?' I should have thanked her first, but I needed to know where they'd been.

'Um, a customer must have handed them in and Sam put them in the office. I just checked in there in case—'

'Okay.' I tried to make sense of this. I was always so careful so couldn't see how they had fallen out of my bag.

'Anyway, I'm about to leave so I'll bring them to you now. You live off Garratt Lane, don't you? I can be there in ten minutes, just——'

'No! I mean, don't put yourself out. I'll walk back to the library. Meet you there?' I had never invited Maria to my flat and recently she had started to drop hints about coming over, but each time I'd managed to avoid it actually happening.

She fell silent for a moment. 'Right. Fine. But I'll meet you at the coffee shop. I have to lock up now and it's too cold to stand around outside.' And right then I made a silent promise to myself to make it up to her.

Thanking her, I wrapped my thick wool coat tighter around me and began to trace my steps back towards work. I walked fast, even though I knew Maria would take a while doing all the checks before she closed up. I just wanted my keys back in my hands. I didn't expect her, or anyone else, to understand it but any disruption to my routine left me vulnerable. I needed order. Everything to be exactly as it should be, no deviations. And tonight could so easily have become one. As it was, I was still thrown off my routine; I should have been inside by now, cooking dinner before logging on to the website and living my vicarious life once more.

When I reached the coffee shop, I peered through the window to see if Maria was there but there was no sign of her. The after-work crowd had claimed every seat, chatting away to each other, in no rush to be at home. Unlike me. I felt a pang of envy, but I knew I could never be like them.

Although I was thirsty, I decided against going inside. As much as I enjoyed her company, if Maria and I sat down together the evening would be gone and I needed to get online. So continuing to brave the cold, fiercer now than it had been just moments ago, I faced towards the library, anxious to spot her the minute she became visible so I could grab my keys and get home.

It was twenty minutes before I saw her, walking as if she was taking a stroll on a beach, in no rush to get my keys back to me. 'Oh, you're out here,' she said, when she reached me. 'I thought we could get a coffee.'

'I'm really sorry, but I need to get home. So tired. But we could go for one next week?' I considered faking a yawn but didn't think I'd be able to pull it off.

Her smile disappeared. 'Okay. But next time, right?' With a gloved hand, she pulled my keys from her pocket and handed them to me. 'Be more careful next time,' she said.

As I walked home, I wondered how much of her comment was made in jest.

It always felt comforting to close the front door and stand for a minute in my hallway; like stepping into a bubble, knowing the world had been shut out. That I was safe. This was my space and I rarely had visitors. It was easier that way.

Of course there were rare occasions when I invited Mum over, but those times were always fraught with tension. Her complaints of London being too dreadful a place for words, and her insistence that I'd be more comfortable at home, were things I had to spend weeks psyching myself up for. She could never concede that my small flat in Wandsworth *was* my home now. There was no other.

A pile of letters sat on the threadbare doormat and scooping them up, I rushed up the creaky stairs, eager to get my evening back on track. Normally I opened my mail before I did anything else, but my growling stomach warned me to fill it up with food, and quickly. So for the first time, I left the envelopes on the kitchen worktop. No letter I ever got was so important that it couldn't wait until later.

Even though I was existing rather than living, I filled every moment of time with something. Idle time was a toxin for me; it meant my thoughts could get the better of me and I'd spent too long letting that happen. Keeping them at bay was my goal now.

Once a week I volunteered at the care home on the next road, reading to the residents after dinner and keeping them company. If I could have afforded to I would have done it seven days a week. Just seeing their faces light up when I walked in was enough to lift me from my fog, to show me that I wasn't a bad person.

But there were still long hours I needed to fill and it was thanks to Maria that I'd discovered Two Become One a few months earlier. Never shy about her search to find a man who would stick around longer than a week, she openly shared the fact that she had found a dating website. On it, the men were all professionals and people broke the ice by talking in chat rooms before deciding whether to meet up.

Hearing Maria talk about it, the idea of meeting someone online filled me with horror. It was like shopping for a partner. How could you know they were who they said they were? How could you be sure what they wanted? The idea was abhorrent to me. I wasn't being judgemental, it was just the idea of meeting any man, anywhere, filled me with anxiety.

But curiosity – or perhaps it was loneliness? – got the better of me one night and I checked out the website, browsing through it until I had worked out what it was all about. I felt safe doing it: I was alone in my flat and nobody could see me, no one could reach me.

Witnessing people's conversations, I envied these people for their carefree attitudes, and was slowly drawn in, within weeks setting up an account, using Mum's maiden name, Harling, and posting a picture that I was convinced nobody from my past would recognise me from. In it, my hair, now lighter than it ever had been, covered a lot of my face and I was turned to the side. It was the best I could do if I wanted to talk to people on the site. But that was all I would allow myself to do. If I couldn't have my own life then at least I could live in a fantasy one.

The incident with my keys almost forgotten, I sat on the sofa, balancing my laptop on my knee, a cup of tea on the coffee table. Although it was easier to use the computer at my tiny kitchen table, I was too exhausted to sit on a hard wooden chair.

I entered a chat room and read the lines of conversation, staying silent. But, as was usual, my presence was announced in bold blue letters and a string of welcomes followed. As tempted as I was to respond, just this once, I ignored them and waited for the conversation to start up again. There were seventeen people in the room and they were asking each other what jobs they did and where they lived. I watched as two of them, a woman called Melissa and a man called Rich, disappeared to their own private chat room. There it was. So easy for other people.

There were more visitors than usual that night; Friday was a day that highlighted loneliness more than any other, a day people's single status stared them in the face. But I had taught myself immunity to that feeling. It was all a matter of perspective, and what was being alone when there was so much worse out there? That didn't mean I enjoyed it, though. I would have loved to approach someone, respond to the messages I was constantly sent, be normal. I had intended to start up conversations but so far my hands froze whenever I went to reply to a message.

Cradling my mug to warm my hands, I browsed through profile pictures, making up a story about who I believed each man to be. Of course, I was never right when I compared my ideas to the details they provided, but it helped pass the time.

A ping erupted from the laptop and I didn't flinch. I was used to being sent private messages and that's what I knew the sound was. But when the envelope flashed in the corner of the screen, I saw it was from a moderator. I knew they lingered around, making sure chat rooms were safe, but I had never been contacted by one. Perhaps they would tell me that I was no longer welcome on the site, that I wasn't playing the game, getting involved, so they could do without my business. Taking a deep breath, I clicked the envelope.

Moderator34: Hey, u ok?

Confused, I exhaled and reread the message. I wasn't getting kicked off. He or she was only asking if I was okay. But why? I had no idea if this was normal. Without thinking, my fingers began tapping the keyboard.

LeahH: I'm okay. Thanks for asking. How are you?

It was all I could think of to say.

Moderator34: Just worried about you!

I've noticed you on here before but you don't seem to want to talk to anyone??

So this was it. I *was* getting kicked off. Quickly, I tried to think of an excuse for my lack of communication.

LeahH: Sorry. Bit shy.

The response came back immediately.

Moderator34: Believe me, you have no reason 2 b shy.

Your photo is beautiful.

I am male by the way, in case you were wondering...

LeahH: Are you allowed to say things like that?

Moderator34: Probably not but figured you were worth the risk

I should have stopped there. This had already gone too far. I wanted to type back that he was wrong, that I was one person who was not worth any kind of risk, but I didn't. Instead I continued our conversation, allowing myself to bask in a few minutes of feeling normal, firing questions at him, without having any idea why I was so interested. I didn't even know what he looked like.

He told me his name was Julian, he was thirty-six and lived in Bethnal Green. Begging me not to judge him by his job, he revealed that he was a civil servant and worked in Whitehall.

When he turned the questions on me, I began to get nervous. I looked around my flat, wondering just how much I wanted to share with this stranger. My home was crammed from floor to ceiling with books, leaving little room for furniture. I made do with just a sofa and coffee table just so I could buy more books and not worry about where to put them. I could see the whole flat from the sofa because the kitchen and lounge were open plan. I always left the bedroom and bathroom doors ajar. It wasn't a conscious decision, just something I always did.

I wondered what Julian would think of it here. Would he know straight away that I lived vicariously through the characters in the stories I read? Or the people in the chat rooms?

Ignoring my reservations, I continued talking to Julian and he began to intrigue me. His sense of humour jumped off the screen, his words creating a vivid picture of him. He seemed different to anyone I'd come across on the site so far, more natural, as if he wasn't trying to do anything or be anyone other than himself. He was funny and charming without being creepy or desperate, and it made something in me ache. With sadness or longing, or a mixture of both.

I had to snap out of it. Nothing like this had happened to me in all the time I had browsed through profiles and lurked in chat rooms on Two Become One, and I didn't like how I was starting to feel. Making an excuse that I had to go, I closed the website, not bothering to log off, and took my mug to the kitchen.

Although it had left me feeling empty, the encounter with Julian had distracted me from thinking about tomorrow. I knew nothing would happen other than my head swimming with memories, but every year was still as painful as those that had preceded it. As if no time had passed.

After making myself another cup of tea – a small comfort given the day I'd had – I took it over to the window, kneeling down so I could look out at Allfarthing Road. This was another way I spent my evenings when I wasn't at the care home: watching life pass by outside my window. With a deep sigh, I told myself, as I did every night, that this was how it had to be. The difference was that now a tiny part of me wanted to fight against my sentence. I wanted to feel alive.

It was only when I was washing up before bed that I remembered I hadn't opened my post. The pile remained on the kitchen worktop, and grabbing it, I sat down at the table. There were only three letters, and I binned the first one without opening it. I had no interest in special offers from a catalogue I'd never ordered from, or even heard of. I also ignored the letter I recognised immediately as a council tax bill; my payments were made by direct debit so I had nothing to worry about there.

It was the final envelope that puzzled me. It was pastel yellow and felt like a card. Strange. The only cards I ever received were from Mum on my birthday and at Christmas, but my birthday was months ago and it was too early for Mum's Christmas card. And yellow wasn't a Christmassy colour, was it? Red perhaps, green even, but not yellow.

The foreboding I'd felt walking home returned and I immediately knew I was holding something I wouldn't want to see. But my hand still found the edge of the flap and tore it open. I slid out the card and stared at the glittery blue writing.

Happy Anniversary!

The picture of a champagne bottle with its cork popped, colourful ribbons bursting out of it, silently mocked me. Bile rose to my throat but I still opened the card. Inside, my name was written in thick black marker pen. Leah. There were no other words, only my first name. In writing that looked childish, every letter a different size.

I slipped it back in its envelope and flung it on the table, pushing it away with the heel of my palm, as if it could physically hurt me if I touched it more firmly. It balanced precariously on the edge of the table but didn't fall to the floor. My flat seemed to grow even smaller, as if attempting to crush me, and I had to fight for breath.

My past was catching up with me.

CHAPTER TWO
1995

I turn away from Mum and head towards the huge glass doors of the main block. This is where the letter said to go when I arrived, so I take a deep breath and force myself to move forward. This doesn't feel like a school; it's a hundred times bigger than my old one and every subject has its own building. How will I ever be able to tell the maths block from the English one when they all look the same? Not for the first time, I wish I wasn't old enough to start secondary school. There is no way I'm ready for this.

It doesn't help when, half an hour later, I am just one in a sea of students seated in the assembly hall, listening to the head teacher, Mr Curtis, drone on about behaviour and consequences. I can't take in a word he says because I'm scared stiff, surrounded by strangers who all seem to know each other.

I loathe Mum and Dad for making us move here. I was happy in Derby so why did everything have to change? Don't they care that I will have no friends now? I found it hard enough to talk to people back home so what chance do I have here? Slipping further down into my chair, as if I can make myself invisible, I know for sure I have arrived in hell.

I'm so lost in my thoughts, I don't realise Mr Curtis is calling out a list of names and telling us which teacher to follow to our form room. Has my name already been called? I think I might pass out. Everyone else seems to know what they're doing, why is it only me who doesn't? But then I hear it. Leah Mills. What a relief. I look around and there is a teacher – a woman with short, blonde bobbed hair – lifting her hand slightly to signal her form group. She looks kind enough, but it's not as if I have any choice but to go with her. Apparently, this is the teacher I'll be stuck with for the rest of my time here, unless the woman leaves or dies or something.

I take so long to squeeze through the crammed rows of chairs that, by the time I make it to the aisle, the teacher is strutting off, students tailing her like rats following the Pied Piper. I try to catch them up but even when we reach the classroom I still lag behind. Is this what secondary school is going to be like? A constant struggle to keep up? I hate it already.

Things don't get any better once I'm inside the classroom. The blonde teacher has assigned seats to everyone and I am the only one sitting alone. I am also right at the back, in the corner against a wall, as if I am unimportant and it doesn't matter to anyone whether I'm here or not. I stare at the empty space beside me, it seems to be mocking me and it is all I can do to stop a massive flood of tears from erupting and showing me up even more.

Murmurs die down and everyone turns to the teacher, waiting for her to speak. It seems to take forever, but when she eventually opens her mouth, her voice is soft and unsure. Not at all what I've been expecting. All the teachers in my primary school sounded as if they were talking through loudspeakers, deafening us if we were unlucky enough to sit near them. Perhaps this one is new? She looks fairly young, younger than Mum anyway, so this could be her first time teaching. I should feel sorry for her because if she *is* new then we are in the same position, aren't we? And just because she's an adult, it doesn't mean she isn't scared. But she has stuck me at the back and why did it have to be me out of everyone here? There are at least thirty of us, but Mrs

Whoever-She-Is has picked me to sit alone. I don't think I can forgive her for that.

'Um, I'm Miss Hollis,' she manages to say, and I only realise what she's said because she writes it on the whiteboard too. The next thing I know, everyone is being told to pair up and tell their partners three interesting facts about themselves. Immediately the room bursts into life and everyone chatters away as if they've known each other forever, while I sit by myself, partner-less.

I can't even see Miss Hollis any more; perhaps she's decided she's had enough and made a run for it. I wish I could do that. But no, there she is in the corner, watching the class anxiously from behind her computer. Can't she see I don't have a partner?

Just when I decide I'll have to tell myself three interesting things about myself, a short, plumpish girl turns to me from the desk in front. 'I'll work with you,' she says, smiling shyly. 'Those three can work together.' She motions to the three other students in her row, and for the first time I notice they are all boys. It makes me feel slightly better because at least I'm not the only one sitting in an uncomfortable place.

I introduce myself and watch as the girl screeches her chair around so we are facing each other. She's got nice eyes, huge, dark and shiny, and a small upturned nose like a ski-slope.

'I'm Imogen,' she says. 'And the only interesting fact I can think of is that I've only been here one hour and I already hate this place.'

And for the first time that day – maybe that month – I smile and feel my spirits lift. This girl will be my friend. I know it.

CHAPTER THREE
2014

I had barely slept, but that was only to be expected when the day looming ahead of me was the anniversary. I knew it did no good to dwell on events that couldn't be undone, and usually I didn't because I'd cocooned myself in my new life. Whenever anything threatened to remind me, I pushed it away with ferocity. But this day was always different. It forced me to remember. It *helped* me to remember.

But now I'd opened that envelope, and the floodgates to something I couldn't work out, everything had changed. The card had tainted the day, coating it with something toxic, and giving it a different feel to every other twelfth of November. It wasn't my day any more, to quietly, furtively, remember what had happened, because now someone else has made it theirs too.

Of course there were others for whom time would stand still on this day, but nobody had crossed my path with their pain. Until now.

I wasn't even convinced this was about pain or grief. The card made that much clear. I didn't want to consider what it did mean, though, so before I went to bed I'd stuffed it in my underwear drawer, covering it up so I wouldn't see it every morning. Throwing it out would have made more sense, but I couldn't do that. Not until I understood what it meant.

Shutting things out was something I'd been forced to learn, so that's what I did. I got up when the alarm beeped, showered, and ate muesli with too many raisins in it for breakfast, trying to pretend the day would be just like it had the previous years.

It was easy to keep up the charade at work. When I arrived the computer system had gone down, which meant chaos, everybody running around in a panic, and it fell to me to try and investigate the problem. I seemed to be the only member of staff with anywhere near decent IT skills. I knew before I removed my coat that I wouldn't be able to help – I was no computer genius – but I gave it a try. At least it helped me erase the memory of what lurked in my drawer at home.

Maria kept me distracted with her chatter, thankfully not mentioning my reluctance to have a coffee with her the day before. I opened my mouth several times to try and explain, try and make her understand, but each time the words died before they could form. So instead I went out of my way to help make her day easier, rushing my own tasks so I could help her with hers.

Listening to her speak of how she now didn't think things would work with Dan, I marvelled at how resilient she was. She was thirty-nine, but never let the constant rejections and disasters put her off finding someone. Her soul mate, she called it. I had no clue how she bounced back each time, but admired her for being able to. 'Do you really believe there's one person out there who is destined only for you?' I asked her once, watching her eyes light up at the thought of it.

'Of course, why? Don't you?' She seemed incredulous that I had no such notion.

'I think we just make do with someone we find and make it work,' I said, but the truth was I had no idea. If Maria was right then was Adam my soul mate? I couldn't imagine this to be true, but where did it leave me if it was?

Despite my love of books, sometimes I thought it strange that I'd chosen to work in a library when I constantly craved solitude. There was a buzz there, although a quiet one, a constant murmur of activity and hundreds of people passed through the doors each week. But despite there being some regular visitors, most of the faces were unfamiliar and I liked that. It made me feel removed from them, even though I answered their queries and helped them with whatever they needed. They came and went and didn't affect me in any way.

In the short time I had known her, I had grown fond of Maria. Just hearing her voice lifted my spirits, even though we lived in different worlds, and she never pried into my life. I knew she had questions she wanted to ask me but she never did. So I overlooked her furtive glances when she thought I wasn't looking. She was only trying to work me out.

Maria tapped me on the shoulder and I swivelled round to face her. 'That guy's really fit,' she said, pointing towards the IT technician we'd had to call in when I'd had no luck identifying the problem.

I studied his face and could see what she meant; his unblemished skin and wide smile were attractive. It made me wonder if Julian from the website looked anything like him. But what did it matter if he did? I could never let someone into my life, no matter how lonely I might get or how good being held would feel.

Shrugging at Maria, I watched as a frown spread across her forehead. She probably wondered how I could be so immune to the man's good looks when she was blushing.

For the next few hours, Maria and I both went about our work, but I was becoming distracted, both anxious and looking forward to going home. The anniversary night loomed ahead of me, but I didn't dread it. Not any more. It was something I needed to do. But another motivation for wanting time to pass quickly had crept in. As soon as I'd finished what I had to do, I would log on to Two Become One and see if Julian was around.

Later that evening, I made cheese on toast, slicing up a huge tomato and laying the pieces over it. It wasn't exactly a decent meal, but I never ate much on this day.

When I'd finished my food, I got everything ready and sat cross-legged on the floor, in front of the low coffee table. The lights were off but I'd opened the curtains, bathing the room in light from the lamppost across the road.

Even though something felt different – something *was* different – I carried on and lit each candle. To anyone who'd been able to glimpse me through the window it must have looked like a strange type of séance, but it was nothing like that. It was reflection.

I stayed silent and still, my eyes closed so I could live through it again, until experience told me the wax on the candles would have melted down.

As I cleared up, putting the candleholders back in the kitchen drawer, it was harder to ignore that things had changed this time and were out of my control. And once I'd acknowledged this, I was even more certain about going online tonight. Normally I wouldn't have considered doing this afterwards – I usually just read a book until I fell asleep on the sofa – but my anxiety was rising and I needed a distraction.

Julian.

He was a stranger to me, and I had no idea what he looked like, but he hadn't been far from my thoughts all day. It was puzzling because I'd trained myself to keep a distance from everyone, especially men, so I wasn't prepared to have those feelings.

I wasn't even certain what the feelings were. Perhaps curiosity? It had been such a long time since I'd even held someone's hand, so wasn't it natural that I'd miss human contact?

I grabbed my laptop from the kitchen table and took it to the sofa, immediately logging on to the website. But there was no guarantee that he was online this evening, so what was I supposed to do? I decided to hang around and wait, visit some chat rooms and hope that if he was on he would notice me. It was then I noticed I had a new message. Assuming it was from someone I had no interest in talking to, I clicked on it with no enthusiasm. But then I saw it was from Julian, and he'd sent it only two minutes ago. His message was short, but before I'd even read the words I noticed the picture he'd attached.

It was tiny so I clicked on it, expanding it to fill my screen. And there was Julian, smiling a white, toothy smile and throwing his head back as if he'd been captured mid-laugh. I stared at it for a moment, taking in all his features as well as the background. It looked like he was in a field somewhere, sitting at a picnic table.

He wasn't what Maria would call fit, but there was something I immediately liked about him that I couldn't explain. Maybe it was the fact that I had already seen glimpses of his personality from our conversation. It was impossible to know whether I'd find him attractive if I'd seen his picture anywhere else.

Most of all I liked the fact that he was nothing like Adam. His hair was light, his eyes blue while Adam had been dark with brown, almost black, eyes. This was good.

I quickly read his words, unable to stop myself smiling or the excitement swelling in my stomach.

Hey, LeahH, how's it going? You disappeared on me the other night!

This is me, by the way, just so you know I'm not a 3-headed freak!

With Julian's photo staring at me from the laptop, within minutes all my caution had evaporated and I knew I had to talk to him again.

Ignoring the issue of me rushing offline the other night, I kept my message simple and casual: *Hello again.* Like dipping only my toes into the water so I could quickly draw them out again if anything went wrong. After all, I had no idea what Julian wanted from me.

Pressing send, I held my breath for what seemed like minutes. I waited to hear the ping alerting me there was a message in my inbox, but it didn't come; the only sounds to be heard were the rain pelting down outside and a distant hum of traffic.

After five minutes and still no ping, my disappointment began to swamp me. Julian must still be online so why didn't he reply? He was the one who had found me.

To distract myself, I left the laptop on the coffee table and made a cup of black coffee. I needed to give this up, I couldn't let a man become my focus, especially one I barely knew. I should turn the laptop off and go to bed with my book, forget the whole thing. I was reading *Rebecca* for the hundredth time but still loved it as if I hadn't read a word before. That would take my mind off everything.

Why did I think I could do something different like reaching out to someone, even in such a small way? My life couldn't change.

But when I finished my drink and picked up the laptop to log off, a small blue envelope flashed at the top corner of the screen. Julian. I clicked on it, almost spilling the mug of coffee I was still holding because my chest felt as if it would fold in on itself.

Hello. Hope I haven't scared you with my photo!

When I recovered enough to compose myself, I realised I had no idea what to reply. Was he flirting with me? This was all new to me, it had been years since I'd spoken to a man in this way – not since Adam – but I knew I had to keep talking to him. But he was a moderator so what did that mean he was doing? Perhaps he introduced himself to a lot of the women on here and he was just passing the time. After thinking about this for a moment, I realised I didn't care because I was doing exactly the same thing. I could never have a relationship with him so what I said or did wouldn't matter. Without further thought, I began typing, letting my fingers take control. I needed this. I needed to be someone else, even if only for this night.

No… Thanks for sending it. Nice to put a face to a name. If that is your real name. And face!

It was weak. A child could have managed something more effective, but I didn't have time to come up with anything better. I couldn't take the chance that Julian would get bored waiting and log off. His reply came quickly and he invited me to a private chat room instead of sending messages back and forth.

Moderator34: I can assure you that is my face. If it was fake do you really think I'd choose someone who looked like that?!

LeahH: Why not? It's a nice photo…

Moderator34: glad to hear that, I'm wiping sweat from my brow as we speak

LeahH: Shouldn't you be working? Checking chat rooms for inappropriate behaviour or something?

Moderator34: just needed to know you'll still talk to me

LeahH: Anytime…

Moderator34: well nice 2 speak again, LeahH, better get back to it now but c u around I hope

LeahH: See you...

Even as I stared at our trail of messages, repeatedly reading each line, I found it hard to believe I had spoken to Julian again, even if only with the written word. Granted, we hadn't said much this time, but it was something. And now I knew what he looked like, I was even more excited about what I was doing. Despite everything, it felt right.

Later, I deviated from my ritual for the second time that evening. I had to; I didn't want to think about the card. Although I'd already showered that morning, I ran an extra hot bath, filling it with Radox so that the bubbles almost overflowed. It seemed callous, given what day it was, but I needed to erase it from my mind. I wanted to try and relax, to forget the card and forget the day, because for the first year since it had happened, I felt the need to escape.

I climbed into the bath, sinking down so that the water immersed every inch of my body and only my face was uncovered. Lots of books I had read made reference to water being able to cleanse away a person's sins, but as I lay there watching the bubbles gently fizzle out, I knew there was no way I could be absolved of mine. And my life was my penance.

It was only on that day I ever let myself cry. Ducking my head under the water, I kept it there for as long as I could manage to breathe; I didn't want to feel the tears on my face. At least that way they merged into the water, leaving no trace behind.

Something woke me, hours before my alarm was due to go off. Living in London, I had become accustomed to noise, so much so that I barely noticed it, but this sound was all wrong, not part of the nightly soundtrack I was familiar with. But I'd been asleep so couldn't identify it. I closed my eyes again and tried to drift off, reluctant to get up and check things out when it had already taken me three hours to fall asleep.

I heard nothing more, but the fact that I'd been woken by something niggled away at me. I had to investigate. There would be no hope of sleep if I didn't.

As it was so small, it didn't take long to search the flat. Everything was as it should be. But then, remembering the card, I decided to check the downstairs hall. There hadn't been any mail for me when I'd got home from work, but something compelled me down the stairs.

I didn't notice it at first – the only light in the flat came from the bedroom – but as I got closer I clearly saw the white envelope, standing out against the dark grey doormat like a sign post leading me towards it, my name emblazoned across it in the same writing as the card, with the same black marker pen.

It's hard to say what I felt at that moment. Perhaps I'd been expecting the card to only be the beginning of something. But in that case I should have taken it as a warning to ignore the new envelope. If I didn't open it, it couldn't hurt me. I could take it upstairs, rip it to pieces and dump it in the recycling bin so that I would never know what was in it.

That's what I should have done. Instead, I grabbed the envelope, ripping it open as if it was a lottery cheque. I pulled out a photograph. A road at nighttime. A road I knew well. I didn't need to see the small sign at the bottom of the photo confirming it was High Elms Lane.

I sat on the stairs, my eyes fixed on the photograph, even though I didn't want to see it. The only thought in my head was a mixture of fear and confusion that it had taken so long.

But rather than let fear paralyse me, I raced back upstairs to the bedroom and pulled the card from my underwear drawer.

Taking it to the kitchen, I dug out the lighter I had used only a few hours ago to light the candles. Then, holding both items above the sink, I lit the corners of each, and watched them blacken and crumble.

Only when I had removed all the charred pieces from the sink did I climb back into bed and pull the duvet over my head, telling myself nothing had happened. That it had just been another ordinary anniversary.

CHAPTER FOUR
2014

On Monday I made my way to Fulham. I had an appointment with Dr Redfield and probably would have rescheduled, as I usually did, had it not been for the card and photo. I may have destroyed the evidence, tried to tell myself nothing had happened, but erasing the memory was impossible.

As I walked along Fulham Palace Road, I tried to remember the last time I'd kept an appointment with Dr Redfield. I had a vague memory of wearing a loose top because the shoulder kept falling down, and I was conscious of constantly hiking it back up, so it must have been during the summer. And now the end of the year was approaching. Would she see right through me? Would she know I was only going now because she was the only person I could mention what had been happening to? But I didn't suppose it mattered. She was not a friend whose feelings I had to worry about; she was paid to listen.

It always astonished me that Dr Redfield worked from home, letting people into her private family house. It was a beautiful three-storey terrace house on Rigault Road, and if I'd owned it, I wouldn't have let people like me anywhere near it. She worked out of a downstairs room that had been converted into an office, but other rooms were visible from the front door, so what was to stop someone strolling around, prying into her life?

I hated to think how much Mum was forking out for my sessions. I'd been having them on and off for over ten years and I knew she was dipping into the inheritance Dad had left her. Many times I'd tried to persuade her I was fine without Dr Redfield, but she wouldn't listen. My sessions were only monthly – or meant to be at least – but it still added up, so I worried how she was managing. But Mum would never discuss it. To her, financial affairs were not something to burden your children with. Even if that child was now an adult, and responsible for everything bad that had happened in your life.

Dr Redfield was already standing at the door, watching me, when I walked up the path. As always, she was dressed immaculately, this time in a pencil skirt, cardigan and pretty black and white scarf tied in a knot around her neck. I could never tell her exact age, but she was probably fifty-something yet better dressed than I was. My clothes weren't dowdy, just nondescript. Jeans, slightly fitted t-shirts or jumpers, boots or trainers. Nothing that would make me stand out, but nothing that would point me out as a slob either. It was all about blending in.

'Don't worry, I haven't been standing here long, I just saw you from the window,' Dr Redfield said, smiling and beckoning me inside. 'I'm glad you're here, Leah, it's been a long time, hasn't it?'

I looked at my watch and it was only five to ten. But Dr Redfield wouldn't mind about giving me an extra five minutes; she was kind and considerate, which only made me feel worse for cancelling so many appointments. Following her into the office, I sat down on one of the black leather armchairs while she set about making me a cup of tea. Despite the infrequency of my visits, she always remembered I liked to have tea during our sessions.

'So how have you been?' She sat on the other chair and took a sip of whatever she had made for herself.

I wondered if she made her patients drinks to make us feel more like we were just having a cosy chat rather than a counselling session. But whatever the case, it worked. I told her I'd been fine but she scrunched up her eyes and frowned.

'Have you been going out at all? Meeting people?' By people she meant men. She considered it an issue that I hadn't let anyone near me for so long, but it should have counted for something that I was okay with that. That it was my choice. Until Julian. But I wasn't going to mention him, or the fact that I'd been scouring the website for weeks, because nothing had happened. And there was no way it ever could.

'No, I didn't mean that kind of fine. Just, well, I suppose I meant fine for me.'

Dr Redfield nodded, waiting for me to continue. Both her hands cradled her mug and she crossed her legs, pointing them towards me. No doubt she was an expert in body language, every position she took up deliberate, a means to an end. But I didn't mind. I was just grateful she didn't make notes. She might do afterwards, of course; how else would she remember everything about all her patients? But she at least had the courtesy to wait until the session was over.

When I didn't speak she continued her questioning. 'How's work going?'

'It's fine. I can cope with it. It doesn't cause me any problems, at least.'

She nodded again. 'You're still at the library? That must be enjoyable for someone who loves books as much as you.'

Again I was impressed with her memory, and wondered if someone could learn to retain more information. Although that wouldn't help me; I needed less information cluttering my head.

'It gives me a quiet life,' I said, shifting in my chair. I began to grow uncomfortable with her line of questioning. She knew all this about me already. She knew my job at the library was the only one I'd ever had. That since I'd given up on university, there was nothing else for me. It was as if it was our first session and we were starting from scratch.

'And the care home? Do you still volunteer there?'

I nodded. 'As much as I can. I love being there, keeping the residents company.'

Dr Redfield smiled. We had talked about my voluntary work before and she had told me how pleased she was that I did it, how selfless it was. I'd tried to explain that I got just as much out of it as the residents but she told me not to be hard on myself. That I was doing a good thing. I'd wanted to ask her if she thought it made up for anything but I'd kept quiet, fearing her answer.

After an eternity of similar questions, which I went along with because I liked her a lot, I owed her, Dr Redfield threw something out that I wasn't, but should have been, expecting. 'Can I ask what you did yesterday? After work?'

I stared at her but she held my gaze, her eyes widening, showing me we both knew exactly what she meant. I hesitated at first, but why had I gone there if not to reach out to her and get some advice? She didn't usually tell me what to do, preferring that I made my own decisions, but she could at least guide me. So I told her about the card and photo, and she listened, storing it away in the filing cabinet inside her head, to be referred to again next session.

'Well, I suppose it could have been instigated by the date. Maybe that will be the end of it.' She drummed her fingers on her mug. 'However, if it continues I would have to think that this is something a bit more serious than someone just trying to upset you.'

I thought about this for a moment. I hadn't wanted to consider that this might continue. At least not beyond the twelfth.

The post had already arrived when I'd left that morning and there had been nothing further, so it was easy to convince myself it was over. But after Dr Redfield's suggestion I was far from sure.

'Well, what do you think I should do?'

She paused, biting her lip before answering. 'I think it's too early to go to the police because there's nothing obviously threatening in either thing.' She frowned. 'At least not to anyone else.' She didn't have to tell me this because there was no way I would go to the police, even if I had been directly threatened. No way in hell.

It was making me anxious talking about the subject so I tried to dismiss it. 'I'll just see what happens,' I told her. 'There's no point getting carried away, is there?'

I could tell she was disappointed, but Dr Redfield was good at taking a hint, and quickly moved the conversation on to Mum. They had met a few times through mutual friends and, as far as I knew, got on well, even though Dr Redfield had to keep the relationship professional. But even if they had become friends, I trusted her. I might not have always been eager to attend my appointments, but I knew she would never let me down. Despite what she knew about me.

'Do you visit her often?' she asked, placing her mug on the desk. I was still holding mine, even though I'd finished the last drop some time ago.

'As much as I can,' I said, but then reconsidered. 'Not enough, though.' The truth was, I hadn't seen Mum for over two months, and she only lived in Watford, less than an hour away. My visits were usually fortnightly but lately I had been putting them off, with no idea of why.

'I see,' Dr Redfield said, and for the first time that day I saw judgement flicker across her face. She understood everything I had done, but couldn't forgive me neglecting my mother. Of course she would never say this, but she didn't have to.

'I'll go again soon, though,' I said quickly. And I was surprised to find that I meant it. I suddenly missed Mum, despite things being strained between us.

Then it was Dr Redfield's turn to shock me. 'Have you ever spoken to your mother about what happened?'

I was not prepared for this question. She didn't usually broach this topic so abruptly, normally coaxing me into bringing it up myself. This was all wrong. I shifted in my chair to give myself time to get my thoughts in order. 'No. But then I think she finds it difficult to talk about. And I don't want to push her.'

'But she does love you, Leah. So maybe you should give her the chance to talk about everything.'

'How do I even begin to talk about ruining her life?' This was no exaggeration, not me being difficult or petulant. I had brought chaos and disorder to a world Mum always kept neat and tidy, as if she was the housekeeper of more than just our home.

Dr Redfield tried to assure me this wasn't the case, but not even she could convince me I was wrong. I glanced at my watch. We had ten minutes left. Ten minutes in which she'd want me to talk about something it hurt me to revisit. 'Is it possible to live with guilt?' I asked her, finally putting my mug down and clutching the strap of my bag instead. 'Even if every day it threatens to suffocate me?'

Her eyes widened. Me bringing this up would be a strong signal we were making progress. 'I think it's an unhealthy emotion to cling to. But inevitable given your circumstances.' My circumstances. Is that what she'd labelled this? Is that how I was supposed to think of it? 'Don't be hard on yourself, Leah. Make a life for yourself and live it. A full life. That's all you can do. You can't erase the past but you can make sure your future isn't dictated by it. Punishing yourself won't change anything. And you've done that long enough.'

I wanted to tell her that I was happy with how I lived. My actions didn't affect or hurt anyone around me, and I was free in a way she could never understand. But I was beginning to doubt this myself. I nodded, assuring her I would start by visiting Mum. It was a small offering, but seemed to appease her.

When our time was up, I shook Dr Redfield's hand, promising to keep my appointment next month. I wanted to. I didn't want to let her down, but something told me it would be a while before I was back there.

Once I was outside, I stood for a moment on the pavement, breathing deeply, trying to shake off the session. I always did this, it was just another ritual I couldn't explain but needed to do before I could head home. But this time, walking away I didn't feel clear. I decided to head across the bridge to East Putney station to give me time to shake off the conversation Dr Redfield and I had just had; it had left a bitter taste in my mouth.

Stopping on Putney Bridge, I leaned against the railing, watching the boats glide past on the Thames. If such a place existed, then this was my safe place. When I had first moved to London, it had taken me a long time to adjust, but coming here always comforted me. It felt like being in the middle of everywhere, surrounded by hundreds of people, but still somehow invisible.

Droplets of rain began to fall as I stood there so I didn't stay for long. I only had the morning off work, and needed to get some food before I started. I'd told Sam I had a doctor's appointment, which was true, she just didn't need to know what kind of doctor it was with. Walking off, I wished getting drenched with rain was all I had to worry about.

I passed many people as I walked, but the only ones I noticed were those clutching each other's hands, or wandering along with arms wrapped around each other, oblivious to the rain. I tried to imagine being part of a pair, attached so firmly to someone that their life was entwined with mine, but I struggled to picture it. There would always be a shadow over me, and it could only be made worse by someone being part of my life.

Yet somehow when I thought of Julian, I couldn't, or didn't want to, address any of that. Going with the flow, people called it. That's what I would do. It didn't matter if nothing came of it, I would just enjoy talking to him. Even if there was a cyber wall, as well as many others, between us.

Thinking of Julian – as strange as it seemed considering I barely knew him – helped me put the morning with Dr Redfield behind me, and by the time I stepped off the train at Wandsworth Town, I felt better.

I still had half an hour until I was due at work, so I stopped at the café by the library and ordered a ham and cheese ciabatta and a hot chocolate to warm me up. It wasn't too busy that morning so I didn't feel the need to flee. I pulled out *Rebecca* and read in peace until my phone beeped, alerting me that it was time to get to work. I always had to set the alarm if I read before work, otherwise I'd find hours had passed without me once glancing up.

I might have loved my job but all afternoon I was once again impatient to get home, to see if Julian was around. Somehow I knew it wouldn't be difficult to talk to him again, that I'd find things to say, that he'd make me feel comfortable. I don't know what made me so certain of this but it felt as if I knew him already.

It was nearly half past nine by the time I'd finished visiting the care home and the minute I was through my door I wasted no time logging on to the website. Once again, my stomach growled in protest at my neglect, but I ignored it and didn't even get myself a drink, although my throat was parched. Deviating from my routine was starting to become a habit. But I soon discovered there was no message from Julian, and no alert inviting me to a private chat. Disappointed, I shut my laptop and decided to distract myself by making some food. I couldn't help thinking life had been simpler before Julian. Before there was anything to be disappointed about.

I enjoyed the ritual of cooking, the carefully planned steps that, if followed precisely, meant nothing would go wrong, nothing should change course or throw anything unexpected at me.

Dr Redfield had talked about this once. About how I needed structure and ritual because I was scared of the unexpected. She was right.

But tonight I didn't feel like cooking, so I foraged in the cupboard and found a packet of Uncle Ben's egg fried rice.

While it was in the microwave, I had a few minutes to spare so, with Dr Redfield's words from earlier today swimming around my head, I picked up the phone to call Mum. She probably wouldn't be home, but at least I could leave a message.

But I was wrong. Rather than being out, she was just back from her book club and sounded out of breath, unable to keep the shock from her voice. 'Leah, are you okay?'

My heart sank. She thought I was only calling because something was wrong. In a repeat of my earlier performance with Dr Redfield, I assured her I was fine, grateful she was not one for pushing. She had no energy left for any trouble, and I could sense her relief, even before she let out a deep breath.

I listened while she rattled off a list of all the activities she had planned for the weekend, wondering how she had time to sleep. We were mother and daughter, yet our lives were polar opposites.

We were polar opposites. Mum was rarely alone, while I craved solitude. I understood her need to be surrounded by people; it was a way for her to block out Dad's death, and everything else, but I had honed better techniques, and learnt to block it out without needing anyone else to distract me.

Until now.

The microwave beeped and, even though I was sure Mum could hear it, she seemed upset that I had to get off the phone. 'Will you come soon?' she asked.

I told her I would and that I loved her, ignoring the growing dread I felt at the prospect of going back to Watford.

Before bed, I checked Two Become One again, but there was still no word from Julian. I hovered for a while in a chat room, reading a conversation about a reality TV show I'd never heard of, but he didn't appear. He'd probably found someone else to talk to, maybe even met up with someone, so wouldn't be interested in talking to me any more. But wasn't this to be expected? I had fooled myself into thinking there was something between us, but I couldn't have been more wrong.

I loathed myself for daring to think I could be anywhere near normal. That I could be like Maria, and take my chances with someone. I should have known that wasn't possible.

As I shut down the website I noticed an email in my inbox. I never got anything interesting sent to me, but I always checked my emails, quickly moving them to the trash bin when they invariably turned out to be spam.

That's what I thought I was looking at when I clicked open the mail from a sender called *reepwhatyousow@gmail.com*. But again I was wrong. The page was blank apart from a hyperlink. I would normally have dismissed it but the name stood out, as if it was written in bold, flashing capital letters. I hadn't seen it, or even heard it spoken, for years. I stared at it for a moment, then holding my breath, clicked the link.

When it took me to an archived newspaper report, I quickly shut it down, feeling as if my chest would collapse. There was no way I could read that article. No way I could live that time again.

But the woman's picture accompanying the story was now firmly embedded in my mind.

CHAPTER FIVE
1998

The bell is still sounding as I race out of the maths block. I'm not alone; already kids are erupting from all the buildings, as desperate as I am to be free, even though it is January and bitterly cold outside. I never rush out when English is my last subject because I always want to talk to Mrs Owen about the latest book the class is reading. It is *Lord of the Flies* this time and I love it. I easily identify with Piggy because I'm always on the edge of things too, never quite fitting in. But at least I have Imogen. This place would be a worse kind of hell without her.

I suppose, in a way, we have Corey now as well. Somehow – I can't remember how it happened – in Year Eight he attached himself to us, and now we consider him a friend. Well, I do anyway. I can't vouch for Imogen because lately I've had the feeling she wants Corey to be more than that. Perhaps I will ask her about it later. We're having a sleepover at her house so there will be plenty of time to talk about anything we like.

And now, as if I've conjured him up just by thinking of him, Corey appears and taps me on the shoulder. 'Hi,' he says. 'You walking home?'

'No, waiting for Imogen. We're going to hers.'

'Oh,' Corey says, frowning.

I wonder if he is waiting for an invitation. 'It's kind of a girl thing. I'm staying the night.'

Corey looks around as if expecting Imogen to appear any second. 'Okay. You meeting her here?'

'No, by the art block. Walk with me if you want?'

He shrugs. 'S'okay. I'll catch you both on Monday.' And with that he is off, almost gliding towards the gates, with his bulging rucksack bouncing on his back.

It is strange that Corey has rushed off so quickly, but I don't have time to dwell on it too long. The art block is on the other side of the school and Imogen might think I'm not coming if I don't hurry.

As I expect, she is already there when I arrive, sitting on the steps with her head buried in her hands. She does not look happy. It is only now I realise how stupid it was of us to arrange to meet here when the maths block is right near the school gate. But that doesn't matter now, we are together and the weekend is just beginning.

'About time, Leah,' she says, looking up.

I open my mouth to apologise but then I notice Imogen is smiling, her face a different picture now that I'm here. She jumps up and grabs my arm. 'Come on, I've got *so* much to tell you.'

Imogen's mum is still at work when we get to her house so we have the whole place to ourselves. It is a luxury I never have at my own house because Dad works from home most days. He's an architect so doesn't need to be in the office much, and when he does have to go anywhere, Mum always arranges it so that she is home instead. I liked having the company when I was younger, but I'm fourteen now so need my own space. They just don't get it. So now I intend to make the most of any second when there are no parents around, even though I like Imogen's mum.

We sprawl on the two large sofas in the living room, stuffing ourselves with microwave popcorn while we talk about school.

'I hate Miss Hollis,' Imogen says, throwing a piece of popcorn in the air and catching it in her mouth. 'She couldn't even get a word in at form time today, could she? Nobody listens to her and it's just such a waste of time. Have you noticed how the other forms get all the notices passed on and we don't find anything out? It's because she can't shut everyone up long enough to tell us stuff.'

I nod and swallow some popcorn. It is true. I don't hate the woman as much as Imogen seems to, but it is starting to annoy me that we are wasting so much time during form period. And it has been like this since Year Seven. 'You'd think she'd have learnt how to teach by now,' I say.

Imogen snorts. 'She'd have more chance of flying to the moon without a rocket.' A giggling fit overcomes us both and we end up spraying popcorn all over the sofa and floor. It lasts until Imogen's mum gets home.

Mrs Bannerman is tall and neat, her body made up of elegant angles. When I was younger, I thought if goddesses existed then she was what they would look like. The woman had seemed mythical, almost perfect, with her deep melodic voice and sounds that rolled effortlessly off her tongue. But I've grown up since then, and now I know she is just another mum. Not at all like my own, or Corey's, but still a mother. And at this moment she is annoying the hell out of me.

She has already made us dinner and insisted on eating with us, which is fine as she's gone to the effort of cooking, but now she joins us on the sofa and we are forced to listen to her moaning about how Imogen's dad never does anything for her. I can't understand her claim because she is a beautiful woman, even if she does talk too much. What chance do Imogen or I have if men don't even appreciate the beautiful ones?

Once this thought occurs to me, it gnaws away and I want to grab Imogen and run up to her room so we can be alone to talk about all the things that are bothering me. One glance at my friend shows me that she must feel the same because she raises her eyebrows, shrugging in apology.

When we finally escape from Mrs Bannerman's tirade, it is nearly half ten and we will be expected to go straight to sleep. We will just have to whisper, though, because I have no intention of wasting this sleepover actually sleeping. Not when I need to grill my friend about Corey and tell her some very personal things. Things I don't want any parent hearing. Or any other person for that matter.

Imogen has set up the blow-up mattress next to her bed and is already cocooned in her duvet when I emerge from the bathroom, my mouth tasting of mint. The only light in the room comes from the small round bedside lamp, and I let it guide me to the mattress before flopping onto it and pulling the thick woollen sheet around me. I've stayed at Imogen's so many times since we met and find it strange that nobody has ever thought to buy a spare duvet. But I don't care tonight; I am just glad to be here.

'Sorry about Mum,' Imogen says, pulling out a bag of Haribo from under her duvet and offering me a sweet. 'She just gets lonely cos Dad's always working. She likes to have company.'

I pull out a fizzy cola bottle and stuff it in my mouth, but it tastes foul mixed with toothpaste. 'It's fine,' I lie. 'We can talk now, can't we?' One thing I have learned is that friendships need sacrifices, and I feel good that I have made one tonight. 'I saw Corey after school. I think he was looking for you.' I study Imogen's face, trying to gauge her reaction. But she only sighs and continues chewing one of the many sweets she has shovelled into her mouth, so it is impossible to know what she's thinking.

Finally she speaks. 'Do you think he's nice? You know, in that way?'

I sit up, almost choking on my sweet. 'I *knew* you liked him. You do, don't you?'

Imogen pulls the duvet over her face. 'Shuddup! I don't like him. Not really. As a friend of course...' She trails off and I lean over to drag her duvet back down. I take in my friend's features, and for the first time wonder if Imogen is scared to admit she likes Corey because she doesn't think she is attractive. I have never dwelled on Imogen's appearance because to me, she is just Imogen. My friend. The girl who saved me from loneliness. So how she looks or dresses doesn't matter. Imogen has always been fairly plump but it isn't something people immediately notice. Out of school, she usually wears jeans and t-shirts, but all the girls do so that isn't a problem, even if Imogen's are always slightly ill-fitting. Her hair is thick and blonde and that is bound to be a bonus. Don't all the boys love blonde hair?

I run my fingers through my own dark hair and thank God I don't care what boys think of me. I can't name a single one in our school who I find attractive and not for the first time I wonder if there is something wrong with me. What if I'm not attracted to boys at all? I consider this for a moment but shake it off. There is no way I like girls, so it must be just that there is no one cute enough at school.

'Okay, I do like him, but *please* don't tell him,' Imogen says.

'I knew it! But why not? Why don't you want him to know?'

She scrunches up her face. 'Oh come on! Look at me! Why the hell would Corey be interested in me?'

'Because you're friends. And you're great. A beautiful person.' As soon as I blurt it out I regret it. I may as well have just said it doesn't matter about her size because she's got a great personality. What am I thinking?

But Imogen laughs. 'Thanks for trying, but no. I don't want him to know. I like things how they are. It's nice with the three of us hanging around together, isn't it?'

I have to agree. We have all become close and it means that nobody else in school matters. Maybe other people have tons of friends and flaunt their popularity as if their lives depend on it, but we don't need anyone else because three is better than two, better than one. 'I won't say anything. But you should think about it because what have you got to lose?'

Imogen laughs again. 'Um, only my dignity and my friend. No biggie.' This is what I love about her; she knows how to laugh at herself. 'Anyway, it's easy for you to say, you're gorgeous!'

Now it is my turn to chuckle. 'Hardly. Look how flat my hair is. And it's greasy and hangs like a curtain.'

She scrunches her face again. 'Yeah, okay. Anyway, don't you like anyone? What about Tommy?'

'Hutchinson? No way! He's disgusting.'

Imogen reels off a list of all the eligible boys we know but none of them garner anything like a positive response from me. 'I give up!' she says eventually. 'You must be a lezzie.'

And with that, we both burst into uncontrollable giggles until Mrs Bannerman bangs on the wall and urges us to keep the noise down.

'I forgot your parents' bedroom is right next door,' I say. 'Do you ever hear them doing it?'

'Uggghhh! No way! That's sick.' Imogen smiles as she says this. 'Anyway, there's no way they do it any more. My mum's nearly forty!'

Rolling onto my stomach, I turn my head so I am facing Imogen. There are so many things I want to talk to her about, but even though we are close, I find it difficult to get the words out. There are thoughts and worries floating around my head all the time that I hardly dare think about, so to bring them up in conversation seems an impossible task. Instead, I guide the conversation back to Imogen. 'Do you want to? With Corey I mean? Do you ever think about it?'

She giggles but then appears to register that I'm being serious. 'I don't know. I suppose. I do dream about him sometimes. That we're doing it. And then when I wake up it feels like we really have done it and I swear I actually blush—'

'There's something wrong with me!' I am so desperate to get the words out, I forget to whisper.

The smile drops from Imogen's face as she tries to make sense of my abrupt interjection. 'What? Are you ill or something? What is it?'

'No…not…I didn't mean like that. It's just that everyone in school is always talking about sex or thinking about it or whatever but…' I trail off, unsure how to put my thoughts into words that Imogen might understand. 'Well, I never do. Never.' I look up at my friend, who is now peering over the side of the bed, chewing another sweet.

'Oh. Well, that doesn't mean anything, does it? I'm older than you, remember, so maybe those feelings will come later? You're not fifteen for ages.'

I have thought about this but it is of little comfort to me. I just want to feel normal. To feel something. *Anything*.

'And most of the boys in our school are crap, aren't they? Except Corey, of course. And Jason isn't bad. Or that Dwayne.'

None of this is helping. In fact, it is making me feel even more of a freak. I should at least be able to find one boy attractive if Imogen can like three. Probably more than three.

She stops chewing. 'I know we were joking about it earlier but are you sure you're not, you know, into *girls*? It wouldn't matter, I wouldn't care…'

I shake my head. 'No. I'm not. I'm just not into anyone.'

'Give it time, Leah,' Imogen says, resuming her chewing.

'You're right, it's probably just that there's nobody I like at school.' I don't add that I'm not particularly interested in any singers or actors on TV either.

But for the next hour, at least, I am distracted from worrying when Imogen suggests we listen to music on her headphones. We select 'I Believe I Can Fly' and put it on repeat while Imogen mimes the words, standing on her bed and using her pencil case as a microphone. I wish we could live in this moment forever, that we didn't have to worry about school or parents or boys or anything. Why can't it always be like this?

Eventually Imogen gets tired and curls up in her duvet, leaving me alone in the dark to worry about what is wrong with me.

CHAPTER SIX
2014

It was inevitable that things would catch up with me, but still I wasn't ready to face up to them. My life had ticked along for years without any interference from anyone, but now it was clear someone wanted their presence felt.

I could ignore the card, but it was impossible to forget I'd been sent that newspaper story. Impossible to see her name without shuddering, and without being right back there again. And her face. Her haunted eyes silently accusing me.

Thankfully, the library kept me busy as usual, allowing me to shove all other thoughts to the back of my mind. But I was fully aware the distraction would be temporary. And that I'd eventually be forced to confront the intrusion.

It was Maria's day off and an influx of students from the university flocked in just before lunch. They were noisy and unruly, more like primary school children than young adults, and I glowered at them until they eventually calmed down and set about the research project they'd been given. It was only later I discovered their own library had been flooded so they'd been forced to descend on us.

At two p.m. they finally drifted out and then Sam appeared, apologising for leaving me alone. She offered to cover me for a late lunch break, but just as I grabbed my bag, wondering whether to brave the weather and sit outside to eat, I felt someone behind me.

Spinning around, I found myself face-to-face with a thin man wearing glasses. He looked about my age and didn't seem to notice I was trying to leave the front desk. Removing his glasses, he began explaining he had several boxes of books to donate to us. 'I wanted to check you'd take them before I hauled them in from the car,' he said.

I looked over at Sam, but she had already walked off to help someone on the computer, so I knew I wouldn't be eating soon.

Turning back to the man, I asked him how many boxes he had, dreading the answer he would give me.

'Five. Is that okay? Will you take them?'

Stretching my face into a smile, I nodded and put my bag back behind the desk. Whoever this man was, he was doing a kind thing and I was grateful to him. Our funding was always being cut so we depended heavily on donations. Even if he told me he had a hundred boxes I would still help him unload.

He chatted as we walked to his van and I learned that his name was Ben. He told me he worked for the RSPCA and pointed across the car park. 'That's why I've got the van,' he said, waving his keys in front of me. 'Lucky, really. I'm moving house in a few weeks so needed to have a huge clear-out.'

I couldn't understand how anyone could get rid of books – I would sooner throw out furniture – but I didn't want to seem ungrateful by criticising him.

Ben did most of the talking, and I was in awe of how comfortable he was conversing like this with a stranger. He seemed nice enough, but I still squirmed inside, anxious for the task to be over so I could say goodbye. But he was in no hurry, chatting as if we were old friends, and by the time the boxes were neatly stacked by the counter, I had forgotten my hunger.

'Oh,' he said, standing back to appraise the neat stack we'd created. 'I've just realised how much extra work I've given you.'

I told him not to worry, dipping my hand into one of the boxes and pulling out a thin hardback book. I turned it over so I could see the front cover. Whatever the book was would tell me more about Ben than anything else could. Staring at it, I was surprised to find it was *Of Mice and Men*, one of my favourite books. And the edition I held in my hand was the same version I'd read at school. I couldn't help my outburst. 'I *adore* this book, you can't get rid of it! Don't you like it?'

Ben's eyes widened. Perhaps he was shocked that I'd spoken so effusively. Or maybe just that I'd spoken more than two words. 'Oh, I love it, but I've got another copy and there's no need for two. I read it at school and it's haunted me ever since.'

He was echoing my thoughts and it was rare I found common ground with anyone. 'Me too. It is the kind of novel that stays with you, isn't it?' As soon as I'd said this I regretted it. Feeling like an idiot, I put the book back in the box and turned away from him.

'I would have said the same thing,' he said, forcing me to turn back to him. And in that moment I liked this man. Not in the same way I liked Julian, nothing at all like that, but somehow Ben had put me at ease.

I thanked him and told him I had to get back to work, walking over to Sam without turning around. Behind me I could hear Ben trooping off and I felt bad that I'd ended our discussion so abruptly.

By the time I left work and began my walk home, I'd forgotten all about Ben and his donated books. Without the distraction of the library, I was once again consumed with worry over the card, photo and newspaper article. I was so used to having nothing to think about, other than what I should cook myself for dinner, or what book to read to the care home residents next, that worrying about anything else made me more uneasy than I already was.

Opening my front door, my eyes dropped to the pile of envelopes scattered on the doormat. I was about to step over them and head upstairs, when my desire for routine took over. Sweeping them up, I took them upstairs to examine.

I inhaled deeply when I checked through the letters, but they were only bills and a bank statement. I'd had no emails either so perhaps it really was over; whoever was trying to torment me had become bored and moved on.

Convincing myself things were getting back to normal, I whistled as I cooked macaroni cheese and heated up some frozen garlic bread. I thought about Julian and tried to imagine what he was doing at that moment. Probably heading home from work or meeting friends for a pint. Or he could be out with some woman from the website. I pushed away the twinge of jealousy I felt. He wasn't mine, so I had no right to care who he was out with.

I'd forgotten to set the oven timer, so the garlic bread was burnt around the edges, but I tucked in anyway, starving after missing lunch.

I was still eating when the phone rang so I ignored it. It had to be a computerised call, a robotic voice telling me I was owed Payment Protection Insurance or something similar that I'd never taken out. It wouldn't be Mum; we'd only spoken yesterday so there was no reason for her to call again today, even if she was always worrying about me. Anyway, if there was an emergency she would leave a message. I waited for the beep but the caller hung up. Not Mum then. She would never miss an opportunity to make me feel bad for not answering.

I washed up – there was no room for a dishwasher in my tiny kitchen – and left the plates to drain by the sink. Looking around, I decided it was a good thing Julian would only ever be in my flat on the laptop. He would never have to wonder how I could live like this, with books taking up space where there should be furniture, and hardly any modern appliances. But I made do with what I had, and preferred to spend money on my reading habit rather than flashy gadgets.

At least I had my laptop; a link to the outside world that I could control. With it I could decide whom to let into my life, and right at that moment I wanted to let Julian in. Just to get a message from him and know that he was still around in some way, would have made me feel better.

Luck seemed to be with me that evening because, as soon as I logged on, a message appeared inviting me to a chat room. I was both scared and excited; I hadn't thought through what I would say to him. Everything was blank and no words came to me. But my desperation – for what? A man I barely knew? – won in the end and I started typing.

LeahH: Hi stranger…

I bit my lip and waited, the seconds it took him to reply feeling like hours.

Moderator34: hey, Leah, how r things?

With anyone else it would have irritated me the way he shortened his words, but with Julian it didn't seem important. Not when someone as seemingly great as him was talking to me. And not when, for the first time in years, I had dared to take a chance and started to let someone in.

Leah H: Good thanks. With you?

Moderator34: not great. work stuff. boring. but glad you're online.

I felt the usual excitement at Julian's compliment and wondered if I should return it, say something, anything to cheer him up.

LeahH: Anything I can do?

I cringed at my own words, but it was too late to take them back. How was I coming across to him? He really would know I didn't have a clue now, that I was naïve and inexperienced with men.

Moderator34: Just talking to you is enough

For an hour and a half our messages flew back and forth, and I soon began to feel comfortable, typing without worrying, Julian continuing the conversation each time I thought it was about to end. It was true that sometimes we became like the people we surrounded ourselves with, because the more messages that passed between us, the more a sense of humour that had long been buried in me started to resurface. I liked how Julian made me feel. I couldn't explain it, but I definitely liked it. Needed it.

During our conversation, I told him everything I could let myself reveal about my life. I played down the part about being a loner, of course, and anything that had happened prior to leaving Watford, so as far as he knew, I was London born and bred.

It was nearly ten o'clock when we finally said goodbye. Although we'd talked all this time, nothing had been said by either of us about meeting up or even talking again online. But whatever had passed between us was enough for me. I couldn't think beyond talking. I would let things be as they were.

Feeling at peace, I made a cup of tea to take to bed. Today had been okay. There had been no surprise mail and I'd just spent hours talking to Julian. These things might seem too insignificant to bring happiness to most people, but to me they were huge deals.

And then I made a big mistake and checked my emails on my phone. Most were junk mail but then I saw one from *reepwhaty-ousow@gmail.com*, the subject line once again blank.

Knowing it was from my tormenter – that's what I'd resorted to calling him or her, for want of a better word – I should have deleted it, but something compelled me to click on it, and then it was too late. There were a few lines in the body of the message this time, but that only made this correspondence worse than the others. Much worse.

Do you really think any man could be interested in you after what you've done?

I reread the email. The words weren't going to change, but maybe reading it again would help me make sense of it. The problem, though, was that it made too much sense. I knew exactly what these words meant and I also knew that this was not going away.

And then it hit me that whoever this was knew about the website. They must do. Those words could only be about me talking to Julian.

I hadn't felt helpless in a long time. I'd made sure I was never put in a position where I would be, and up until then it had worked. So I was unprepared to feel as if the ground had been knocked away from me. I considered replying to the email, telling whomever it was exactly where to go, but that would only encourage them. They would see they were affecting me, and that was the last thing I needed. No, that was not an option.

Could I call Mum? I'd kept her out of it so far, not wanting to drag her back into my mess, but at least she might understand. I scrolled down to her name on my mobile, and was about to press call but something stopped me. I could hear her words in my ear: the panic, the fervent plea for me to stay with her for a while, the resignation in her voice when I refused. I couldn't put her through that. One thing she would never understand was why I needed to live here, away from her home. It was possible to commute to work from Watford, so she would never have accepted that as an excuse.

I carried on scrolling until I reached Dr Redfield's name. She had given me her mobile number years ago but I'd never used it. I wasn't even sure it was still her number, but I was out of options. After only a couple of rings, her voicemail kicked in. I hurriedly explained what had happened, not knowing what I expected her to do, only that I couldn't deal with it alone.

My mind was empty of Julian as I paced up and down my living room in the dark, trying not to trip over books, waiting for the phone to ring. Half an hour ticked by but Dr Redfield didn't return my call. I couldn't blame her; she had a life of her own, and didn't have to be at my beck and call. Especially when I didn't even bother to keep my appointments.

Eventually I gave up waiting and headed to bed, knowing I wouldn't sleep. I felt a lot of things as I lay there with my eyes closed. Fear, sadness, anxiety. But most of all I was angry that the life I had carefully constructed for myself was falling down around me, forcing me back to a time I couldn't let myself remember.

CHAPTER SEVEN
2014

I was not one for clichés or platitudes, but the one about never knowing how you will react in a certain situation is one I knew to be true. I thought I could handle anything, after all I'd been through, but the email knocked the wind out of me. In a way I had been violated, someone had shown me they were watching what I was doing, keeping tabs on me somehow. I shuddered at the thought of this.

And the next morning I did something I'd never done before. I called Sam and told her I was sick.

She was silent as I listed all my symptoms. Fever, nausea, shakes. It seemed like flu, I told her. I was only glad our conversation was being conducted over the phone, otherwise she would surely have seen through my feeble lie.

As it was, after the shock, I think Sam believed me. She offered her sympathy and told me not to hurry back. It felt despicable to accept her kindness, but I was used to lying by then. I was an expert at bending the truth and keeping things hidden, and my small lie about sickness was nothing compared to the lie that I myself was.

With work dealt with for the time being, I left the house and walked to the care home, a carrier bag full of books swinging from my arm. I was immediately greeted by Mick and Elsie, both of them sitting in the foyer coffee shop, their eyes lighting up when they spotted me. For at least a few hours I would be able to focus on them and forget all that waited for me at home.

Back in my flat that evening I had no clue what to do, how to deal with my tormentor. It was possible my computer had been hacked, but I would wait to see what happened next. My instincts screamed at me to ignore it all, surely whoever it was would give up eventually? But I was uneasy about doing this; someone had gone to a lot of trouble to dig up my past so I doubted they would give up easily.

Maria texted to ask if she could call and I welcomed the distraction. Hearing her news might take the edge off, and maybe she'd need help with something.

'You poor thing,' she said, when I answered. 'It was weird you not being at work today, but sounds like you've caught something nasty. Where do you think you picked it up from? I don't think anyone at work's got it. Not yet anyway.'

I tried to make my voice sound weak, riddled with cold. Thankfully, Maria didn't dwell on my illness too long, and in no time she was filling me in on work. I hadn't missed much, but then what did I expect? It was rare that anything exciting happened at the library. That was exactly why I liked it there.

Maria asked if I'd eaten and when I said no she tutted, insisting I needed to have something, even just soup.

'I'll be fine. I'll probably get my appetite back tomorrow.'

She tutted again. 'Do you think you'll be in tomorrow? Because you know you should probably just rest. If it is flu, you'll be knocked out for ages.' There was something in her tone. Disbelief? I told myself I was just being paranoid.

I agreed that it was doubtful I'd be better, and she fell silent for a moment. But it wasn't long before she was launching into a story about a man she had spotted in the library that morning. 'I'm going to give him my number next time he comes in,' she said, and I laughed, once again admiring her confidence, her resilience.

'Anyway, I better go,' she said, and I felt a wave of disappointment. It surprised me how good it had felt to talk to her, even if that feeling was alien to me now. 'Get better soon.'

Maria's talk of food reminded me I was hungry, but I didn't want to move from the sofa, even just to travel the short distance to the kitchen. My mind was firm; I would not budge until I'd thought of a way out of this mess.

It was already dark outside, so I had no way to judge how much time had passed, but eventually a seed of an idea came to me. Although I had initially dismissed the idea of replying to the email, if I chose my words carefully, perhaps there was a way I could get through to the person behind it. Try to find out what they wanted, without letting them think I was worried.

The laptop sat on the kitchen table, but before I had a chance to move, the doorbell chimed. I froze. It rang so rarely that I always forgot how piercing the sound was, how incongruous in my usually silent flat. Sighing, I headed for the stairs, convinced whoever was out there had got the wrong door and that it was my neighbour they were after.

Maria was the last person I expected to see standing on my doorstep. But there she was, shuffling her feet and rubbing her hands together. I blinked, sure I was hallucinating from lack of food, and that when I opened my eyes she'd be gone, in her place the familiar scene of the empty concrete garden and the road beyond. But then she spoke.

'Oh, Leah, you sounded so ill on the phone I would hate myself if I didn't come over to check on you.' She held up a Tesco carrier bag. 'And I've bought some ingredients so I can make you some soup. You've got to eat, haven't you? Well, come on, are you going to let me in? You don't look right, you know.'

I was overwhelmed by her kindness. Until it dawned on me that I had never given her my address. I opened my mouth to ask but she beat me to it. 'Sam had the pay slips in the lunch room and I saw your address on yours. Sorry, but I really wanted to come and see you.'

I stepped aside and she sauntered in, as if she had been there many times before. Following behind her, my mind a jumble of thoughts about the email, Julian, having someone other than Mum in my flat and everything else that was not as it should be.

'Oh this is…nice,' Maria said, when we reached my front room. 'Love books much?' She gazed around, taking it all in, trying to match my flat to what she already knew about me. I don't know what conclusion she reached but I'd put money on the fact she never pictured me living anywhere like this. Alone, yes, but not somewhere so basic and soulless.

'It'll do for now,' I said, sitting on the sofa. 'I'll get something better eventually.'

Maria continued standing. 'Hmmm. You should see my place, it's a right shit tip! You should come over for dinner.' Her words were lies to make me feel better but, either way, I was grateful for her tact. 'Anyway, you just stay here and relax, I'll find my way around the kitchen…if you don't mind?'

I shook my head, sure I wouldn't be able to say no and make it sound like the truth. I was supposed to be ill and, whatever else I felt, I was grateful for her kindness.

She was already in the kitchen, calling across to me. 'I know soup's a bit dull, but it's meant to be good for flu-type things and, well, I wasn't sure you'd want anything else.'

From the sofa, I told Maria that soup was fine and listened to her banging around in my drawers and cupboards, biting my lip because it just didn't feel right. Perhaps if we'd known each other a lot longer I wouldn't have felt so strange, but it had only been a few months, and the truth was you could know someone for years but not *know* them. I, of all people, knew that. It would be easy to tell Maria I felt a lot better, even help her make the soup, but I knew I wouldn't be able to face going into work the next day when I had my emailer to sort out. So I kept up the pretence.

We sat at the kitchen table to eat, and I stared at the French stick Maria had bought to dip into our soup. I longed for a piece but stuck only to the soup to preserve my lie. If I wanted the day off tomorrow I couldn't have Maria suspecting me. I didn't think she would blab to Sam if she thought I was faking it, but how could I really know when our friendship – if that was the right word – was so new.

'You're lucky, you know,' Maria said, dunking her bread in her soup.

I almost laughed because that was one word I'd never been able to attach to myself. 'What, to have a couple of days off work? I'd rather go in,' I said, knowing that wasn't what she'd meant, 'than be stuck at home ill.'

She stopped chewing. 'I mean, what are you? Twenty-seven? Twenty-eight?'

When I told her I was thirty her eyes rolled upwards.

'Do you know how lucky you are? You've got the best years still ahead of you and every chance to meet someone.'

All I could do was nod. That was exactly how it looked to other people. I seemed normal enough, looked okay and could hold a decent conversation, so why wouldn't they assume I could easily find someone to settle down with? On the surface, perhaps the best years were ahead of me, but I couldn't tell Maria, or anyone else, that my past had erased any chance of a future.

'So have you,' I said, attempting to deflect the conversation away from me. 'You just can't let it stress you and make you seem...'

'Desperate? Yeah, I know. But it's hard not to when you *are*. I'm bloody thirty-nine, Leah. *Thirty-nine!* She laughed then, but I knew it was just for show. I'd quickly realised that her inability to settle down with anyone bothered Maria.

'Stop looking,' I said. 'That's all you have to do.' I sounded like I knew what I was talking about and felt like a fraud. No man had been near me since Adam, and the little I had learnt had been from my time on the website, or from Maria.

She nodded and looked around the kitchen, something passing across her face that I was sure was annoyance. Had I spoken out of turn? She was always so open about things that I'd assumed no topic of conversation was out of bounds.

'You're right,' she said eventually. 'Anyway, are you feeling any better? You seem to be. Shall I make us some tea or coffee?'

While Maria boiled the kettle, I ignored her protests and washed up. I needed something to help pass the time because as much as I liked her, I needed to be alone to work out what I could do about my problem. I had no idea how long she intended to stay, and I hated the uncertainty her unexpected visit had brought. As if my life wasn't already in a state of flux.

'I'll just have this coffee then I'll have to get home,' she said, as if she could sense my thoughts.

We took our mugs to the sofa and while I sat drinking mine, wondering how it could taste different just because someone else had made it, Maria took it upon herself to browse through my books. It shouldn't have mattered; there was nothing there I had to worry about, but I still balked at the intrusion.

When she trotted off to use the bathroom, I took our mugs to the kitchen. Mine still had at least a quarter of the cup left but I tipped it down the sink and doused it in washing up liquid, my mind already assessing my options for how to deal with the messages I'd been getting.

Maria crept into the kitchen so quietly that when she spoke I jumped, almost dropping my mug in the sink. 'I would have done that.'

I spun around. 'No, don't worry, it's fine. Thanks for coming over, though, and for dinner, it was really kind of you.'

'No trouble at all. Just hope you feel better soon.' Her eyes narrowed as she said this, forcing me to look at the floor.

'Any man would be lucky to have you, Maria. And you will find him. Didn't you say to me there's someone for everyone?'

She shook her head. 'Well, I must have been drunk. Anyway, I'll let myself out, you just get some rest.' Heading out, she scanned my flat again as she walked to the top of the stairs. But before she reached them she turned back around, frowning. 'You do seem a bit better, though. That's good, isn't it?'

Once she'd left, I paced the flat, unable to shake off Maria's visit. I knew it was irrational; she was a friendly work colleague and nothing negative had ever passed between us, but something had been different that evening, and I couldn't pinpoint what. Perhaps I was still shaken after the email, and that had put a slant on her visit? Or it could have been that it was too strange having someone in my flat after so long on my own.

But it had been nice to have company and I wondered if I could do it again. It was too much to hope that I could ever invite a man here – like Julian – but maybe I had taken a small step, even in the midst of the chaos that was unfolding. But still, no matter how I justified things, Maria had definitely not been herself and it could only be because I'd upset her with my frank words.

I couldn't think about that now, though; I had an email to write, and my words needed to be chosen carefully. With the laptop balanced on my knee, I logged in to my Hotmail account and opened the message. I hadn't intended to read it again, I'd just meant to click reply, but there were the words, taunting and mocking me, and I couldn't tear my eyes away.

Do you really think any man could be interested in you after what you've done?

And seeing them again, every intention I might have had to keep calm and work this out evaporated. Anger coursed through my body and my fingers flew to the keys as if they were one step ahead of my brain. How dare they? It may have been true but that was for me to think, nobody else.

I read my words again.

Yes, I do. Get over it.

There was still time to press delete, abandon the whole email and rethink my strategy, but, of course, that's not what I did. Within seconds I was staring at a message telling me my email had been sent.

It's hard to say what I felt afterwards, as I sat staring at the screen. It wasn't regret, just anxiety because I wasn't used to acting so spontaneously. I preferred to think things through carefully, weigh up all the possible outcomes. This seemed to have become a habit of late; I had done the same with Julian. Well, it was too late to dwell on that now. On any of it.

Thinking of Julian, I logged on to Two Become One. Even if he wasn't around, reading some chat room conversations might help distract me from the mess I was making. Plus, if he was online, there was no better way to get back at whoever was emailing me than to prove his or her words wrong. Even though I didn't believe that, or that Julian could be interested in me for that matter, I needed to hear from him.

He wasn't online but when I checked my inbox, he had left me a message. It was short, but his words lifted me out of the fog I was in. They couldn't have been more different from those of my emailer.

Missed you this eve. Was hoping to chat! Speak soon.

I replied straight away, given that there was no thought needed for what I would say. I was following my heart for the first time since Adam and it felt good. Scary but good.

Will go on tomorrow evening, hope to chat then!

I studied my reply for a moment, making sure it didn't seem desperate or needy. I had learnt from Maria that men detested that. When I was certain it was okay, I sent it, logged off and went to bed.

It was no surprise that I couldn't sleep again. I tried to think about Julian and how if I was a different person we might have been able to meet, but my thoughts were flung back to the emailer. I wasn't sure what effect my reply would have but it was too late to worry about that now.

CHAPTER EIGHT
1999

As usual, Miss Hollis can't be heard above the cacophony of voices in the classroom. Imogen and I sit at the back, our heads buried together, trying not to be overheard by any of our classmates.

'Wait,' I say. 'Tell me that again. Slowly.' Although I have heard exactly what Imogen said, I need to make sure because this is a huge deal.

'Last night,' she whispers. 'Finally. It was weird but good weird not bad weird, I mean I liked it, course I did cos it's Corey.'

I should have seen this coming; she has done nothing but talk about wanting to lose her virginity with Corey for months now. But it is still a shock. Not a bad one, not really, because she is my friend and I want her to be happy, but I just feel sad. For myself. That there is no hope of me ever losing anything with any boy. I am also surprised because I thought Imogen was going to wait until her sixteenth birthday. But I will just have to be happy for her, especially after everything she does for me.

'That's great,' I say. It's not hard to mean it when I see the excitement on her face. 'Do you feel…different?'

She shrugs. 'A bit. Kind of. Yeah, I think I do.' But I doubt this. Surely it must all be psychological because it wasn't like it physically made you any different. At least not on the outside. But I am no expert so I keep my mouth shut; I have never even kissed a boy.

The door swings open and Mr Faulkner, our head of year, strides in. We call him Sergeant Faulkner because he bellows commands at us as if we're in boot camp, but he's not all bad. And his strictness is far preferable to Miss Hollis's inability to take control.

Behind him, following him into the room is a boy I have never seen before. He is wearing our uniform so must be a student here, but up until now I thought I knew everyone in our year, by face if not by name.

The room falls silent and Miss Hollis quickly stands up, probably trying to make her presence felt now that Mr Faulkner is here. The head of year scowls. I bet he is angrier with her than he is with us; we are just doing what kids do, it is Miss Hollis's job to keep us in order.

'Year Ten, this is Adam Bowden,' Mr Faulkner says, his voice loud enough to shatter glass. 'He's joined us from another school and will be in this form, so let's all make him feel welcome.' Beside him, Adam Bowden slouches and stares at the class, looking as if he couldn't care less whether or not he is made welcome. I wonder how he can be so confident. If it were me standing there I'd be hiding behind Mr Faulkner, wishing the floor would swallow me up.

But not Adam Bowden. No. He just stares at each of us in turn, from underneath his floppy dark hair, nodding his head as if making secret judgements about us, before strolling to an empty seat at the back. He doesn't even wait for Miss Hollis to allocate him a seat. I am impressed. Impressed and a little startled by this boy's behaviour.

He turns to Imogen and me as he slumps in his chair and raises his eyebrows, smiling as he does so. It's not a mocking smile, but quite a friendly one. And this is when I realise that, whoever this boy is, I think I like him.

Once he's delivered a lecture about the school field being out of bounds when it's raining, Mr Faulkner leaves, letting the door slam behind him, and we all stay quiet, waiting to see what Miss Hollis will say, if anything.

'Um, excuse me, Adam? You'll be sitting here.' She points to an empty seat in the front row. It's Nicholas's seat but he hasn't been in school for ages and no one knows where he is.

Adam's reply is firm and confident, matching his appearance. 'No thanks, Miss. I'm fine here.' He rests his head in his hands and stares at her, daring her to object.

For a second, Miss Hollis looks shocked. She nervously eyes the class, as if expecting someone to back her up, but most of the students are now beginning to chuckle.

And then she surprises us all.

'Come back here. Now.' It isn't quite a shout, but is louder than I have heard her speak before.

Scanning the room, I see most of the class is open-mouthed, staring at Miss Hollis. I'm not even sure who she's talking to, but then she turns to the new boy who frowns and shrugs, but makes no move to give up his seat.

Miss Hollis stands firm. 'I didn't say you could sit there, you need to wait for me to tell you where to sit.' This is unheard of. She is challenging a student. In all the years she has been my form tutor she has never spoken like this to anyone. It must be her time of the month.

All eyes turn to Adam Bowden. 'I'd like to stay here, Miss,' he says, as if it is his right. He speaks politely but the smirk behind his words betrays his true intention. I normally dislike challenging behaviour, but there is something different about Adam. He is too confident to be just another dumb idiot, using bad behaviour to disguise academic weakness. Again I am impressed.

'Get out!' Miss Hollis screams. 'Now! Get out!'

For a moment, Adam looks stunned, but he quickly recovers and breezes out, not looking at anyone he passes, the way he did just a moment ago. But no matter how surprised he is, it is nothing compared to the bemusement I – and the rest of the class, I am sure – feel witnessing Miss Hollis shout like this. She may as well have transformed into a dragon and breathed fire because that's how we all stare at her until she goes out to deal with Adam Bowden. Even when she has followed him out into the corridor, closing the door behind her, nobody dares speak above a whisper.

I don't see the new boy for the rest of the morning, but at lunchtime he is all Imogen, Corey and I can talk about. We sit on the steps of the art block, shivering because we don't want to go to the canteen or put on our blazers. Lunchtime is the only time we have a reprieve from wearing them so we can't miss an opportunity to shed our shackles, no matter what the weather.

'He was in my history class this morning,' Corey tells us. 'But Miss Hollis wasn't being weird to him so they must have sorted it out.'

'She's not allowed to be weird to any of us, she's a teacher,' I say, biting into my cheese baguette. 'Anyway, you should have seen it, she humiliated him in front of the whole class. On his first day!' Now that I've had the morning to think about it, I am sure that's what happened. Humiliation. Nothing more, nothing less. I would have been mortified if it had been me, but Adam Bowden had handled it well.

Imogen nudges Corey. 'So you sat next to him? What's he like?' I'm glad she is the one asking these questions. If I had to ask them myself they would both know how I feel. Or think I feel.

'He's okay, I like him. Clever, I guess. Why?' Corey shoots Imogen a glance that I can only interpret as asserting his ownership, or something not quite so dramatic but meaning more or less the same.

'I dunno, he just seems cool. But not like that.' Imogen grabs Corey's arm and keeps hold of him while she eats her crisps.

I watch them both, finding it hard to believe so much has progressed between them over the weekend. But I don't feel envious, at least not in a substantial way, because Imogen and Corey are my closest friends. Besides, there is hope on the horizon in the form of Adam Bowden. I repeat his name in my head and it sounds good, as if it fits me somehow. And he smiled at me, didn't he? Or did I imagine it? I can't be sure now, but after consideration I tell myself he definitely did.

I wish Imogen and I were alone now so I can share my thoughts with her. There is no way I can say anything in front of Corey; other things, yes, but not stuff about boys. Particularly one he sat next to in history. But I decide I will call her later. This is too important not to share at the earliest opportunity.

The three of us are so engrossed in our conversation that by the time I look at my watch, there are only four minutes left before the bell is due to ring. I have English next and there is no way I can be late so, jumping up, I shout something about catching them later and rush off, every second swearing I can hear the bell. Today we are due to finish *Of Mice and Men*. It's my favourite book so far, but I suspect things will not end well for George and Lennie. I think how amazing it is that one writer can control the destiny of all their characters, as if they are God. Perhaps I will write a novel one day, and enjoy the unfolding of lives from my mind.

Being so engrossed in this idea, I collide into someone outside the English block with a heavy thwack. Stunned, I quickly look up to apologise to whomever I've smacked into. But when I see who it is, the words drop from my mouth.

Adam Bowden.

My insides burn as I struggle to say sorry, but then it is too late because he is saying it for me. Was it his fault? I am sure I was the one who barged into him, but there he is, apologising profusely and asking if I am okay.

'I'm fine,' I manage to say. 'Thanks. Sorry.' He pats my shoulder and even when he removes his hand I can still feel the weight of it.

'You were in my form group this morning, weren't you?'

I nod. 'Yeah, sorry about what happened. Miss Hollis is a right fruitcake.'

Adam smiles. 'Yeah, I've heard she never talks above a whisper so don't know what the hell happened this morning. She must hate me.' He shrugs his shoulders as he says this, obviously not caring one way or the other. 'So what's this one like?'

'Mrs Owen? Oh, she's nice. Strict but nice.'

Adam nods, but there is no way to tell what he is thinking. I wonder what impression he has of me. Isn't it a good sign that he is here talking to me now, when the bell is about to go and the rest of the class are already lined up inside? But then again, that doesn't necessarily mean much. Adam doesn't seem one for sticking religiously to school rules.

'We'd better get in,' I say, just as the bell pierces the air and there is a flurry of activity from latecomers.

'If you say so,' he says. But when I look up at him, not sure how to take his comment, he is smiling. I can't explain what I feel at that moment, I only know I have been waiting to feel it for a long time.

CHAPTER NINE
2014

Four days passed and there was no reply to my email. I didn't know whether I was relieved or disappointed, but tried to tell myself my lack of fear had worked. That I had confused the emailer so much that he or she had decided to back off. Perhaps my computer hadn't been hacked after all. I had taken the words to be about Julian, but it was possible this person knew I was single and assumed I wanted someone in my life.

I shrugged off the thought that this was too easy, that whoever it was had an agenda and wasn't likely to give up on it just because I'd responded in an unexpected way. But still, four days was long enough for me to convince myself it might be over.

On the other hand, I hadn't heard from Julian either, and this puzzled me. He had been the one to send me the last message, and all I'd done was respond to it, saying I'd be online the next evening, but we had missed each other. Still, I couldn't fathom why he hadn't at least left a message and why all was now silent on his end. There were, of course, a number of harmless explanations for his lack of response: a work trip, holiday, parents struck down by illness. Any one of these was plausible, so I convinced myself it would be okay. He would respond when he could.

I went back to work and everything felt normal again. Maria seemed pleased to see me and continued to fuss, checking I was okay at regular intervals. I assured her I was fine, and felt grateful that if I'd upset her that night at my flat she had obviously put it behind her.

It didn't take long to bury myself in work and forget the outside world existed. During my break, I sat in the coffee room with some hot water and lemon because, ironically, I had started to notice the telltale signs of an impending cold.

My back faced the door and I was so engrossed in *The Catcher in the Rye* that I didn't realise Sam had come in until she coughed to get my attention. 'I'm glad you're here,' she said, closing the door and walking towards me. 'Can we have a quick chat?'

My first thought was that she had uncovered my lie about being sick. But how? Even if Maria had suspected I was being dishonest I was certain she wouldn't say anything to Sam. And even if she had there was no evidence. But there was no other reason I could think of for Sam wanting to talk to me on our own with the door closed. Unless a customer had made a complaint about me.

'You've been at the library a long time now, Leah, haven't you?' Sam began, and I held my breath, waiting for her to get to the point. 'Well, something's come up that I wanted to discuss with you.'

'Okay, of course. What is it?' I tried to sound upbeat but she was trying to get rid of me, I was certain. There was nothing else it could be. I couldn't lose my job. It was the one thing that kept me going. The thought of not working there made me feel faint; it wasn't just a job to me, it was my life.

'A position has come up for a senior librarian and I think you'd be perfect for it. It would mean a lot more responsibility, but nothing you couldn't handle. What do you think?'

It took me a moment to digest Sam's words, but when I did I wanted to hug her. Not only was my job safe but she was talking about promotion. Before that point, I'd given no thought to my career or future, I was just living day to day, getting through each one as best I could. But now this. I couldn't speak for a moment but when I recovered all I could say was, 'Yes, I'd love that. Great. Thanks.'

Sam chuckled. 'Of course there will have to be an interview, but that's just a formality. I've got to have all the correct paperwork.'

'That's fine,' I said, still not believing what I was hearing. Things like this didn't happen to me. And then something occurred to me, plummeting me back to the ground. 'What about Maria? I know she's only been here a few months but she worked in a library for years before she came here, didn't she?'

Sam bit her lip. 'Let's just say I don't think Maria has the commitment you do. But that goes no further than this room. Anyway, she's welcome to apply. It's fair and open competition, after all. Just don't forget to fill out an application form, I'll email it to you this afternoon.' And then she breezed out, leaving me questioning again whether I'd invented the entire conversation.

As I walked back to the front desk, I could see Maria deep in conversation with a man in a black jacket. I couldn't tell who he was but there was something familiar about him.

'There she is,' Maria said, pointing at me as I got closer. The man turned as she said this and I realised it was Ben, the man who'd donated so many books to us the week before. I hoped there wasn't a problem. Perhaps he had changed his mind about the donation? That would be awkward; the books were already logged in the system and some of them were out on loan so there was no way he could have them back.

But as I got closer, the huge smile on his face assured me this couldn't be the case.

'Hi,' he said, holding up a large carrier bag. 'Found these when I was unpacking.'

I took a closer look and saw the bag was bulging with books. Again, I was torn between gratitude for Ben's donation and annoyance that he could so flippantly part with something so important.

I thanked him, turning away from Maria's raised eyebrows.

'I'll take my break now, Leah,' she said, patting my arm. 'You can look after this gentleman, can't you?' It was obvious to me what Maria was insinuating and I only hoped Ben hadn't picked up on it. All the poor man had done was mention me, and that was only because I'd been here the last time he came in.

Thankfully, he was busy shuffling through his bag. 'I've got some DVDs too, if they're any good?' he asked, as Maria walked off, turning back for one last look.

I told him it all helped, but was distracted by Maria's silent assumptions. I needed Ben to leave quickly. He was nice enough, but I didn't want Maria trying to match me up with anyone.

We talked as I unpacked the bag – one of those huge Sainsbury's bags for life – and he told me he had a cat to rescue in a flat on Garratt Lane. The tenants had gone on holiday and left it locked inside so he was waiting for the landlord to turn up with the keys. I liked the passion that emanated from him as he talked about some of the animals he'd rescued. I got so caught up in his stories that I didn't notice the queue forming behind him until someone coughed loudly, just as Sam had done earlier.

'Oh, I'd better let you get on,' Ben said, standing aside. 'What time do you have lunch?'

I was taken aback by his question. 'Um, one ish, why?'

'Let me take you for a coffee and sandwich to say thanks.'

Behind him, the man who had coughed sighed and tapped the book he was holding. I ignored him because the words *no way* screamed in my head, but then something occurred to me. I could use the hour with Ben as practice. If I was ever to have the courage to meet up with Julian then I needed more experience being around men. I couldn't see this happening, wasn't even sure Julian would want it to, but what was the harm in familiarising myself with male company? With other people in the queue starting to tut, I didn't have time for an internal debate. I told Ben that would be fine. No song and dance, just fine.

I didn't have time to dwell on what I had agreed to until the queue had died out, but by then it was too late. I was meeting a man I hardly knew and had no romantic interest in for lunch. What was I doing?

'It can't do any harm,' Maria said, when I told her what had happened. 'He seems nice so what's the problem?'

Her question was one I had no way to answer. 'I just don't see the point. He'll think I like him or something if I go for lunch with him, won't he?'

'Not if you make it clear you don't. I can't see a problem. Just go and have a sandwich and a nice chat and leave it at that. Unless you—'

'Unless nothing! I'm not interested. Not like that.'

'Okay, okay, I get the point. Just have some fun, that's all.'

There were just under two hours before Ben would be back, and I spent them walking around the library, tidying up books that people had left scattered around. No matter how many times I did this check, the books always got messed up again the next time I looked, but at least it gave me a chance to think.

I couldn't understand what was happening to me. In the last few days I had done so many things that were out of character, out of the frame of my life, as if I was on a rollercoaster I was powerless to stop. First, there was Julian and my inexplicable desire to keep up contact with him. Then, there was the email I had replied to without having a clue what it would accomplish. And letting Maria, someone I didn't know that well, into my home, allowing her to see part of me I had not shown anyone. But now I had agreed to go for a coffee with Ben, and I was not prepared for it. In fact, as much Julian had stirred something within me – the desire to change my life – it terrified me. It meant I was giving up control, and that was a risk.

Mulling it over in my head, I couldn't see anything too negative that could come from having lunch with Ben. The worst that could happen would be if he wanted more than friendship, but I had no right to assume his motivation for asking me. He seemed friendly, so why not take him at his word that he just wanted to thank me? And we had got on well, hadn't we? It wasn't often I felt comfortable talking to anyone so maybe it would be okay. I might actually enjoy myself.

But when one o'clock came and Ben turned up, I couldn't shake off the feeling that I didn't deserve to be going for lunch with him. My karma was disrupted; I should be sitting alone in the break room with my Marmite sandwich finishing *Catcher in the Rye*. None of this was right.

'Are you ready?' Ben said, brushing droplets of rain from his jacket sleeves. He looked different and I couldn't immediately tell why. Then I noticed he wasn't wearing his glasses and I wondered why. 'You'll need an umbrella!'

We ended up at Caffè Nero and it set me at ease. After all, if Ben had taken this to be anything like a date it was unlikely he would have brought me here. But despite this, I was too nervous to eat, so made an excuse about being so hungry earlier that I'd had to eat my sandwich before he came. I ordered a hot chocolate, though, and despite his protests, I insisted on paying for everything.

'So did you save the cat?' I asked him, when I returned from ordering.

His eyes lit up. 'Yep, she now has a new temporary home and an adoptive father.'

I frowned. 'That was quick.'

'Well, actually it's me. We're so short of space at the kennels that I decided I'd look after her until we can find her a permanent home. I've just bought new leather sofas but sod it, animals are more important than furniture, right?'

I nodded, although I wasn't sure I would have made the sacrifice he had. I wasn't a cat person. Or a dog person. Or an any animal person, but that didn't mean I wanted any harm to come to them.

'So,' Ben continued. 'You know so much about me already and I know nothing about you except you work in the library. Surely that's not fair?'

And there was the thing I dreaded, the reason I didn't do things like this: intrusion into my life. I searched my mind for something, anything, I could say to him so he would assume I was just a normal woman, but there was so little I was able or wanted to share. 'Well, you also know I'm addicted to books.'

'You and me both.'

'Yes, but I don't give mine away.' I hadn't meant to say this or sound rude but Ben's eyes widened.

'Well, you can blame Pippa for that. She needs all the space she can get.'

Pippa. So he had a girlfriend. Relief flooded through me and my shoulders relaxed.

I was about to ask him about her but got distracted by the server bringing over our drinks and the cheese and pesto toasted sandwich Ben had asked for. When I saw it I wished I'd ordered something to eat myself.

'Want some?' Ben asked, catching me staring at his food. 'No meat in it, of course.'

Shaking my head, I smiled because somehow it didn't surprise me that Ben was a vegetarian. I distracted myself from hunger by sipping my hot chocolate while Ben munched his sandwich.

The more we talked, the harder it became to keep up my guard. Ben was nice. Probably too nice, but I wasn't complaining. I began to feel at ease, almost forgetting myself. As if I was watching two characters on television. The past drifted away and there was no future to worry about, only the moment we were in. It wasn't a romantic or sexual feeling, more like the comfort of family. Or at least what family should be like.

And then came the question that hurled me back to reality. 'So do you have a boyfriend?' I thought of Adam then. He was the only person who'd had the title of *boyfriend* so I had no other frame of reference. It seemed ludicrous; it was so long ago and I was nothing more than a girl, yet it remained a fact.

Shaking my head, I tried to make light of his question. 'No, much too busy reading for all that.'

Ben rubbed his chin. 'Yeah, I suppose it's better to live in someone else's world sometimes, eh?'

We both laughed, but he had no idea how close he had come to the truth. How close he had come to me.

'I'd better get back to work,' he said, looking at his watch. 'Got to drive out to Acton this afternoon for a training course. Thanks for having lunch with me.' He looked at my empty mug. 'Even though you didn't eat.'

He insisted on walking me back to the library, and by the time we got there we were both drenched. My phone vibrated in my pocket and I fished it out, my wet fingers leaving a trail of water on the screen. The screen showed me I had a new email and I knew who it was from even before I could read anything clearly. Wiping away droplets of rain, I opened the email and read the reply.

Don't go getting any ideas. There's no way he wants anything more from you than to pass his lunch hour.

My knees felt as if they would give way, but I quickly recovered and looked around us. Someone was watching me, they had to be. Someone had seen me go for lunch with Ben. But there was nobody paying us any unusual attention. Nobody even looking in our direction.

'Leah? What is it?' Ben reached for my arm.

I shrugged him off. 'I'm…It's fine. Just work needing me back. Sorry, got to run. See you.'

'Wait, here, take this.' He pulled a business card from his pocket. 'In case you want to talk about books or something. Or find an animal in distress.'

I took it out of politeness, trying to still my shaking hands, but couldn't say anything. And as I walked off, I could feel Ben watching me, wondering what the hell had just happened.

After that I couldn't concentrate at work. Maria could tell something was wrong, but I dismissed her concern and told her I was probably still getting over my illness. I could tell she wasn't buying it, though, and tried hard to avoid her for the rest of the afternoon, making excuses for needing to be anywhere she wasn't. But I could feel her eyes on me whenever she made an excuse to be close by.

When it got to six o'clock, I gathered up my coat and bag and rushed out of the library, straight into the piercing cold. All I could think about was getting home to lock my door and plan what I should do next. I had never walked home so hastily, and took nothing in around me but the ground at my feet. It was still raining but I barely noticed that either.

Inside my flat, I bolted the front door, scooped up the mail on the floor and rushed upstairs, my breathing only slowing once I sank onto the sofa. I didn't even remove my coat, and my bag was still slung across my body.

My laptop was balanced on the arm of the sofa and I grabbed it and logged on to Hotmail. I knew the words wouldn't have changed but hoped seeing them again would strip them of their toxicity. The meaning of them would never alter, but perhaps I could change my perspective and find a way to deal with it.

But no matter how long I stared at the two sentences, nothing changed the fact that someone had been watching me in the coffee shop with Ben. Things had escalated, which meant the police might take the messages seriously, but I couldn't go to them. No way. Whoever was doing this could be face-to-face with me and I still wouldn't be able to ask a police officer for assistance. Which left me no alternative but to deal with it on my own.

I didn't feel like eating, even though I'd had nothing since breakfast, and was about to go to bed and read when I thought about Julian. Perhaps he would be online, or might have left me a message? Either one of those things would help erase thoughts of my emailer.

Logging on, I tried to forget how likely it was that someone was watching all my activity online. There was no way of knowing whether Julian was moderating the website that evening, but when I checked my messages I found one from him. A sliver of excitement passed through me, vanquishing all my fears. It was only a short message, asking if I'd be online the next day, but it was still a glimmer of light in the darkness that enveloped me.

CHAPTER TEN
2014

It was always difficult going back to Watford. I sat on the train, huddled against the window, telling myself I was doing it for Mum. Repeating it in my head like a mantra until I was almost convinced it would be okay. Surely if I was doing something good then karma would repay me somehow? Perhaps even end the email messages? But I knew that was too much to hope for; one good thing wouldn't make up for the terrible acts of my past.

I had picked a late morning train, assuming it wouldn't be busy, and I was in luck; only two others sat in my carriage, both of them men in suits with their heads buried in newspapers. I was inconspicuous, alone with my thoughts.

Through the window, I watched trees replace buildings as we headed out of London. The train journey was only twenty minutes to Watford Junction but I would have preferred it if I'd had to go across the country. Even to Scotland. Anything that would delay the moment I'd have to step onto the platform and once more face the place that used to be home. Home was not just a title for where you slept, it was meant to be somewhere that comforted you, not just the house but the whole town or city. A place where memories were built and cherished. Watford would never be that place for me again.

Nothing about the house had changed since I'd lived there, and as I stood on the doorstep, I could have been twelve again.

Or fifteen. Even nineteen. The years all blurred into one, just as they did every time I visited. But I didn't want to be the person I was at any of those ages. Apart from to see Mum, I didn't want to be there at all.

'Oh, you're here, I didn't think you'd make it.' Mum stood holding the door open. She seemed thinner and her black trousers and purple blouse hung loosely on her. I'd only been here a few weeks ago so was shocked at the difference in her. But no matter how she was feeling, Mum always dressed smartly.

I had no clue why she was greeting me with those words when I'd phoned barely two hours ago to say I was on my way. I explained this but she raised her eyebrows. 'Well, you haven't been for a few weeks and I just know how busy you are at work. Anyway, come in. You haven't got a bag with you, aren't you staying?' I'd also told her it would be a short visit, just for some lunch perhaps, but nothing I'd said seemed to have registered. Mum heard only what she wanted to hear.

Following her into the house, I shuddered as I stepped into the hall. I replayed the mantra in my head. I was there for Mum. As was the case outside, nothing had changed inside either and it always disorientated me. Many years had passed since I'd lived there, but with every visit it was as if time had frozen, or rather Mum had frozen it. Why wouldn't she want anything to be different? She could redecorate or rearrange the furniture, anything that would give the place a new feel. Why would she keep the past trapped in there with her? Only one thing was noticeably absent: my father's presence.

In the kitchen, Mum asked if I wanted tea or coffee. I wasn't thirsty but didn't want to disappoint her by refusing, so asked for tea. I told her I would make it for us and when I'd finished we sat at the table, uncomfortable in each other's presence. Thankfully, Mum was always good at filling silences, and she did so then, rambling about a ballet performance she'd been to see a couple of nights before.

I watched her as she spoke, and realised she was the one thing in the house that *had* changed. Her face, so identical to my own, was now haggard, her skin folding over itself, even though she was only fifty-five. She had covered her face in a layer of foundation – something I never bothered to do – but it couldn't mask the stress lines. I looked away, unable to stare at something I was responsible for.

When she'd finished recounting details of the ballet, Mum suggested we go for a walk. 'Just to Cassiobury Park, Leah. I know it's cold but it's not far and you've got a thick coat, haven't you? We'll be fine. Fresh air will do us some good.' She was talking as if she rarely left the house when, in fact, the reality was the opposite. The truth was, she wanted me to see more of Watford again, to get used to it, to appreciate my hometown.

There was no reason I shouldn't go for a walk. Cassiobury Park held no memories for me, other than feeding the birds with Mum and Dad as a small child, but there was always the chance I would bump into someone. I may have buried the past, somewhere deep inside me, but there were plenty of others who would not have. Could not have. And seeing me would only reignite their rage. The harassment I was being subjected to was proof of that.

I turned to Mum. Even though her lips were pursed, something about her face begged me to do this for her. I weighed up the odds: it was nearly lunchtime on a freezing cold weekday, so what were the chances of me bumping into a familiar face in a park? I had to go, for Mum's sake.

'Okay, maybe just quickly?'

Her lips remained tight as I said this, but her eyes brightened.

Mum chattered away as we walked, grilling me for details of my life. I tried to answer her questions by shedding a positive light on things, but it was the same each time I saw her; she was never satisfied with my answers. Staring at the ground, because I didn't want to see anyone I knew, I told her the same as always. No, I didn't have a boyfriend. No, I hadn't been anywhere nice lately. Yes, work was fine. I mentioned the prospect of promotion and her face lit up, for a moment all the spidery lines becoming less visible.

'It's not guaranteed,' I warned her, but she was already too excited to let my caution bring her down.

We reached a path, on either side of the pavement the trees leaning across so it looked as if they were kissing in the middle, above our heads. I never paid much attention to my environment, but it struck me as beautiful so I asked Mum if we could sit for a moment. I had spotted a bench further along, and with nobody around, it seemed safe to stop.

Her face brightened. 'Of course, it's lovely out here, isn't it?'

And I surprised myself by agreeing with her. So far, this walk had been harmless. There weren't many people around, and those we had passed paid us no attention. But I still eyed everyone with suspicion; people I didn't recognise might still know who I was.

Mum hunched her shoulders and wrapped her arms around herself. 'I used to come here with Dad,' she said. 'After.' She turned to me and narrowed her eyes.

This was the first time in years she had mentioned anything to do with what had happened, and I was shocked into silence.

But my reticence didn't deter Mum. 'We'd sit for hours and just talk about everything. Hoping to make some sense of it all, I suppose.'

I didn't need to ask why they couldn't talk at home; they would have needed to speak without any chance I would over-hear them. I remained quiet, letting Mum get everything out in the open. So many times I had longed for her to talk about it but she always clammed up, telling me to leave it be. Perhaps that was why she had forced Dr Redfield on me, so that I would have someone else to unburden myself on. But things were different now. I was fine. I didn't need to talk about anything. Except what had been happening lately. With Mum's newfound loquaciousness on the topic, I wondered if she could help me.

'So what did you come up with?' I asked, trying to swallow the lump that had formed in my throat.

She looked away, staring straight ahead and clicking her nails. It was a habit she'd always had but she did it more when she was under pressure. 'Well, to start with we blamed ourselves. I mean, children learn from their parents, don't they? So we reasoned that somewhere along the line we had influenced you somehow.'

'No, Mum, that's not true,' I said, shaking my head. There was no way I would let her take the blame for this. I alone was responsible for my actions.

Mum turned to me. 'We spent so much time going over what we could have done differently, but then we realised there was nothing. You were your own person and we felt that we'd guided you, done everything we could for you—'

'You did.'

'Let me finish. Now I've started I want to get everything out in the open. Please, just hear me out.' Her voice was stern, making me feel like a child again.

I nodded but turned away from her. Hearing her words was bad enough, but I didn't want to see the expression on her face.

'We felt that we were good parents, Leah,' she continued. 'And when he died from his awful heart attack, your dad still had no clue why you did it. I still don't now.'

I could give no answer to this. I had tried to work it out many times afterwards but none of it was easily explainable. I had loved Adam and didn't want to see him hurting. Changing before my eyes. Becoming increasingly unrecognisable the more time passed. But perhaps it was not as simple as that. It could be I wanted to believe this just to ease my conscience – because even worse than that was the thought that, beyond fear, there was no other reason.

Mum stopped clicking her nails and turned to me. 'Anyway, my concern now is for you. There's no point going over it all, it's in the past and nothing can be changed. Are you happy? I don't see how you can be, being on your own all the time. Why do you insist on punishing yourself like this?'

And now we were back to a conversation we'd had many times. My isolated lifestyle irked Mum, despite how many times I'd protested that I was fine. I don't know what made me choose that moment to open up to her; perhaps it was because she had been candid with me, for a change. 'Mum, I am okay, but...'

'What is it? I knew there was something. What's going on, Leah?'

I began to explain everything that had happened, but quickly realised I would need to tell Mum about Julian and Ben too, otherwise the emailer's later messages would make no sense, be out of context, just as I felt opening up to Mum. She didn't flinch when I mentioned Julian, but I told her we had met on a website for book lovers and skirted over my feelings for him. Ben was easier to explain because we'd met at the library and there was nothing between us. Mum stayed silent, letting me finish my story while she intently watched me.

When I got to the end, she reached for my hand. 'Oh, Leah, I wish you'd told me this before. Why do you always have to keep things from me? You're such a closed book. I wish you could see it's not good for you.'

Of all the things I was expecting her to say, this wasn't one of them. Although she had never been good at dishing out sympathy, I assumed this situation was important enough for her to at least try and understand. Try and help me. 'It only started a few days ago,' I said, trying to smother my annoyance. 'And I'm here now, telling you everything.'

Mum let go of my hand and once again stared ahead of her. A young mother walked past, clutching her toddler's hand, and she smiled at us, obviously assuming we were having a nice chat. Mother and daughter. Years ahead of her and her own girl. But at that moment I felt more as if we were strangers than members of the same family.

'Yes, I suppose it's more than you normally do, and I should be grateful for that. Anyway, the only thing you can do is ignore this person. They're just trying to upset you. Stop replying to the messages. I'm sure it will all go away, once the anniversary is further behind you.' You, she had said, not us. That summed up Mum's feelings about it all; it was my problem to deal with.

I wanted to ask her who she thought it could be, but she chose that moment to stand up. 'We'd better get back, hadn't we? I'll make us some lunch, would you like that?' And as quickly as it had started, the conversation was over.

Somehow I managed to nod, even though I was confused by Mum's attitude. She was always telling me to be more open, yet when I had been, about something so personal too, she brushed me off and moved on, filing the problem away in a neat compartment and forgetting it existed.

And as we headed home, Mum twittering on about her friend, Nancy, who needed an operation, I had never felt more alone. That was what happened when you let people in.

Back at the house, Mum made cheese and ham sandwiches and we sat at the dining room table, a setting far too formal for the occasion. There was no more mention of my predicament, and Mum didn't question me further about Julian or Ben. Instead, she asked me about Maria and whether or not I thought of her as a friend.

'In a way,' I told her. 'But I haven't known her that long. It's more of a work friendship.'

Mum peeled the crust from her sandwich. 'I see. Well, friendships take time to grow, don't they?' And then she changed the subject once again and told me she was planning to go to Derby next weekend to put flowers on Dad's gravestone.

'Come with me, Leah. You haven't been for so long, I think it would be good for you.'

It was strange she had chosen to have him buried there, in the town they had both lived as children, yet she had stayed put in Watford. But I could never bring myself to ask her about it. I assumed the main reason was because she didn't want to say goodbye to the memories of Dad. But there was another alternative: perhaps Watford was as tainted for her as it was for me so she didn't want him laid to rest here.

'I have to work on Saturday,' I said. 'But I promise I'll come next time.'

After we finished eating, I helped Mum wash up – she didn't believe in putting the dishwasher on unless she'd had a houseful of guests, so seemed to forget she had one – and then told her I had to go. I was expecting a protest but she only nodded and told me to call when I got back home.

'I want to show you something before you go,' she said.

She led the way upstairs and with each step I found it harder to control my breathing. I never went up there on these visits, never wanted to see my room, which Mum had left unchanged since I'd moved out. But she opened my bedroom door and stepped in, urging me to follow. What choice did I have? I couldn't make a scene. I tried to remember how I had left it, but couldn't picture it. Was there anything in there that would remind me of it?

I walked in and what I saw stunned me. The room wasn't mine. The walls had been stripped of my blue wallpaper and painted lilac. Over by the window, a double bed replaced the single one I'd had, and a matching wardrobe and chest of drawers lined the other walls. There were no posters, clothes or CDs; it was void of everything I'd ever owned. I turned to Mum and she didn't acknowledge my shock.

'I thought it was for the best,' she said. 'Now you might actually want to stay here once in a while.'

The train journey home allowed me time to think, to get my jumbled thoughts straight and try and make sense of everything. For years I had wanted Mum to change things in the house, but it had still been a shock to see my room so different. But it was a good thing. I could see myself staying there now, for Mum's sake. And now she had done the hard bit, there was every chance she would redecorate the whole place.

But once I was home, hatred for my emailer overwhelmed me. Every positive step I tried to take was ruined by his harassment. There was no way I would let this anonymous person interfere with my life; I was minding my own business, doing no harm to anyone, so what right did anyone have to shake my world? Although there was little I could do to prevent further correspondence, I would not sit timidly by, letting him think I was cowering in a corner.

So after making a strong black coffee, I sat at the kitchen table with my laptop and replied to the last email.

I don't care what you want, but what you need is help.

I didn't add any more, those words were enough to at least give me some control back. They made me sound strong, as if all the messages and everything else I'd been sent had no impact on me. I doubted it would stop anything, but it at least felt good to humiliate whoever it was.

After that I decided I would remove all thoughts of the emailer from my mind, at least until they said something else I would have to confront. I logged on to Two Become One and loitered in a chat room. There was still no message from Julian, but maybe he was moderating tonight?

But I couldn't get interested in the conversations I was reading, and was about to log off when a message pinged onto my screen.

Moderator34: was beginning to think you'd abandoned me. U r never on here!

LeahH: We just seem to keep missing each other!

Moderator34: Well, we r here now. So tell me about ur week

LeahH: It's been long. Just work stuff, nothing major

Moderator34: then let me take you out to take your mind off it

I read Julian's last line again, wondering if there was any way I could have misinterpreted it. But there was no ambiguity; he was asking to meet up. I had longed for this to happen, but now that it had, my stomach sank. There was no way I could do it. And saying no would mean an end to our conversations; the one thing that had begun to cast some light onto my existence. But as I began to type, I realised I didn't necessarily have to say no.

LeahH: Would love to. Will be away for the next two weeks but how about after that?

Julian's reply sprang up so quickly that I barely had time to work out where I was going on my fictional trip.

Moderator34: no problem. going anywhere nice?

LeahH: Just to Italy with my mum. She's alone so I thought it would cheer her up.

Julian: ur a very kind lady

If only he knew how wrong he was. That Mum and I hadn't been on holiday together since I was a kid. That she would never want to now.

LeahH: Just doing my job of being a daughter!

Julian seemed to like my story, and it distracted him from working out that I was stalling. It was difficult enough to trust people online so I didn't need him worrying about whether or not I was genuine. That made my lie about Mum easier to live with.

He began telling me about his family: two sisters and a brother, parents both alive and still married. I soaked up every detail, imagining what it would have been like to have siblings. Would things have turned out differently? Perhaps I wouldn't have been so desperate for Imogen's friendship in the first place if I'd had a clan of brothers and sisters to offer me company.

It got late as we continued speaking and was nearly midnight when Julian announced he'd better get some sleep. He had an early meeting the next day and needed to be refreshed. But before he said goodbye he asked me for my email address, so that we could communicate more easily. At first I felt excited that things were progressing, so I gave it to him. What harm could giving it to him do? After all, my tormentor already had it, and most likely access to my computer, and that was the worst-case scenario. I had considered getting a new laptop but couldn't afford it at the moment. Let him or her see how happy I was. That I had met someone I could make a go of things with.

But after Julian and I said goodbye, it dawned on me that there could be no meeting up for us.

Which meant there would be no more Julian.

CHAPTER ELEVEN
1999

'Where's Corey?' I ask Imogen, as we walk to my house. In the last couple of months they have become inseparable, so it is strange seeing Imogen without him. I don't mind, though; it means I get to see a lot of Adam. And now we are on the cusp of something, I can feel it. I have sworn Imogen to secrecy and made her promise not to say a word to Corey, or Adam himself. Only I will know when it's right to mention it.

'He said they'd meet us at yours. At about eight. Your mum's still going out, isn't she?'

I nod, filled with excitement at the prospect of an evening without my parents. It is their wedding anniversary today and this is the only reason Dad convinced Mum I'd be okay on my own for a few hours. 'Yep. Won't be back till at least ten.'

'I can't believe she's actually leaving you alone,' Imogen says. She stops and takes my arm. 'I need to ask you something and I know it's taking the piss, but do you think I could be alone with Corey for a bit this evening? We're hardly ever by ourselves and never get a chance to—'

'That's fine,' I say, not wanting to hear any details. It is hard now to hear about Imogen's sex life when I still haven't even kissed a boy.

'Hey, maybe if you and Adam are alone something might happen?'

This is an interesting idea. It is always the four of us together, or just Imogen and me, so I've never been alone with him. The possibilities are endless, aren't they? If Imogen and Corey keep to themselves this evening, I might get a chance to tell Adam how I feel. Buoyed by this idea, I pull at Imogen and we resume walking. There are only four hours until the boys get to my house, and I need to look decent.

'I thought they'd never get going,' Imogen says, jumping onto my bed and flinging her arms up. 'Now we can finally get ready.' She pulls a carrier bag from her school bag and carefully removes some neatly folded clothes. I join her on the bed to get a closer look at what she's brought. It is a brand new glittery top and some new dark jeans and I smile to think how being with Corey has made her put more effort into her choice of clothing. She hasn't shed her plumpness, but it makes no difference to Corey and I love him for that.

'Now, what are you going to wear to impress Adam?' she says, springing up and heading to my wardrobe.

When we've both changed, and hastily applied some make-up Imogen has stolen from her mum, we go downstairs to wait for the boys. 'Are you sure Adam's coming too?' I say, even though I have checked several times already.

'Yeah, so just relax.'

But this is easier said than done when I feel as though I'm about to puke all over my new sparkly tunic top. I join Imogen on the sofa and watch her as she shovels salt and vinegar crisps into her mouth. They must be left over from her packed lunch because I'm sure we don't have any in the house. She offers me one but I shake my head. How can I eat when in less than ten minutes I will have a chance to be alone with Adam?

I should probably use this time to plan what I will say to him, how I can bring up such a huge topic, but my mind won't let me form any ideas. So instead I listen to Imogen tallying up how many times she and Corey have done it, and wonder if it will ever be me saying the same thing to her.

The boys turn up late – over half an hour – but I don't care because I'm so happy to see them. An attack of nerves makes me forget to offer them something to drink, but thankfully Imogen does it for me.

'No thanks, I've got Coke,' Adam says, pulling a can from his pocket.

'Me too,' Corey says, mirroring Adam's action. It is not the first time I have noticed Corey copying Adam, and I glance at Imogen. But she hasn't seemed to notice and is pulling Corey towards her.

'Give it a break, you two,' Adam says, grinning.

Corey immediately breaks away from Imogen's grasp and apologises to Adam, but she doesn't seem to mind.

We hover in the hallway for a moment, unsure what to do with all this freedom, until Adam comes up with an idea. 'Let's listen to some tunes,' he says. 'I've got the new Robbie Williams CD.' He reaches in his pocket again and pulls it out, waving it in front of us as if it's a wad of cash. I don't tell him I'm not keen on Robbie Williams, but smile and lead the way upstairs.

'Wait!' Imogen says. 'I thought maybe me and Corey could just be alone for a bit.'

Adam opens his mouth to respond but Corey beats him to it. 'Maybe later. Let's go and listen to Robbie.'

As we all traipse upstairs, Imogen lags behind, disappointment etched on her face for the first time today. I feel for her then; she's been looking forward to being alone with Corey all day.

'So this is your bedroom. It's nice,' Adam says, walking into my room. I feel myself blush, even though it's not really me he has complimented. At that moment I am glad I didn't opt for girly pink walls, as Mum suggested; my choice of pale blue is much more grown-up.

Adam locates my CD player and loads the disk, not even asking if I mind him doing it. But I am too drunk on this weird feeling to care. He could start throwing my things around the room and I would probably laugh. It should bother me that I'm losing my head over him, but after so many years of feeling nothing for any boy, I am grateful to finally feel normal.

Plonking themselves on the floor by the stereo, Adam and Corey chat away, hardly listening to the music, and beside me on the bed, Imogen hugs my pillow, no doubt anxious for the last song to play. Once again I feel bad for her. After all, it is rare for her and Corey to have a chance to be alone, but I am also happy. I don't even mind if I am not left alone with Adam tonight; I am enjoying watching him, and for now that is enough. Besides, I still haven't worked out what the hell I will say.

'This is the last song,' Adam announces, and Imogen's face brightens. 'Great album, isn't it?' I bet she's hardly heard a note.

We all nod and show enthusiasm, particularly Corey, but I wonder if any of us are being genuine.

'I'm trying to get my mum to let me go to his concert in the summer, but so far she's not giving in.' Adam stares at the floor. 'I'll get through to her, though. When she sees my marks for this term she'll have to let me go.'

This is another thing about Adam I admire. He barely listens in class but gets As and Bs in everything. I, on the other hand, study hard to get my As. And other than for English, it is a real chore. But it's what I have to do to make something of myself after school. I want to go to university – maybe Adam and I will end up at the same one? – and have a career. I don't want to be like Mum: a housewife who could have done more with her life.

Imogen joins Corey on the floor and whispers something to him. He shakes his head in reply. It's not hard to guess what she's asked him and I feel for her at this moment. I don't doubt Corey loves her, but being in Adam's presence is intoxicating; it doesn't matter whether you are male or female, it just feels good to be around him.

'Did Adam tell you what he did today? To Miss Hollis?' Corey says, clearly trying to distract Imogen from her attempts to whisk him off.

'Bitch,' Adam mutters, pulling out his CD and carefully placing it in its case.

'What happened?' Imogen asks.

Adam huffs. 'We had a test last week and she gave us back our papers today. She was handing them out and saying how well Simon and Elliott did for getting eighty-nine per cent and how proud she was of them—'

'Yeah, and then Adam looks at his paper and he's got ninety-six per cent! We checked with everyone later and that was the highest mark. What a bitch!'

Imogen and I both agree that Miss Hollis has been out of order not to praise Adam when he's done better than everyone in the class.

'So guess what he did?'

Adam stands up. 'I'll tell it, Corey. At break I went to her classroom, didn't really know what I'd do, but then I saw she had all her next lesson's notes up on the whiteboard.' He pauses for dramatic effect. 'So, I rubbed it all off and threw out the lesson plan that was on her desk. She had loads of stuff written on it, it was practically an essay so there was no way that didn't mess up her next class.' Adam doesn't gloat as he says this;

instead he reports the facts in a serious tone, as if he is reading the news.

'Oh my God, Adam, good one!' Imogen says. 'But does she know it was you?'

We all turn to Adam and he shakes his head. 'There's no way she could know, it was ages after our lesson, and I didn't say anything to her about not mentioning my mark. As far as she knows, I have no idea about her bitchy act this morning.'

I force myself not to frown. 'But she does know you hate her, so be careful,' I say. I don't agree with what he has done, but this is all I dare to say. If I disagree with him then surely he won't like me?

Adam doesn't seem bothered by my comment. 'Don't worry, Leah, I know what I'm doing.'

'Yeah, Adam's got more tricks to play on her,' Corey says.

'Like what?' Imogen asks, seemingly forgetting her plan to be alone with Corey.

Not wanting to hear what Adam is planning, I go downstairs to get some drinks. I still like him – of course I do – but that doesn't mean I have to agree with everything he does, like Corey and Imogen seem to. Mum and Dad always disagree on things but they're still married so it's not a deal-breaker. No, I still want Adam as much as ever.

While I'm grabbing a bottle of lemonade to take upstairs, I notice the time on the oven clock. It's already five to nine so we have less than an hour left before the boys have to disappear. They have been here before, of course, but never without a parent being home. Mum would have a heart attack if she came back early and found them here. I'd never be allowed out again. But Adam is worth this risk.

When I get back upstairs, Adam is alone in my room, sitting on the bed with his back against the wall. He's wearing loose jeans and a red hooded top tonight and I always find it strange seeing him out of uniform, even though I should be used to it by now.

'Where are Imogen and Corey?' I say.

'I told them to have some time alone,' he says, casually, as if he commands the world. 'They're in the spare room. That's okay, isn't it? Come and sit with me.' I'm about to tell him that's not a spare room, it's Dad's study, but think better of it.

For a second I wonder what he would do if I refused to sit with him. Became one of the first people – other than Miss Hollis – to resist him. But, of course, I could never do this, and before I think any further, my feet are urging me towards him. I flop onto the bed and push myself up to the wall, but make sure there is a gap between us. I don't know how close he will want me.

I have to tell him now; this might be the only chance I get before we break up for summer. Adam has told us his parents are taking him to America for three weeks to visit family, so if I don't open my mouth tonight then it will be too late. He could start to like someone at school – please don't let it be Dionne – or he could meet someone in America. I can't let that happen; he's meant to be mine. And then I have an idea. I can test him out by asking if he likes any girls at school. If he says yes, I will know not to expose my feelings and therefore preserve my dignity.

But just as I open my mouth to speak, Adam beats me to it and launches into a tirade about how much he loathes Miss Hollis. I listen for a few minutes, to let him get it out of his system, but eventually I am exhausted by his rant. It is already quarter past nine and I don't want to waste any more time.

This no longer seems the right moment to ask about girls, so I decide to find out more about Adam's family instead. He rarely talks about them and all I know is his mum and dad are still together and he has an older brother who lives in New York.

'What's your brother doing in America?' I blurt out, as soon as he pauses for breath.

'Jeremy? Oh, he's at uni. On a basketball scholarship. Lucky sod. I wish I could play.'

'Can't you?' I ask, relieved I've distracted him from talking about Miss Hollis.

'Um, well, a bit. Not that well, though. Not like him. He taught me a lot but I guess I'm more academic.'

It is funny to hear Adam describe himself this way. Even though everyone knows how clever he is, he plays it down and hates anyone mentioning it. But I like it. I'll never tell him that, but I do.

'Well, when you've finished school maybe you could go and live out there or something?' I don't know why I say this, Adam moving away is the last thing I want, but perhaps I am testing the waters.

He turns to me and I see something in his face I can't work out. Sadness? Anger? A mixture of both? 'No, my parents would never go for that. They've already said I've disrupted their lives enough by us having to move to Watford.'

Adam has never told me this, but I know from Corey that he had trouble at his old school in London so had to come to ours. I want to ask him what happened – what trouble could such a bright boy have got into? – but he'd tell me if he wanted me to know.

'Mum and Dad are always giving me grief,' he continues. 'Just because I refused to go to a private school. I mean, what the hell? Why would I want to end up a snobby arsehole at one of those places? No way, I'm happy where I am. Even if some of the teachers are cunts.'

I balk at his language. I've never heard him use that horrible word before. Luckily he doesn't seem to notice; the whole time he's been speaking he hasn't looked at me once. Instead, he plays with the zip on his hoody, pulling it up and down as if he can't make up his mind what to do with it. Not wanting to hear another rant about Miss Hollis, I ask Adam what he wants to do when we leave school.

'Uni of course,' he says, as if I've asked a stupid question. 'I want to be a lawyer.' He looks at me now, so we're clearly on a subject he feels comfortable with.

I'm surprised at his answer. I had no idea what Adam wanted to do, but it seems out of character. Not a stupid idea, though, because he's clever enough, it's just not something I can picture Adam doing.

'That's great,' I say.

'Well, what about you?'

I shrug. 'Definitely uni. But then I'm not sure. Maybe a teacher. Or journalist.'

'Yeah, I can see you being a journalist,' Adam says, smiling. He says nothing about my teaching idea. 'Hey, I wonder what Corey and Imogen are doing,' he says, grinning.

I feel my face redden, just by what he is referring to. 'Well, they better hurry up because you and Corey have to be out of here in less than half an hour.'

Adam snickers. 'That's plenty of time for Corey,' he says, and we both erupt into laughter. I love being like this with him, sharing a joke which is only for us.

Now is the moment. I have to ask him about girls. Taking a deep breath, I begin. 'Adam…'

But he interrupts me again. This time, pulling me towards him and kissing me on the lips. It is a strange sensation, not at all what I expected it to feel like, but nice anyway. His mouth is soft and smooth and I melt into him, trying to pretend I know what I'm doing.

CHAPTER TWELVE
2014

The next day was Saturday and it had snowed overnight, covering the ground in a crisp white blanket. Staring out of my window, I shivered at the sight, even though I wore a thick towelling dressing gown and fleecy pyjamas. Winter already seemed as if it had lasted all year, and I longed to feel warm air on my skin. Across the road, three children were making a snowman, wide smiles stretched across their faces, their laughter piercing the air. I thought of the others then, how that was us once, a time long ago buried, and wondered what the future held for these three.

I should have been working but Sam had called to swap my days off. Although I needed the time at home – I had a list of things to do that seemed to be growing rather than shrinking – I wanted to be at the library. With people around me. At a distance, but still there. But when I thought about it, I was probably better off here because out in public I could easily be spied on. Here I was out of reach of prying eyes.

Despite my determination last night not to let the emailer get the better of me, I now felt uneasy, as if I was just waiting. For another email. For something worse to happen, because now I was convinced it would.

I had no plan, no idea about what to do, other than to wait for another assault and take it from there. My hopes of involving Mum had been shattered by her attitude yesterday, and there was nobody else except Dr Redfield I could talk to, so that was what I'd have to do.

But her phone went to voicemail when I called. I left a message, telling her I needed her advice quite urgently. I added the *quite* because I didn't want to worry her unduly when she must have had other patients with more pressing issues. After leaving my message, it was just another waiting game I was forced to play.

This was not the only thing bothering me. Julian had asked me to meet up with him, and although I had stalled him for now with my story of a holiday with Mum, two weeks would pass quickly and then what? I was conflicted: if I put him off any longer he wouldn't waste another second on me, but how could I start something with him when it would only mean sharing who I was? I needed time to think carefully about this, one mistake could have awful consequences.

Sitting on the floor by the radiator, which was only emitting a tiny amount of heat, I pushed thoughts of Julian aside for the moment and loaded up my laptop, preparing to check my email. There could well be another message and I would have to find a way to deal with it. But when I logged in to Hotmail, the only email I'd received was from Sam, reminding me to apply for the senior librarian position.

She had attached an application form so I spent the next hour filling it out, trying to be as thorough and detailed as I could, selling myself even though I felt every persuasive word I wrote was a lie. Sam had told me it was just a formality, but I still wanted to put in all my effort, to convince myself that maybe I would get the job on my merits, not just because Sam wanted me to have it. I wasn't sure whether Maria was also applying, but hadn't dared bring up the subject.

Once I'd completed the form and read it through twice, I emailed it to Sam and tried to forget about it. I knew better than to get my hopes up, just in case, but couldn't help thinking the money would come in handy. Maybe I could redecorate the flat, or buy some new clothes. I couldn't remember the last time I'd gone shopping for anything other than food or toiletries, and I found the idea exciting. I'd probably order online, though; the thought of crowds was abhorrent to me, no matter how tempting the reward.

It was getting late by then and I still hadn't heard from Dr Redfield. After a quick shower, I grabbed a bowl of cornflakes and sat at the kitchen table, my hair dripping, trying not to think about anything but eating my breakfast.

But no matter how much I tried, I couldn't push away the thoughts of Julian intruding into my head. How was it possible that a stranger could have me obsessing so much? I had never even met him. Yes, I'd seen his photo, but photos were only a tiny percentage of the real person. And what if I did meet up with him and he didn't like me? There was no guarantee of anything so wasn't it better to stay in this fantasy world?

I could tell him I wanted to keep things as they were, just until we knew each other better, surely he would understand that? But then again, that was a crazy idea when he moderated a dating website and had access to all the single women on there. There was nothing to stop him contacting one of them, just as he had found me. I didn't like this feeling. It was like losing control and I'd had enough of that in my life. Not since Adam had I been so distracted by anyone or anything and it felt strange, much like everything had lately.

But no matter how much I hated the feeling of helplessness, I would try to meet up with him. Even if it didn't work out, at least I would know I had tried.

I cleared away my cereal bowl and coffee mug and as I began washing up, my phone pinged with an email. I took a deep breath and opened my inbox. It was Julian.

Hope you still want to meet up?

I replied straight away, telling him I did, and then spent the rest of the morning wondering how the hell I would be able to keep the promise I had made to him and to myself.

To try and distract myself, fool myself into believing my life was as it should be, I tidied and cleaned my flat. There wasn't much to do because I had so few belongings, other than books, so when I'd nearly finished I was still no nearer an answer.

I began dusting the tops of the last shelf of books when I noticed *Of Mice and Men*. It made me think of Ben and how nice it had been hearing someone else enthuse about the novel as much as I did. And that led me to an idea. A crazy one, one I was opposed to in many ways, but one that would help me find the confidence to meet up with Julian.

Ben's business card was still in my coat pocket and I was relieved to see it had his mobile number on it. I didn't want to have to call his house phone and end up speaking to his girlfriend. What was her name? Pippa. That was it.

He picked up straight away. 'Ben? Hi, it's Leah. From the library.' I was surprised how easy I found it so far.

There was a moment's hesitation before he spoke. 'Leah? Hey, how are things? Everything okay?'

It shouldn't have surprised me that Ben was so kind and friendly on the phone. Both times I'd seen him he'd been nothing but amiable. But I wasn't used to talking to men so didn't know what to expect; anything would be a surprise. This made me even more certain I was doing the right thing. I checked what his plans were that afternoon and when he said he had none, told him my idea.

'Lunch? Yeah, that sounds good. How about the West End? I know it's cold but the snow's stopped and it's not a bad day, is it? The sun's out, at least.'

This threw me. I had been hoping to meet up in Wandsworth, or at least Putney, and didn't want to venture further than that. I never went to the West End; it was too crowded and the thought of it terrified me.

I was about to protest but realised it was the least I could do for Ben if he was willing to meet me at such short notice and help me out when there was little in it for him. Besides, Julian lived in Bethnal Green so I couldn't expect him to come all the way here. I had to look at this as training.

I told Ben I'd meet him at one o'clock and he suggested we meet outside Waterstones in Piccadilly.

'There's a roof terrace café there and it's got a great atmosphere. Plus, it's always nice to have a browse through the books, isn't it?'

Trying to hide my concern, I told Ben that this would be my treat, cutting him off when he tried to protest. I told him we'd sort it out later and was about to hang up before I remembered something. 'Pippa won't mind, will she?'

'No, course not. She'll probably be grateful to have the house to herself!'

Although it would take me longer, I decided to get the bus straight to Piccadilly Circus. That way I could at least avoid the crowded tube and stay huddled in the back corner, avoiding eye contact with other passengers.

I sat upstairs, my head buried in my book – I had just started *The Color Purple* and, although I had read it before, I couldn't remember much of the plot – and was so engrossed it in I barely noticed people getting on and off. So far, it was all going well, and I shoved any thoughts that someone might be watching me to the back of my mind.

Ben was right; the café was nice and surprisingly not too full. We sat at a table at the back and talked about what books we were reading. We both ordered salmon and I was surprised to find I felt relaxed. Would it be this easy with Julian? Somehow I didn't think so. It was easy to feel at ease with Ben because I wasn't attracted to him, I wanted or needed nothing from him other than company. There was nothing riding on our lunch, whereas everything depended on my date with Julian. It had the potential to change my life.

Thinking of this reminded me there was someone out there determined that I shouldn't be able to do this. But, once again, I pushed it aside and focused on Ben.

'How long have you been with Pippa?' I asked, poking my fork into a chunky chip.

Ben's face lit up, convincing me he loved his girlfriend and I had nothing to worry about. It was easy to hide the truth behind words – I should know – but there was no faking what I saw in Ben's expression. 'Oh, six years now. She's great. My family all love her too and that helps, believe me.' He fell quiet and I wondered if he'd had a bad experience before he'd met her. 'How about you? Are you happy being single or are you looking for someone special?'

An image of Adam flashed before me but I blinked it away. Things always came back to Adam. I had no idea how to answer his question, but before I could speak, Ben frowned and his glasses tipped further down his nose.

'I'm really sorry, you don't have to answer that. It's none of my business. But I do have to say, I'm surprised you're not attached.'

I wanted to say *you wouldn't be if you knew me*, and the words were at the edge of my mouth, desperate to spill out, but I couldn't do that to Ben. Instead, without thinking, I told him about Julian.

'That sounds promising,' he said, once I'd finished filling him in. 'You should definitely meet up with him. Don't worry, what's meant to be will be, so if you're right for each other then the date will go well. Nothing you can do to control it.'

I thought about this carefully. Did I believe in fate? That everything happened for a reason? I didn't think I could believe that, otherwise what did it mean for those I had hurt? For me?

Shaking my head, I placed my knife and fork together. 'I don't think I believe that. It's too easy. I think we're in control of what we do.'

Ben watched me for a moment. 'Well, maybe. But if that's the case, you have to make things work with this man. If that's what you want, of course.'

After lunch, we browsed the books and Ben bought three crime thrillers. 'I'll be bringing them to the library soon,' he said. 'Unless you want to borrow them?'

I told him I mostly read classics or literary fiction and a frown crossed his face, but he said nothing. I didn't want to appear judgemental, so quickly added that I needed to branch out and explore more genres.

When he'd paid for his books, we walked outside and Ben told me he was walking up to Oxford Circus to get the Central Line. I said I would get the bus from just across the road so we said goodbye, Ben directing me to keep in touch.

I changed my mind once he'd gone and I was left alone in the crowds, and decided to attempt getting the Tube to Earl's Court. I could then get the train straight to Wandsworth Town. I needed to know I could do it. It was a small step, but who knew what it could lead to?

On the platform, I let three trains go because the carriages were too crammed. I just needed a corner, somewhere where there wouldn't be a body encroaching onto me. Even if it meant I would let several more go before that chance came.

I hadn't paid attention to anyone else on the platform, so there was no way I could have foreseen what happened next. There was nobody close to me and when someone barged into me, knocking me to the edge of the platform I had no time to stop myself falling. I heard a scream, and then I was lying flat on the train track, the cold metal digging into my cheek. I didn't have time to feel fear, or anything else, because immediately someone was dragging me upwards and over the platform edge, back to safety. I felt nothing. As if I was watching it all happen to someone else.

'I think it was a woman who did it,' I heard someone saying faintly, as if they were a mile away. 'But it happened so quick. Is she all right?'

I couldn't tell if it was the same person speaking and I didn't care, I just closed my eyes, hoping that when I opened them again I'd be in my flat and none of this would have happened.

A gush of wind forced me back, followed by a Tube train grounding to a stop. It was barely seconds since I'd been lifted from the track.

Someone ushered me to a seat and gradually things came into focus. I didn't think I was badly hurt because I could stand up and walk, but drops of blood from my cut face splattered onto the floor.

Then an Underground employee was checking me out, asking if I was okay, telling me they were calling for an ambulance.

'No!' I almost screamed. 'I'm okay. I'll be fine. I just want to get home.'

But my plea fell on deaf ears as he mumbled something about paperwork and following procedures. I finally convinced him to let me see a first-aider instead and he trotted off to fetch someone, moaning to himself.

While I waited, I felt questioning eyes on me. I stared at the ground, waiting for everyone on the platform to be replaced with new bodies, people who had no notion of what had just happened. It was only then I realised something was wrong. My bag wasn't hanging across my body. I hobbled to the edge of the platform and peered over, but it wasn't on the tracks where I had just fallen. Even if the train had crushed it there would still be some evidence left. I patted the front pockets of my coat and was relieved to feel my keys and phone. I didn't usually keep either of them in my coat but thanked God I had that day, for whatever reason.

Fate, Ben would say.

The Underground man reappeared with a woman carrying a green first-aid case. They spoke between them for a moment, each of them glancing in my direction. When the woman told me to follow her, I went without argument. It was better than the alternative.

'So what happened?' she asked, as we walked, her eyes flickering to the gash on my cheek.

'Someone accidentally knocked into me and I fell,' I said, trying to sound believable. There was no way I could tell her I'd been mugged. That would mean police involvement, statements, police stations. All things I never wanted to think about again. Anyway, this was London; people got mugged all the time, and when did they ever catch the culprits?

Other than my purse, there was nothing much of value in my bag and although it would be time-consuming, cancelling my debit card would be fairly straightforward. And I was alive. Maybe only by a few seconds, but Ben would say I was never meant to be crushed by that train. But as I let the woman clean up my wound, I wondered whether I had been deliberately singled out.

At home, I lay on the sofa with a blanket, shaking from the low temperature in the room and from fear. I tried to reason with myself: the incident was a random mugging, nothing more than coincidence. But every time I thought this, a louder voice told me it had been deliberate. There were no coincidences.

Eventually I concluded that if I didn't speak of it to anyone, not even to myself, then perhaps I could fool myself into thinking it hadn't happened. What good would come of dwelling on it? I was okay.

I took some sleeping pills I found in the bathroom cabinet and went to bed, willing sleep to catch me quickly.

CHAPTER THIRTEEN
2014

Over the next two weeks I heard nothing more from the emailer. I tried to remain cautious but somehow, this time, it felt as if it was over. I had even convinced myself that the mugging was definitely random.

I emailed Julian every day, pretending to be in Italy with Mum, and he replied to each one, long accounts of everything he was up to at work and at home. Even though we had not yet met, through his words I had begun to know him. And it strengthened my resolve to meet up with him, and find out for certain if this could be something real.

Of course I still wondered whether I could actually have a normal life. Go out with a man and enjoy myself without the heavy burden of guilt weighing me down. It seemed too much to hope. But I had to take a chance. Julian was my chance. Even though I knew I didn't deserve it, my compulsion to see him in the flesh grew stronger.

The trouble was, even though I knew what he looked like – I'd stared at his photo long enough to memorise every feature on his face – every time I pictured him it was Adam's face I saw.

We agreed to meet on the Saturday I was supposedly back. Julian picked Hammersmith for our meeting point, and although it was further than I wanted to go, I could get a couple of buses there easily enough. I was determined not to let the mugging put me off meeting him, not when I had made such progress.

Since arranging the date and time, I had decided I would not try to change myself. I would dress in my usual jeans and not fuss too much with my hair. I had to be myself, otherwise what was the point? With Adam I had never tried to change myself so I wouldn't do that now.

But that Saturday evening, as I was about to leave, I changed my mind and wished I had some decent clothes to wear. Something that showed I was making an effort. But it was too late now. At least it was cold outside; if I kept my coat on all night he'd never have to see how dull my wardrobe was.

My mobile rang in my pocket as I walked to the bus stop. Ben's name flashed on the screen and I immediately answered, happy to hear from him. He said he was calling to wish me luck, but couldn't speak long. He was taking Pippa out.

When the call ended, I realised I had come to think of Ben as something like a friend. Sort of. I hadn't told him about the mugging or anything else, but he was someone I was starting to believe I could rely on. A bit like Maria. I never thought I'd be able to call two people friends, but any normal person would consider the two of them to be just that. I only hoped that Julian could be even more.

On the bus I realised there was one small flaw in my plan to meet Julian: we were meeting at the entrance to the Tube, but what if he wanted to go to a pub for a drink? There wasn't much else we could do there so I could hardly argue against it. What would he think of me if I politely refused and suggested somewhere else, anywhere but a pub? Surely it would make him wonder about me? This was just one of the paranoid thoughts that raced through my head as I sat hunched against the window, willing every passenger who got on not to sit next to me.

Heading through the shopping centre, swarms of people rushed past me in all directions, disorientating me. It was too busy and I began to panic. What was I thinking meeting a man I hardly knew? No good could come of it. I turned around, ready to head back up to the bus terminal. But then I felt a hand on my shoulder.

'Leah?'

It was Julian.

And now it was too late to turn back.

Although I recognised him immediately, he looked different from his photo. Not worse, or better, just different. I was so used to seeing him in two dimensions that it was odd seeing him standing before me in the flesh. My first thought was how different he looked to Adam. Julian was almost blond and quite pale, while Adam had been dark, his skin permanently tanned as if he lived somewhere exotic.

Julian smiled at me, waiting for me to speak. I had to say something before I ruined everything. Before he realised he'd made a grave mistake.

'Hi, yeah.' I held out my hand, not sure that was the right thing to do in this kind of situation. No amount of planning could have prepared me for that moment, the awkwardness I would feel meeting a stranger. A man. Who wasn't Adam.

'So this is weird, isn't it?' Julian said, reaching for my hand and shaking it with a hard grip. Maybe he felt as uncomfortable as I did, but I doubted he was as inexperienced as I was. 'All the way here, I planned what to say when I saw you, but I've forgotten it all. Anyway, thanks for meeting up.'

I couldn't believe he was thanking me; I was the one who should be grateful. Julian might just be the person to help me have a normal life.

'It is a bit strange,' I said, letting go of his hand. 'Where would you like to go?'

'Well, I don't know this area that well. What do you recommend?'

Now was my chance to get him to go anywhere other than a pub, but other than coffee shops I couldn't think of a single place to go.

'How about a walk?' I wasn't sure where we would end up but walking had to be better than sitting somewhere while Julian sized me up. He agreed it was a good idea and told me to lead the way.

I knew only one direction to go from there and that was towards Fulham. We could just keep walking, and if we ended up at Putney Bridge then at least there would be a decent view to discuss.

'But if we're going out in the cold we'll need something to warm us up,' Julian said, winking. I didn't know what he meant until he led me into Costa to buy hot drinks.

As we walked up Fulham Palace Road, both of us clutching our takeaway cups, I began to relax. The man beside me no longer seemed like a stranger. He was the Julian I had been talking to for weeks now, his nerves forgotten. And I was the person I had created. It was easy to forget who I was as I hung on to every word that left his mouth, but it was harder to shed thoughts of Adam every time I wasn't looking at him.

'You know, I've never gone on a walk for a first date,' he said, bringing me back to him. 'Not that I'm complaining. It's refreshing to do something different. There's only so much I can take of bars and pubs. Even restaurants.'

The further we walked, the fewer people were around and I felt even better. It might not have been a conventional date but I had taken a chance and it felt good.

'Are you hungry?' Julian asked, stopping outside a fish and chips shop. Being sick with nerves all day, I hadn't eaten much and didn't want to now, not in front of Julian. I was only just getting my head around talking to him.

'Not yet, but maybe soon?' It was the best I could offer.

He seemed disappointed. 'Course, that's fine. I'm just a bit of a pig, that's all. Always thinking of my stomach.'

I gave him a nudge. 'You're not a pig, it is probably dinner time.'

The frown on his face was soon replaced by a smile and it made me feel good to think I had put it there, no matter how trivial our conversation was. It was a start.

As we walked, I realised it didn't feel strange being with Julian. I no longer felt the burden of my inexperience, it had been lifted from my shoulders. This felt right. I stopped worrying about what I was saying and felt free to be me. As much as I could allow myself.

'You intrigue me, Leah,' Julian said, as we headed along Fulham Palace Road. 'I have to say, I don't think I've ever been fascinated by someone before. I mean, I've had relationships, of course, but I just kind of fell into them. But when I started talking to you…I don't know…I just couldn't stop. I felt like you were someone I had to know.'

I couldn't reply. His words had lifted me up, sent my head spinning. Eventually I pulled myself together. 'I know what you mean. It was the same for me.'

He smiled at that and turned to me, grabbing my hand. I felt shocked by the feel of his skin against mine, but I didn't flinch. It felt good.

He smiled. 'Thank God you said that. For a minute I thought I'd messed up big time.'

By the time we reached Putney Bridge I no longer felt cold. Julian's hand still clutched mine, and I basked in the warmth it spread to my body. It was funny how certain people could make you feel so comfortable, so at home. I supposed Maria did too, and Ben. But it was Julian's company I hungered for.

He seemed impressed with the view, guiding me over to the railing in a place I'd stood many times before on my own. This was better, this was how it was supposed to be. Because it was dark, the twinkling lights made the river even more spectacular and as we leaned over the barrier, Julian cuddled against me. Once again I was startled by the feel of his body against mine, but I welcomed it and kept my nerves to myself, relishing the moment.

'This is great,' Julian said. 'You won't find views like this where I live.'

We stood together staring out at the river, and I concentrated on the feel of Julian's arm against mine. But if I continued staring ahead, it wasn't him standing next to me, it was Adam. Someone I didn't want to think about. There was a seemingly decent man next to me yet all I could focus on was the shadow of someone I would never be able to see again.

'I was thinking,' Julian said, and I turned to him, forcing Adam to vanish. 'How about we grab some ingredients, go back to yours and I'll cook us a meal? I'm no Jamie Oliver but I can knock up a decent curry. I would say my place but it's a bit far.'

Normally I would have said no. I would have thrown out a million excuses for why he couldn't come back, but thoughts of Adam still lurked in the back of my mind and I was caught off guard. I didn't want to blow things with Julian and how would he feel if I said no? He would definitely think I had something to hide and I'd never see him again. Maria had just been round and that hadn't been too bad so maybe I could handle it? I had to try. And this would show my emailer that I was stronger than ever.

'Okay. But I have to warn you, my flat's in a bit of a state at the moment so…'

'I won't even notice. I'll be too busy cooking.'

And once again Julian had put me at ease.

It was a strange feeling having him in my flat. Maria being there had helped, but this was different. He was a man and he wasn't Adam. And he was in my kitchen, cooking a more extravagant meal than I had ever tried to attempt. The smell of Thai green curry filled the flat and it seemed so out of place there, just like Julian. I wasn't even sure I was hungry but didn't want to offend him.

I had lost count of how many times I'd apologised for the state of my flat, but Julian brushed each one off, assuring me his flat was not fit for human eyes. Hadn't Maria said something similar? I knew he was lying. Nobody so well groomed would live in a mess.

Julian had bought a bottle of wine, but standing in line at Tesco's had given me plenty of time to come up with an excuse not to have any. Antibiotics, I told him, trying not to feel guilty at his visible disappointment. Instead he'd rushed off and bought me some elderflower juice. 'The next best thing,' he had said.

We sat at my tiny kitchen table and once the food was in front of me I no longer felt nervous about eating. And one bite of it assured me it tasted as good as it looked and smelt. There had to be a catch; how could the man seem so perfect?

'I think Jamie Oliver should be worried,' I said, enjoying watching the smile spread across his face at my compliment.

'Next time I'll do steak,' he said. 'That's if…you want there to be a next time?'

I nodded but couldn't speak, pretending I was swallowing a mouthful of rice.

I knew it would have to come crashing down around me, that there would be something to stifle my joy. Since we'd got back to the flat I had succeeded in pushing away the constant images of Adam that refused to leave me alone. But if it wasn't his face I could see, it was his voice, replacing Julian's with no warning.

It got worse after dinner. At Julian's suggestion we moved to the sofa with our drinks. It had only two seats, which meant we were close enough that our legs were touching. I tried to focus on Julian's words: something about his job, but I wasn't really there. I was back in my old bedroom at Mum's house, with Adam. Then in Adam's bedroom.

Julian didn't seem to notice I was distracted, or that his leg was pushing into mine, and he suggested we watch a film. I didn't have any DVDs, or even a DVD player, so we flicked through the TV channels and noticed *Independence Day* had just started. I had no interest in the film, but it was nice being there with Julian.

'Are you comfortable?' he asked, settling back.

I nodded, but of course, I wasn't. Not any more. I hadn't expected to feel Adam's presence so heavily and it was becoming harder to push aside. Julian was nothing like him, and we were much older, yet it felt the same.

'You can lean on me,' Julian said, pointing to his shoulder. At first I wasn't sure I wanted to, even though I was attracted to him. If I moved any closer he would feel even more like the ghost of my past.

But I did. And a few minutes later I felt Julian's soft lips against my forehead. The sensation had been alien to me for so long, my body didn't know how to react and I froze. Julian must have noticed my body tense and he stopped suddenly, turning back to the television.

He didn't kiss me again after that. Instead, he said he needed some coffee and asked if I wanted one. When I said I'd prefer a green tea, he smiled and headed off to the kitchen.

'I think I'll have one of those too,' he said. 'Make up for that unhealthy curry.'

Coming back to the sofa, we sipped our drinks and continued watching the film.

And that's all I remember.

When I woke in the morning, with light flooding through the windows, I was curled up on the sofa and there was no sign of Julian. I knew he wasn't in the bathroom, it was too quiet. Too still. I checked each room, just to make sure, and that's when I noticed the kitchen was spotless, everything he'd used to cook washed and put away. Even the mugs we'd used for our tea. And with no note or message or anything, it was as if he had never been in my flat.

CHAPTER FOURTEEN
1999

'Can Adam come over today?'

Mum nods but doesn't look up from her paper, and I can feel Dad's heavy stare on me. He has an important meeting today and won't be home until late. Please don't let him make a fuss.

'Wasn't he only here yesterday?' he says.

'No, Imogen was here. Remember?' I take a bite of the omelette Mum has made and it tastes nice but burns my throat.

It's the Christmas holidays now and Dad has been grumpy and miserable for days. I know he prefers it when I'm at school; the house is all his then and he has peace and serenity, as he likes to point out.

'I just think you're too young for a boyfriend. There's plenty of time for that. What's the rush?'

I'm sick of Dad's hypocrisy. He and Mum were only sixteen when they met so what's the difference? There is one rule for them and one for me and I can't stand it.

'I keep telling you, he's not my boyfriend,' I say. But I can tell them this lie until my throat dries up; they'll never believe it.

'Oh, it's fine,' Mum says, finally looking up. 'I'll be here all day anyway.' I silently thank her for saving me from another day without Adam and glare at Dad. He looks away as if he knows he's in the wrong. I don't know what his problem is; Adam has never done anything wrong – at least that they know about – and is always on his best behaviour around them. Anyway, who cares? Adam is coming over and that's all that matters for now.

We finish our omelettes in silence and then Mum busies herself preparing for her book club this evening. She takes it so seriously and prepares detailed questions for all the women to debate. Sometimes I think I'd like to go, but I need to keep all my spare time for Adam. We hardly get a chance to be alone so when we can, I snap up the opportunity.

I overhear Mum on the phone, calling all the women to tell them the book club will be at our house this evening instead of at Lorraine's. Clearly neither of my parents trusts me.

Dad rushes off to his meeting, and before he leaves he kisses my cheek, but the anger is still there. He will never approve of Adam.

'Why do you have to keep the door open? You're not a baby!'

I look at my bedroom door and wonder if Mum would notice if I pulled it shut. She's downstairs, making cupcakes for her book club friends, and hasn't been up here since Adam arrived. That's the good thing about Mum, she is easily distracted by all the things she has to do. All the things she thinks are important but really aren't. Please don't let me turn out like her.

But then I hear footsteps on the stairs and she calls from the landing. 'I've just got to pop out. I'll be half an hour at the most, okay? Just half an hour.'

I turn to Adam and we both smile.

'Now you're all mine,' he says, springing forward and leaping onto me. My whole body tingles and I pull him into me and breathe in the mixture of sweat and Lynx.

We kiss for a long time, and I get lost in him, forget there is anything beyond us. Then Adam pulls away from me and nestles his head against my arm. 'We should stop,' he says.

But I don't want to. I'm ready. I've been ready for months so why do we have to stop? I tell him this, speaking into his hair because I can't see his face.

'It wouldn't be right, would it? You're not sixteen yet.'

I can't believe Adam is saying this. 'But I will be in six months. And Imogen and Corey—'

'But they're not us. I want our first time to be right. I know it sounds stupid, but I kind of want it to be special.' He raises his head so it's level with mine and we are face-to-face. 'This will be your first time and I want you to remember it forever. To remember me forever.'

Adam's words turn my stomach to jelly. I have been looking at this all wrong. Although I have been thinking of my first time as something special to share with Adam, it's also been something I've needed to get out of the way. So that I can be normal, like Imogen. But we don't need to rush. We've got something much deeper than that, and even more special than what Imogen and Corey have, because it's lasted all this time without us needing to have sex.

'I will remember you forever,' I say, burying my head in his chest.

'Let's go ice-skating,' Adam says, forcing me to topple sideways as he jumps up.

'What? Now?'

'Yeah, come on! We can call Corey and Imogen and tell them to meet us there.'

I have never been ice-skating before and the thought of it terrifies me, but I don't want to say no to Adam. 'I don't know how to skate,' I tell him.

'Don't worry, I'll teach you. You'll be fine.'

'Well, I'll have to call Mum to check it's okay.' Even as I say it I know she'll be happier that we're out in public than stuck up here in my room.

'Okay, hurry up. And call Imogen too.'

I get up to go downstairs and make the calls, and behind me Adam is already slipping on his coat.

It is only when we step outside that I realise the significance of what Adam said just now in my bedroom. He wants *my* first time to be special. He said nothing about it being his too.

Planet Ice is crowded and loud and I love it. I never would have guessed there'd be such a buzz here, but with music blaring from the speakers and everyone in a good mood, I can tell it's going to be a great night. As long as I can keep pushing aside the thought that Adam has had sex before.

Somehow Imogen and Corey manage to find us and we trade in our shoes for ice skates, perching on narrow wooden benches to pull them on.

They've all done this before, so I am the only one wobbling and clutching the barrier as if my life depends on it. Adam tries to help me but it's not long before he's desperate to whizz around on his own and I am left alone, seemingly the only person in the rink who doesn't know what to do.

I manage to make it halfway around, still clutching the rail, when Imogen glides towards me, twirling around and coming to a stop right in front of me. 'I always told you this was fun,' she says. 'You should have come with me all those times.'

I vaguely remember her inviting me to go with her and her mum a few years ago but it never appealed to me. And still doesn't. I love the atmosphere but the skating part I could do without.

'Come on, let me help you.' She reaches for my hand and I clutch her tightly and let her guide me around, already feeling better that I'm no longer stuck to the rail. I beg her not to let go and she promises she won't, so I put my faith in her because she has never let me down before.

'So have you and Adam…you know?' She has to lean into my ear so that she can be heard above the music.

'No, Adam wants to wait.' At least with me, I think.

Imogen slows down and searches my face, perhaps wondering if I'm lying. 'Oh…well, that's not a bad thing. He must really like you.'

I'm surprised by her reaction. For months now she has been hounding me to get it over with. And if I told her I wasn't ready then she would say I was being stupid. I am sure of this. But it is not me making the decision, it is Adam.

'We'll know when the time's right,' I say, forcing myself to believe this.

'Hey, let's go and get some ice cream.' She leads me over to the exit and I'm relieved to be back on the floor. We stand by the barrier and search the rink for Adam and Corey. When we finally spot them they are racing each other, weaving in between bewildered people, with Corey lagging behind Adam.

'Let's leave them to it,' I say, not convinced Adam will be thrilled about being pulled off the rink for ice cream.

Both of us choose mint chocolate chip and Cokes loaded with ice, and even though it's already cold in here, we shovel it down.

'You do still like Adam, don't you?' Imogen asks, once she's finished her last spoonful.

'Course. Why?' I could elaborate on this and explain how he is all I think about twenty-four hours a day. Or tell her that I picture us going to uni together. Sharing a flat. Getting married one day. But I don't tell her any of this, even though she is my best friend. Some things I need to keep just for me.

'Well, you just never talk about him. That's all.' But we both know that's not all. That she has a lot more to say. Imogen and I are still close, and I'd do anything for her, but the older we get, the more different we seem to become. I tell myself it doesn't matter, that mature friendships don't need to be based on listening to the same music or liking the same clothes. Our shared experience is a much firmer base than that. But still it bothers me sometimes that it's happening to us.

Imogen opens her purse and begins counting out change. 'I need another ice cream,' she says. 'Do you want more?'

I shake my head. We're all getting burgers after this so I don't want to stuff myself too much, especially when Adam's paying for mine.

'Please yourself,' she says, trotting off to the counter. She doesn't say it unkindly, but I know something is bothering her.

When she comes back, this time with chocolate ice cream, I ask her what's wrong. At first she pretends to be surprised by my question, but it's not long before she admits there is something.

'I'm just worried you're going off Adam. Or he's going off you or something. And it's always the four of us, so what would happen if you split up? It would be so crap without Adam, wouldn't it?'

I watch Imogen's mouth moving but what she's saying is so bizarre, it's as if she's talking out of sync.

'What? Why do you think that? What's going on, Imogen?' I can't keep the annoyance from my voice.

'Nothing. Nothing. It's just neither of you talk about each other much and…well, it's so different to me and Corey. I'm not trying to say—'

'Adam and I are fine. Okay? Nothing is wrong, I promise. I'd tell you if it was.' And as I say this to my friend, I wonder if she would do the same for me.

What I've said seems to pacify Imogen. She finishes her second tub of ice cream, slurping the remainder of her Coke before pushing the cup aside. Our drinks are so gigantic I don't know how she's managed to finish hers when I'm not even a quarter of the way through mine.

Seeming to have forgotten what we've just been talking about, Imogen launches into a detailed explanation of what Helena Fletcher did on the last day before we broke up for Christmas. But I'm only half-listening because I can see Adam striding towards me, his movements made awkward by the fact he's trying to walk in ice skates. Corey is not far behind, as usual trying to keep up.

'You won't fucking believe who's here,' Adam says, pulling at my sleeve. He doesn't bother sitting on a chair but perches on the table. 'Fucking Hollis. That's who.'

Imogen and I look at each other. This can only mean trouble.

Corey tries to sit on the table as well, but there's no room so he has to make do with the chair next to Imogen. 'Can you believe it? What the hell is she doing here? Doesn't she know students skate here?' His words might be angry but he delivers them with excitement.

We all turn back to Adam, who scratches at his arm. I've noticed him doing this a lot lately but have no idea why he does it. Of course I haven't mentioned it. I don't want him to think I'm picking at him. 'Who the hell does she think she is?' he says. 'And guess what? She's with a *man!*'

Again I look at Imogen, but this time I'm not sure if she's thinking the same thing I am. That it doesn't matter if our teacher is here; we can still enjoy ourselves.

'He must be crazy,' Adam continues. 'Who the hell would want to touch her?'

Silently I lose my patience. I have been listening to Adam slating Miss Hollis for years now and I'm sick of it. At school he talks about nothing else so it would have been nice to have a break for one night. I open my mouth to speak but the words fall away, swallowed up by the thought I might upset him. Instead, I try to be a decent girlfriend and understand his anger. After all, I suppose Miss Hollis is a bitch to him.

'Come and see,' Adam says. 'Skating around like she owns the place. Who does she think she is?' He jumps up from the table, sending the empty ice cream tubs and my Coke hurtling to the floor. He doesn't notice what he's done, and is already heading to the side of the rink.

Corey follows him first, a flash of something I've not seen before on his face. He is enjoying this too much. Imogen shrugs and we traipse behind. Am I the only one who isn't interested in seeing Miss Hollis skating? She is entitled to a private life so why can't we just ignore her?

But to Adam that is impossible, and when we catch up to him he points her out, a snarl on his face. 'There! See. The blonde witch.'

It takes me a while to spot her, but when I do I think Adam is mistaken. The blonde woman gliding across the ice with her arm looped through a man's can't be Miss Hollis. She is too confident, too pretty. Miss Hollis would be shrinking back against the rail, surely? But as she approaches our section of the rink, I realise it is definitely her. A different version of her, but still our teacher.

'Look how much make-up she's wearing,' Imogen says, standing with her hands on her hips. I have never seen Miss Hollis wearing even a scrap of make-up so take a closer look. Imogen is right. Or at least half-right. Miss Hollis *is* wearing make-up but it's not too much and it suits her. The man she is with is much taller than her but it doesn't look strange. In fact, they look quite good together. As if they are happy. She leans into him and he laughs at something she says. Even though Miss Hollis is a million years older than me, I feel a stab of jealousy. I doubt Adam and I look that comfortable together.

'It's so crowded, she hasn't seen us yet,' Corey says.

Adam nods. 'Which is good for me. Come on.'

And then he is off, pushing onto the ice without checking if we're following. Corey does, of course, grabbing Imogen along with him. She shrieks and drops her Coke but nobody notices. It is too busy in here for anyone to notice anything.

I stay where I am because they've all sped off to get a closer look at Miss Hollis. There is no way I will be able to keep up. It's hard to keep track of them as more people are crowding onto the ice. Everything is a blur of colour, masking the white that's hidden beneath the mass of bodies.

Eventually I spot Adam's red jacket and try to follow him as he weaves in between other skaters. Corey and Imogen aren't far behind, and all of them are closing in on Miss Hollis. I don't know what Adam's plan is, but I can't believe he will go right up to her and say something.

After a few minutes I'm staring so hard at the figures on the ice that my eyes begin to blur. Something is happening on the rink but I can't make out what. People are grinding to a halt, pointing and skating around a dark mass in the middle of the rink. Someone has fallen over and it is minutes before they get up. Only then do I realise that it is Miss Hollis, struggling to get a grip on her boyfriend's arm. And that she has only narrowly avoided having her head sliced open by someone else's ice skates.

I look for Adam and the others but I can't see any of them until they appear next to me.

'Wow, did you see that? Miss Hollis fell right on her arse.' Adam's grin is stretched across his face and I'm happy to see it, even though it's there at someone else's expense.

I look back towards the rink and see Miss Hollis's boyfriend helping her off the ice. The evening is over for both of them.

But I'm wrong to think that maybe now Adam will enjoy himself. Seconds later he grabs my arm and tells us all he's had enough and we should get to Burger King.

Adam walks me home afterwards and we stand outside my house, leaning against the overgrown hedge that Dad never gets around to trimming. We are hidden from my parents' view here so Adam wraps his arms around me and kisses me. His lips are cold but I still like it and wish he could come inside with me. When he pulls away, he smiles.

'Did you see that bitch this evening? I can't believe it was so easy.'

Frowning, I ask him what he means.

'Miss Hollis, of course. She fell so easily. I didn't think I'd be able to do it at first, without her seeing me, but it was so crowded and she was so engrossed in that man, so…'

'I thought it was an accident.'

'It was. I just gave fate a bit of a helping hand, that's all.'

'But that person nearly skated into her head.'

Adam scrunches up his face and lets go of my hand. 'Yeah, but they didn't. She's fine. Just a few scratches and a sore arse probably. What's the big deal?'

He grabs me again and pulls me towards him, his lips warmer this time. And I forget all about Miss Hollis because Adam is happy. He is mine and that's all that matters.

CHAPTER FIFTEEN
2014

In the harsh light of day it is easy to mistrust things that have happened the night before. And that is what I did the morning after Julian's disappearing act. My first thought was that he'd stolen something, but my laptop was the only valuable thing I owned and that was on the kitchen worktop, exactly where I'd left it. I never had cash in the flat and the only jewellery I owned – a crucifix necklace that belonged to my grandmother – still hung around my neck.

Maria was always talking about men who only wanted sex, and as soon as they'd got it would never be seen again. But Julian and I had barely touched so that couldn't be it. I wondered if he'd felt rejected when I made no move to kiss him further, but that didn't make sense either. He hadn't exactly tried anything other than kissing my forehead, and he was the one who had stopped, not me.

So that left only one other option. At some point in the evening, Julian had changed his mind about me.

My head ached, and I felt dizzy, as if I'd drunk a gallon of wine instead of just elderflower juice and green tea, but I had no painkillers. As with alcohol, I didn't like medicines coursing through my body. I gulped tap water, but it did little to stem the flood of pain, so I went back to the sofa and rested my head on the arm.

Looking around, it wasn't hard to see why Julian had gone off me. My flat was a soulless shell, showing no personality, and although we had got on well, I wasn't the chirpy, flirty type he must be used to. I was just me. I wanted to tell myself if he didn't like me for who I was then it was his problem, that I wouldn't change for any man, but regret that I hadn't made more effort bubbled inside me.

Across the room, I could see through the window that it was snowing again. Small, delicate flakes that floated past the window and made me shiver. I got up to turn on the electric radiator and checked the time. Half an hour was all I'd be able to leave it on for, otherwise the cost would be astronomical. But things would be better once I'd got my promotion, maybe I'd even think about moving somewhere nicer. With more character and central heating. Even as I thought it, I doubted I would bother. I could change my surroundings but nothing would change me.

I still had a couple of hours before I had to leave for work but was unsure how to fill them. It was Sunday morning so Mum wouldn't be home, and I didn't want to check the website. Julian was probably on there right now, searching for someone else. And for once I didn't feel like picking up a book.

While I decided what to do, I made scrambled eggs on toast and sat at the kitchen table, still in my clothes from last night. Julian's scent still lingered on my t-shirt so I didn't want to change yet. I knew whatever we had was finished before it had begun, but needed a few more moments to let it go.

The scrambled eggs were too runny but I wolfed them down, hoping my head would feel better once I'd eaten. This was how things were meant to be: me eating alone at my tiny kitchen table. I'd been foolish to think anything could change. But at least I hadn't heard from the emailer. Things would be normal again now.

Apart from my headache, I started to feel better by the time I got to work, so the smile I gave Maria as I joined her behind the desk was genuine. I had been okay before I met Julian so there was no reason why I wouldn't be now.

'Sam wants us to put up the Christmas decorations now,' Maria said. It was already the beginning of December so I wasn't surprised by Sam's request. In fact, if anything, it was later than we usually left it.

'Don't you just love this time?' Maria continued. 'The atmosphere. People actually being nice when they aren't normally.' Her eyes narrowed as she said this.

I smiled and pretended to agree with her. Christmas was something I just needed to get over with. I told her we should decorate after lunch, when it might be a bit quieter, and secretly hoped the decorations had been lost, stolen or burnt to a crisp.

For a few hours I replenished and tidied shelves, lost in the job I was doing, letting nothing else infiltrate my thoughts. So when someone tapped me on the shoulder I gasped out loud, and the book I was holding dropped to the floor.

I spun around and Ben stood before me, already picking up the book and handing it back to me. 'Sorry about that. I always seem to do that to people.'

'It's okay. Are you here to see me?'

'Yeah, was just on a call. Thought I'd pop in and see how Saturday went.' I didn't need this reminder. All day I'd tried my best to forget about Julian and now it couldn't be avoided. Before I could answer, Maria popped her head around the shelves, stopping short when she registered Ben's presence.

'Oh, sorry…I, um, just wondered where you were. I couldn't see you from the desk.' She held her hand out to Ben. 'Hi, again.' Her tone became frosty and I had no idea why.

'Do you need me?' I asked, but she shook her head and disappeared again.

When I turned back to Ben he was frowning. 'What was all that about?'

'I'm not sure. Maybe she thinks I'm leaving her to do all the work.' But even as I said this I knew Maria wouldn't think that.

Ben gave a half-smile. 'Oh, sorry. I shouldn't be disturbing you at work. I'll go.'

'She'll be fine,' I said. 'And I haven't had a break yet.'

'Well, I just came in to give you this.' He handed me a small white carrier bag.

Confused, I took the bag and pulled out a book. It was by an author I'd never read before and was clearly a crime thriller. Ben chuckled. 'I thought you should give it a chance,' he said. 'You might surprise yourself.'

I couldn't help but laugh then, taken aback by his thoughtfulness. I may have been happy to step back into my solitary life, now that Julian was out of the picture, but I was still grateful to have met Ben. It had been years since I'd had anyone resembling a friend. I thought Maria was there for me, but there was something I was unsure of. Other than telling me about the men that came and went from her life, I knew very little about her. I still had my guard up with Ben, but the more I knew of him the more I liked him.

But not in the way I liked Julian.

I thanked Ben and promised I'd read it. I had already picked out the next few books I was planning to read but I would read Ben's first. I owed him that much.

He looked pleased. 'I'll ask you questions, just to make sure. Anyway—'

'Oh no.' I had just spotted someone coming into the library. The last person I expected to see.

Julian.

The barrier I'd spent the morning building crashed down and I couldn't help but feel pleased. He had come all this way to see me. But I still needed to know what had happened last night.

I turned back to Ben and told him it was Julian walking towards the desk. He was out of sight then and I didn't dare move. What if he saw me with Ben and thought he was my boyfriend? I had no time to think about what to do because Maria was leading Julian over, a frown on her face as she puzzled over what she was witnessing. For months I hadn't even mentioned a man and now two had turned up to see me. It might have been humorous if I hadn't been so worried about what Julian would think.

'I'd better leave you to it,' Ben said, winking.

But before either of us could move, Julian was there, right in front of me, holding out his hand and presenting me with a bunch of flowers. I couldn't tell what they were – I knew nothing about flowers or plants – but they looked expensive. I had never been given flowers before and didn't know how I should feel. Excited probably. But all I could think of was why Julian was here now, holding out flowers I didn't deserve, when only hours ago I had written him off.

'These are for you,' he said, his face flushing because I still hadn't taken them.

Maria had walked back to the desk already and Ben was hanging back but it still must have been hard for Julian to make such a display.

I reached for them, still unsure what was going on. 'I… thanks. They're lovely. I didn't think I'd see you…After…'

'I'm so sorry about last night. I had to get back but didn't want to wake you. I looked for a pen to scribble you a note but there weren't any in the house. And I didn't have your number.'

Julian looked down at his shoes, but he needn't have bothered avoiding my gaze because I was also too embarrassed to look directly at him. He was offering me plenty of excuses and they all made sense. The only pen I owned was in my coat pocket and we had both forgotten to exchange numbers. But he had my email address, so why hadn't he emailed me? And it still felt strange that I'd fallen asleep next to him.

'I know I could have emailed you,' Julian said, as if he could read my thoughts. 'But I'm such an idiot and only thought of that on my way here.'

'Well, it doesn't matter now, does it?' I said, deciding not to make an issue of it. 'And thanks again for these.' I held up the flowers and breathed in their scent. They would brighten up my flat but I would need to buy a vase on the way home. 'Oh, this is Ben.'

Ben stepped forward and held out his hand to Julian. 'Good to meet you. So, Leah says you're a civil servant? That must be interesting.'

A frown creased Julian's forehead and for a moment he made no move to shake Ben's hand. I held my breath, wondering what would happen, but then he slowly leaned forward and gave Ben's hand a brief, loose shake. 'Yeah, that's right. And you are?'

'Ben. Leah's friend.' I hadn't been called anyone's friend for years and it felt odd. I wondered who the last person to label me their friend was. Imogen? Corey? Adam?

When Julian didn't reply, Ben took the hint and excused himself. I hoped he could sense my silent gratitude and apology as I said goodbye, but I had a feeling, after Julian's rudeness, I wouldn't hear from Ben again.

Once he'd gone, Julian seemed to relax and apologised again for his disappearing act. 'Can I take you for dinner? To make up for it.'

I could feel Maria's gaze on us so I began filling the shelves again. 'You don't need to do that. Honestly, it's fine.'

'But I want to. I just…never mind. Are you free on Friday evening?'

Julian's words filled me with pleasure. Not since Adam had I had even the slightest prospect of a date, let alone a second date. It was terrifying as well as exciting.

Even though I felt that way, for a brief moment I considered saying no. Letting Julian into my life was inviting complications and things had been simple before. But didn't someone even as messed up as me deserve a stab at happiness? It was about time I tried to build a life for myself.

Without further thought I agreed to dinner. I knew I wasn't letting him see how thrilled I was, but I had learnt from everything Maria had inadvertently taught me with her ramblings.

Julian finally smiled. 'Great. I'll meet you at yours then we can go to eat somewhere near you.'

As he said this, I pictured my depressing tiny flat and the two of us sitting watching TV again on my uncomfortable two-seater sofa. Would it be better to go to his? I worried about travel all the way to Bethnal Green, but his flat was bound to be more welcoming than mine. Plus, seeing how he decorated and arranged his furniture would give me a further glimpse of his character. Not that it would make any difference if he lived in a mouldy, decaying shack; I was already hooked.

But when I suggested meeting at his place, Julian's face crinkled. 'Um, we could, but it's being decorated at the moment so is a bit of a mess. Next time, though?'

I nodded, disappointed but also relieved that I wouldn't have to travel to east London. At least not yet.

'I'd better let you get back to work,' Julian said. He leaned forward and for a second I thought he was going to kiss my cheek. Instead, he grabbed my hand and said he would see me on Friday at seven o'clock.

As he turned to leave I remembered something. 'Shouldn't we exchange numbers?' I said. 'You know, in case anything happens before Friday. It seems silly to just talk on email now.'

Julian walked back to me. 'You're right, I completely forgot. That's another reason I came to see you. I'm an idiot.' Dipping his hand in his pocket, he pulled out his phone and tapped in my number as I called it out. 'Now I've got yours I can call your phone so you'll have mine.'

Watching him leave, I took the empty trolley back to the storeroom, avoiding Maria's stare as I passed the desk. She had a queue of customers snaked around the desk so there was nothing she could say at that moment. But I knew her head would be swarming with questions.

I was certain she would find a chance to grill me before I left for the day, and it came sooner than I'd hoped. We had served all the customers and it was nearing closing time when Maria mentioned what she had seen earlier.

'So are you going to tell me what's going on or do I have to guess?' Her words weren't delivered with humour, but they were icy, much like Julian's had been to Ben earlier.

'You've met Ben, remember? He donated loads of books to us. We've…kind of become friends now I suppose.'

Maria narrowed her eyes. 'Friends? Okay. So who is this other guy then? And what's with the flowers?'

I didn't intend to lie, but I couldn't let Maria any further in. She was already asking uncomfortable questions and if she knew about Julian I would never get a break. I would be like her; putting my heart out there to get crushed. The more people who knew about any part of my life, the worse it would get for me. I had already told Ben more than I'd wanted, or planned to, so I couldn't do the same with Maria.

'He's my cousin.' I had done it. And now the lie was out there it was impossible to retract.

'Your cousin? Really? What about the flowers?' Her mouth twisted. She was waiting to catch me out.

'Well, I didn't say anything, but my grandmother died yesterday. He was just bringing them to cheer me up. We were really close, you see.'

That changed everything because suddenly Maria's face softened. 'I'm sorry. You should have told me.'

I wondered if she didn't believe me after all, but just didn't want to seem insensitive, but either way, I needed to steer her off the subject. 'How are things, anyway? What happened with that last man? Didn't you quite like him?'

But Maria did not seem happy at my change of topic. Looking at her scrunched up face, it seemed to blend into Imogen's, reminding me of all the times I'd had to bite my tongue in her presence. It hadn't always been like that, but as we'd got older she had become more volatile. What had I become?

'So do you have any other family? You've never mentioned any,' Maria said, ignoring my question and tapping something into the computer. I couldn't tell if she was genuinely working or just needed a distraction, and I didn't dare peer over her shoulder at the screen.

Thankfully, as I was attempting to form a response, an elderly gentleman shuffled up to the desk and handed her a list of books. I took my opportunity and slipped away.

It was dark by the time I left the library, and most of the snow had turned to ice. I walked slowly, trying to step onto any small patches of concrete that were visible. I pulled the hood of my parka up and focused on the ground, paying no attention to anyone passing me.

So when someone knocked into me, I immediately turned and apologised. I looked up, expecting some sort of response, but the tall figure in front of me just stared at me, a misshapen grin on his face. He also had his hood up so I couldn't see much of his face, but his skin was pasty and dotted with acne.

I should have tried to run then because I knew. I knew something was wrong, but my feet wouldn't move.

The man pulled something from behind his back. A white plastic bottle. Yanking off the top, he held it out in front of him. And then I knew what was about to happen to me.

The liquid in that bottle was acid.

I had heard of men doing this to women, to permanently scar their faces, but I wasn't a beauty queen or model with a jealous boyfriend. But that didn't matter. I had my emailer.

The icy liquid sloshed across my face, feeling as if it had stuck there, permanently frozen. But wasn't acid supposed to burn? Why couldn't I feel the heat? It must be shock. I had heard the body shuts down as a way of coping in these situations.

Within seconds the man had dropped the bottle and run off, negotiating the ice like an Olympic skater. I fell to my knees, tears mixing with the acid pouring down my face.

Gasps and shouts erupted all around me and people crowded around, fussing and hurling frantic questions at me. Someone shouted out that they had seen something being thrown in my face.

'Acid,' I tried to say, but my voice was a rasp so I doubted anyone could hear me.

Then, in my peripheral vision I saw a man scoop up the bottle and lift it to his nose. He took a deep sniff and then nodded. 'It's okay,' he said, either to me or everyone standing around, I wasn't sure which. 'It's just water.'

CHAPTER SIXTEEN
2000

Parents have descended on the school like a swarm of insects. It's chaos everywhere. But like I told Adam, this is good. It means that while they're all busy talking to our teachers, we can slip away at some point this evening and be alone. We'll probably end up in a cupboard somewhere, but I don't care. I need to talk to Adam and it has to be tonight. I've put it off for too long already.

He's late. We agreed to meet at the back of science block at half past five and now it's already ten to six. There is nobody around, but I can hear talking and shoes clanking on the pavement around the buildings. Not Adam's shoes, though. He'll be wearing his trainers so I won't hear him coming. I keep looking in all directions. Knowing Adam, he will creep up on me and try to make me jump out of my skin.

It's cold out here and my denim jacket is too thin for this January weather, but it looks nice, and I'll be fine if Adam hurries up. I try to relax, and really I should be feeling good because my teachers all sung my praises to Mum and Dad this evening. Mr Atler put a bit of a downer on things by saying I talk too much to Imogen in biology, but they soon forgot about that when he told them I'd come first in our last three tests. I don't even like biology, but I want to do well. I want to have a good job after university.

For something to do while I'm waiting, I pace from one edge of the science block to the other, keeping to the back so I'm not seen. I count my steps and when I reach two hundred and fifty-seven, Adam appears like a ghost, gliding towards me, silent in his trainers.

I open my mouth to complain about his tardiness but he beats me to it.

'That fucking bitch.' There is no need to ask whom he's referring to. 'She's gone too far this time, I swear. Can you believe what she's done now?'

Even though I already know, I keep quiet and let Adam deliver his rant. It's always best to let him get it out of the way. I'm used to this now; it's been like this the whole time I've known him. I thought he'd get over the whole Miss Hollis thing in Year Ten but it's only got worse. Neither I nor our looming GCSEs can steer Adam from his path of hatred. I know he's not Miss Hollis's favourite student but I doubt she cares enough to let him take over her life. Yet that's exactly what he's done for over a year now. This is exactly what I wanted to talk to Adam about, so I'm not pleased he's come straight here with another hate story to report.

'She completely slated me to Mum and Dad, making out I was the devil or something. Why can't she just fucking give me a break? I get good grades for everything but she doesn't give a shit.' Adam's voice is loud and shaky; I have never seen him this angry before. But it's more than anger. He is upset.

'Just calm down,' I say, pulling him towards me. But he brushes me off and continues his tirade.

'Now I'm in deep shit. My dad says he won't let me go to America this summer because of it.' His eyes glisten, his breathing heavy in between his words.

Although Adam is distraught, I feel pleased that he won't be going away. I hate myself for having such a selfish thought, but this summer might be the first chance we get to be truly alone. Just the two of us. Without Miss Hollis clouding Adam's every thought and action. I keep this to myself.

'Look, try not to panic. I'm sure your parents are just angry at the moment, but tomorrow they'll see things differently. My dad—'

'No, Leah. This is not like your dad. When they say something they mean it. I can't talk them round like you do with your parents.'

Adam's comment stings but I have to remind myself this isn't about me. I need to support my boyfriend. 'I know…but, maybe if they can see you making an effort then—'

'Do you really think that bitch will give me a glowing report? I get the highest marks in history and it doesn't make a difference. She's had it in for me since day one.'

I want to tell Adam he is wrong, that he just needs to leave Miss Hollis alone and everything will be all right, but, like him, I don't believe it will be. She does seem to have a problem with him, even if it was his fault to begin with. So instead I urge him just to give it a try and see what happens.

Adam falls silent and I focus on the chatter on the other side of the school. I can't make out any words, but the sound is reassuring because it's dark out here. I know he is with me but, with the mood he's in, it wouldn't surprise me if he disappeared.

Eventually he speaks. 'I know what I need to do,' he says, reaching for my hand and leading me over to the low wall.

As soon as we sit down I can feel the cold seep through my skirt. It feels as if I'm sitting on a block of ice. Adam doesn't seem to notice and shuffles next to me.

'I need to take my mind off it all.' He cups my face in his hands and kisses me, and although it feels good, I wonder where he learnt to do this and almost giggle that I'm even thinking this right now. His lips feel dry today but I ignore that and try to focus on the feel of him; moments when we get a chance to do this are rare.

It seems as if we've been kissing forever, and my lips are sore and dry when Adam finally breaks away. He leans in and whispers in my ear. 'I think we should do it. I don't want to wait any more. Do you?'

For a moment I wonder if I'm mistaken and Adam is talking about something else. He hasn't mentioned sex for weeks now, and I thought we were waiting until my birthday. I have got used to this idea, and have been feeling good that I'm waiting until I'm sixteen, but I suppose it's only five months away. Twenty weeks won't make much difference, surely? And if it helps take his mind off all the trouble with Miss Hollis then I need to do what I can to help him.

'Where can we go?' I ask. I'm excited but petrified too. 'My parents will be back home now. So will yours.'

Adam smiles and rests his head on my shoulder. 'We don't need to go anywhere. We've got the perfect place here.'

I look around to see if I've missed something, but no, all that's here is the back of the science block, a low wall and a grassy slope behind us. Beyond that is High Elms Lane.

'Where?' I ask. 'We can't get in the science block, can we?'

Adam stands and pulls me up with him. 'We don't need to go in there. Come with me.'

He walks about two metres and stops. It is only then I notice a gap in the wall, large enough for several people to squeeze into. It's as if the builders ran out of bricks so left a square shape cut out of the block.

I stare open-mouthed for two reasons. Firstly, I never knew about this and, secondly, I can't believe Adam wants us to do it here when it's minus a hundred degrees out here.

'Don't tell me you didn't know about this,' he says, grinning. 'Half the school hang out here at lunchtime. Teachers never come here, though. It's too far for their fat arses to walk from the staffroom.'

Adam's joke can't ease my nerves. We're about to do it. Here. In the freezing cold. He must sense my tension because his voice softens. 'I just don't know when we'll get another chance.'

I want to point out that we'll have the whole summer now, seeing as he probably isn't going to America, but I don't want to remind him what happened earlier. Besides, I want to do this. Maybe it will bring Imogen and me even closer together; I'll finally know how she feels. We've been drifting lately so having this in common is bound to get us back on track.

'Okay,' I say, stepping forward to follow him into the gap.

Adam peels off his coat and spreads it out on the floor before sitting down. 'To cover the ice,' he says. And there is lots of it here, making me wish I'd doubled up on layers. Tripled up, even. Although the more clothes I have on, the more awkward this could be.

I've pictured this moment a thousand times but never like this. We are always in a bed – whose I don't know – and it is warm and comfortable. Romantic. This is just weird. Cold and uncomfortable. But it's Adam. The boy I want to be with forever, so what does it matter? This might be our first time but we'll have plenty more. More chances to make it better.

'You'll probably need to come over here,' Adam says, and I realise I've been standing like a statue, staring at him without saying a word.

I can't let him think I don't want to do it, don't want him, so I kneel down on his coat and cuddle up to him to try and keep warm.

And everything that follows happens so quickly, yet slowly at the same time. Adam fumbles around with my skirt and I am almost paralysed by fear, so there is no excitement, just apprehension. Even when I feel an intense surge of pain, and Adam moves around on top of me, I don't believe we are doing it. I ask him and he laughs. 'Course,' he says. And in that moment I know with certainty that he has done this before.

Afterwards, I can't stop smiling. I can feel Adam's hot breath against my neck and I no longer feel cold. So we've finally done it. I don't feel any different, just very sore. I'm glad we've done it, though; next time will be easier and better, I'm sure of this.

Adam asks if I'm okay and I nod, sure that if I speak my voice will be an embarrassing breathless squeak. Still fully clothed, we cuddle together, both of us lost in our thoughts. I want to ask him if he's happy, but I don't want to be one of those needy, desperate girls.

Thankfully, he speaks first. 'You're special,' he says. I swallow up the compliment and feel weightless. But a few seconds later, Adam jumps up. 'We'd better go. We don't want any teachers finding us here. Especially that bitch, Hollis.'

And with those words everything Adam felt earlier must come rushing back because that dark look appears on his face again. I may have been able to take his mind off it temporarily, but now he's right back where he started, and so am I. With a boyfriend who cares more about his hate campaign against his teacher than he does about me.

As soon as I get home, I rush upstairs to avoid my parents. I'm sure they will know. I might not feel different but maybe I look different? Or walk different? I haven't even checked whether I'm bleeding. But I'm only in my bedroom for a few seconds when Mum calls me down. I keep my jacket on and trudge downstairs to face the music.

They know. I am convinced they know.

'Why did you rush upstairs?' Mum asks. 'We wanted to tell you how proud we are of you. Where did you get to anyway? Have you been with Imogen?'

Mum fires so many questions at me I don't know which one to answer first. But at least she hasn't guessed what I've done.

'Yeah,' I lie. 'We just hung around for a bit.' I glance at Dad and he squints his eyes. He doesn't believe me. But worse than that, there is disappointment painted on his face.

'Dad's going out to get some fish and chips,' Mum says. 'We thought we'd treat you.'

'Thanks,' I say, not feeling hungry at all. 'I'll just go and change. I'm a bit cold.'

'Yes. Well, it is a bit silly to wear such a thin skirt in this weather.' Mum looks me up and down and I rush upstairs before she has a chance to work anything out.

Just before eleven o'clock, Dad knocks on my door and asks if I'm awake. I could pretend to be asleep but curiosity gets the better of me; these days Dad avoids my room like the plague.

'I just want to say how proud I was to hear the way the teachers praised you this evening,' he says, coming in and sitting on my desk chair. 'But keep up the good work, don't get complacent. Your GCSEs are in a few months.'

'I know, Dad. I study every day.'

He nods, unable to refute my statement. 'Just don't get distracted. That's what I'm trying to say.'

Now the real reason for his visit becomes clear. I could stop this now and just promise I won't, but I want to hear what his problem is.

'Dad, I'm not getting distracted. Why do you think that?' I have forced him to show his hand.

'Boys are a distraction,' he says, staring at the floor.

I sit up in bed. 'You mean Adam? Why are you always on his case? He's done nothing wrong, just leave him alone!' I'm shrieking now and it won't be long before Mum rushes in to defend Dad.

'Just calm down and keep your voice down. Do you want the neighbours thinking we're hooligans?'

I do as he asks and lower my voice, but I'm still furious. 'Why have you got it in for Adam?'

Dad looks up at me for the first time and again I see disappointment on his face. 'He's just not good for you, Leah. You need to focus on your GCSEs and getting ready for A-levels, and it's not good for you to be so…distracted.' That word again.

I tell Dad this is ridiculous. That Adam is doing really well in school, even better than me, in fact. But it falls on deaf ears.

'I won't let you make a mistake, Leah,' he says, as he walks out. 'You're not seeing him outside of school again.'

It is strange to hear Dad making this demand. Usually he leaves discipline up to Mum, so I know he is serious. I wonder if there is any way he can know what Adam and I did this evening, but how could he? It's not as if there's a sign stuck to my head advertising that I'm no longer a virgin.

I keep expecting Mum to come and see me but she doesn't, making me think they planned this together and Dad is not the only one who has a problem with Adam.

I turn off my lamp and roll onto my side, letting the pillow soak up all my tears. It's so unfair. I work hard at school and never get in trouble yet I'm being punished for being in love. I feel betrayed. Isolated. They haven't even listened to my point of view. But I don't care what they say; I will never give up Adam.

In five more months I'll be free to do what I want, and I won't have to put up with them any more.

That night, after the tears stop, I fall asleep picturing being with Adam in the summer. Free from the constraints of parents. Our whole lives ahead of us, and a world that's ours for the taking.

CHAPTER SEVENTEEN
2014

I went to work on Monday. Forced myself to shower, dress and walk out of the door, even though all my instincts screamed at me to run back inside, lock the door and shut the world out. But there was no way I could take any more time off work. I had already called in sick after the mugging and didn't want to piss Sam off. Besides, I had the promotion to think about.

But the attack – whatever it was – had shaken me to my core. Yes, it had only been water, but those seconds when I hadn't known had stretched out before me and shown me a glimpse of a life I shuddered to think about.

I could fool other people but I couldn't delude myself into believing I was an innocent victim. I needed to know who I was up against. I wanted a chance to defend myself.

It was only seven a.m. when I reached Garratt Lane. I wasn't due at work until eight-thirty, but I hadn't slept more than a few minutes, so there was little point in staying in bed. Walking helped me think, the action making me feel I was doing something, at least.

I was now convinced my emailer was not about to let things drop. It was as if he could see my every move and hear my thoughts. Why else would he have picked that moment when I was actually feeling quite good? Julian and I had arranged to meet up again and, for once, things had looked up. That's what made it worse. And now, every second I was awake I felt as if there were eyes upon me. Even more sinister was the fact I didn't know who they belonged to.

Pulling up my hood, I constantly checked around me as I walked. I had to expect that anything could happen, and I needed to be prepared. Whoever this person was wouldn't win if they couldn't take me by surprise, would they? But there was nothing out of the ordinary that morning; just the usual workers heading to offices or shops. Nobody gave me a second glance.

Last night had shown me that I had to do something about this; I couldn't just sit by while someone tried to destroy whatever life I actually had. It wasn't a great life but it was mine, and I wasn't going to let someone else dictate it for me.

I reached the café, which was surprisingly quiet, and ordered a hot chocolate and a croissant. Then, after a quick look around, I headed to a table at the back. From my seat I could see anyone who might come in. At that moment only one table was occupied, and I didn't think the two men wearing paint-stained overalls were any threat. They had their heads buried in newspapers and stuffed crusty rolls into their mouths without once looking in my direction. But still, I had to be prepared.

With this new attitude, I felt stronger. It was like a coat of armour, protecting me against whatever was to come, because there would be much worse. I was sure of that. And by the time the waitress brought my breakfast over, I already had the seed of a plan.

I needed help and there was only one person I could ask. I couldn't be sure I wasn't making a mistake, but I was out of options. There was no way I could burden Julian with this, and the help Dr Redfield could offer would be limited. Besides, I still hadn't been able to get hold of her. Maria was out of the question; even though I had no idea what it was, there was something preventing me from opening up to her. So that just left Ben. I would call him at lunchtime.

Biting into my croissant, I watched pastry flakes flutter down my coat and tried to free my mind of all other thoughts.

As the library only opened to the public at nine a.m., it was quiet when I got there. I couldn't see Maria, but her bag was shoved under the front desk and the computer was logged on to her account.

'There you are,' Sam said, making me jump.

I spun around and she was right behind me. I hadn't even heard her. If this was an example of me being on alert then I would have serious problems. She looked different, somehow, and it took me a few seconds to realise she'd cut several inches off her hair.

'Can we talk?' she said. No hello or good morning. Just a command. This wasn't good. She didn't even wait for a reply but whipped around and headed upstairs to her office.

It wasn't often we got to see Sam's office, which was more of a storeroom, and being there didn't feel right. I wondered if she had news about the promotion and decided that must be it. There was no other reason for this unscheduled meeting. But her formal tone puzzled me.

'Have a seat,' she said, pointing to a plastic chair that looked as if it had been stolen from a school.

I had barely sat down before she continued speaking. 'I'm afraid we're not going to invite you to an interview for the senior librarian position. I'm sorry.'

Staring at her, my mouth dropped open and I couldn't think of a thing to say. I hadn't been expecting this; it didn't make any sense. Only days ago Sam had been urging me to apply for the job.

'I, um...'

Sam's expression was stony, but she forced her mouth into a half-smile. 'Of course this doesn't change anything with your current position. I want to make that clear.'

A jumble of questions competed for attention in my head, but I couldn't form a single one. I continued staring at Sam, watching her forehead crease into a frown when I didn't speak. Eventually I managed a nod, and for some reason a thank you came out with it. I was thanking her for snatching away a rare piece of happiness that had come my way.

Downstairs, Maria sat at the computer and didn't raise her head when I appeared. I considered ignoring her but I was at a loss as to why we were playing this game. 'Morning,' I said, trying to make my voice cheerful.

She looked up, startled. 'Oh, I didn't realise you were in. You're not starting till nine, are you?'

I explained that I'd woken up early and thought I'd make the most of the morning, but she didn't seem convinced. She was probably thinking I was keeping even more from her. This shouldn't have surprised her. I was a closed book, probably even one with a padlock.

'Can you watch the desk this morning?' she said. 'Sam's asked me to supervise the study area.' She didn't look at me as she spoke, but clicked away on the keyboard.

I told her that was fine but I needed to do something first. Feeling her eyes on me all the way, I headed off to the toilet, praying I would find it empty.

Locking myself in a cubicle, I sank to the floor and buried my head in my knees. But I didn't cry. There had been too many years of that; I was now a dry well, incapable of the act. I think I wanted to, probably needed to, but my eyes remained dry.

Before Sam had delivered her news, I hadn't realised how much the promotion meant to me, but now it was no longer an option I couldn't seem to shake off the disappointment. I'd had a chance – even a small one – to make my life different, so now what was I supposed to do? Being fully aware that once things happened they couldn't be truly forgotten, I couldn't pretend the opportunity had never existed. Every day now at work would be tainted.

I tried to work out why Sam had changed her mind. I might have taken some time off work, but it was the first time in all the years I'd worked at the library, so that was unlikely to be the reason. Something else had forced her to reach this decision. I was sure of that. I was being targeted by someone. My life was becoming chaotic. Whatever it had been before was preferable to this.

Footsteps shuffled along the floor and halted right outside my cubicle. I couldn't see any shoes underneath the door, but after a moment whoever it was shut herself in the cubicle next to mine. Forcing myself up, I grabbed some toilet paper and pretended to blow my nose. I had to pull myself together, go back out there and carry on.

Back at the front desk, Maria was rifling through her handbag. 'I'm just off upstairs, then.' She still gave me no eye contact. But as she headed off, she turned back. 'Sorry you didn't get the job.' She was gone before I could reply.

Somehow I managed to focus on work for the next few hours. I threw myself into every task, going out of my way to be as helpful as I could. I even vacuumed the floor at the end of the day, even though the cleaners would be in that night. But I knew resentment was inside me, bubbling away, only kept under control by my refusal to give the promotion any more thought. I couldn't let it destroy the pleasure I'd always had in my job. And now on top of that, I had to explain to Maria why I hadn't told her I'd applied for the senior librarian post.

When I stepped outside, I was so preoccupied with wrapping myself up against the bitterly cold air that it took me a moment to notice someone was sitting on the steps, hunched up against the wall.

Julian.

I stared at him, unable to comprehend what he was doing here again. It had only been yesterday that he'd turned up at the library. Unless he'd come to break it off. To tell me that Friday was off and it had all been a mistake. The way my day was turning out, it would be no surprise.

'Leah, hi.' He pulled himself up and walked towards me. Attempting a smile, I prepared myself for his announcement.

'Sorry to, you know, just turn up here again. But I had a day off work and was visiting a friend in Richmond so I thought, well, it's not too far to Wandsworth, is it? And Friday seems like a long way off...' Julian trailed off and waited for me to speak.

'Okay.' I was so surprised to see him there I couldn't think what to say. What did I even look like? I was wearing dowdy black work trousers and my hair needed washing. If he hadn't gone off me already then he certainly would now.

His face seemed to darken. 'You don't mind, do you? I can go if—'

'No, I'm glad to see you. What did you want to do?'

His face brightened when I said this, and he moved closer towards me. 'Actually, I have no idea. I just wanted to see you.'

So it was up to me. It was too cold to stand around here and even going for a coffee was unappealing. I just wanted to be at home. Safe. But then I remembered what had happened last time Julian was there; how could I be sure it wouldn't be strange again? While I loved being there alone, in company the atmosphere seemed to change inexplicably.

'Um, well…'

'We could go back to yours? Get a takeaway or something? It would take too long to get to Bethnal Green and I'm starving!' With Julian's words the decision was taken out of my hands. Just like everything seemed to be lately.

We walked down Garratt Lane, avoiding lumps of ice that looked like they were sprouting from the pavement. Julian talked about his friend in Richmond, and I began to let my guard down. I almost forgot that anyone could be watching me.

As soon as we got back to my flat I saw it through Julian's eyes: full of nothing but books, stark and depressing. I really needed to move, but with no chance of promotion, that was looking unlikely.

Julian chatted away, oblivious to our surroundings. I distracted him further by pouring him some of the wine that he'd left behind the other night, while I opted for apple juice instead. If Julian thought it strange, he didn't say anything.

'You should have let me get the drinks,' he said. 'You've been at work all day.'

We ordered Chinese food and when it arrived Julian paid the delivery man and rushed to the kitchen to dish up. It was strange to see him making himself at home, but I didn't complain. Instead, I nestled into the sofa and went along with it. Again I found myself thinking of Adam. I couldn't recall him ever doing a small thing like this, but then we were so young so how could I hold that against him?

Pushing aside all thoughts of Adam – thoughts that always seemed to surface when I was with Julian – I tucked into my food and let myself get lost in our conversation.

'You know, I could help you decorate in here if you like?' Julian said. 'I'm quite handy with a paintbrush.'

So he had noticed what a state the flat was. I looked up at the yellowing walls, the woodchip wallpaper covering the ceiling. 'I have been meaning to get to it. I know it needs work. It's rented but the landlord did say I could redecorate when I moved in.'

He smiled at me, reaching across the table to stroke my hand. His unexpected touch sent a surge of excitement through my body. 'Oh, I didn't mean because of that. I was just thinking, if I helped paint and stuff then I'd be here more. A lot more.'

'Well, then, I might have to take you up on that offer.'

'And we should actually go out to eat sometime,' he said, grains of rice falling from his fork to the plate balancing on his lap. 'I'd really like to treat you to a nice restaurant.'

'I'd like that.'

There was no dishonesty in my words, but I couldn't picture it. Any of it. I was only just getting used to having him here in my flat. Everything he said made it sound as if we were in a relationship, but I had nothing except Adam to measure this by. Maria would have had the guts to ask where she stood. But all I could do was nod and continue eating, pretending this was as natural to me as waking up in the morning.

When we'd scraped our plates clean, I washed up while Julian excused himself to use the bathroom. I was only in the kitchen for a couple of minutes, but when I went back to the front room, Julian was standing at the top of the stairs, pulling on his coat. So that was it. Another evening cut short. After everything he'd said moments ago.

'I just need to get some more wine,' he explained. 'Back in a sec.'

And then he was gone, and I was left feeling like a paranoid fool. Why did I always have to assume the worst? This was no way to start a relationship, or whatever it was we had. Julian was here because he wanted to be, I needed to accept that and stop being negative.

Rushing to the window, I watched him cross the road and head towards Garratt Lane, until he became a tiny dot. Standing there made me think of my emailer. He or she could be watching me at that very moment, watching Julian leave.

I still hadn't called Ben but I couldn't do it now. Tonight I had to give my full attention to Julian; I could not be distracted by the crazy stuff that was happening to me.

I sat on the sofa again and turned my attention to the television. A soap opera was on, the characters arguing and firing venom at each other. I muted the sound so I could only see their actions, and laughed at the actors' ridiculous facial expressions.

I was so engrossed in watching the characters, and trying to guess what they were shouting at each other, that the soap had ended before I realised Julian wasn't back. The shop was less than five minutes' walk from my flat. My earlier resolve to be positive evaporated and I became certain that he wasn't coming back.

For several minutes I sat motionless, digesting what this all meant. My eyes blurred as I stared at the flickering images on the television. Just like with the promotion, I had been rejected and I would have to accept it, let things get back to normal. But no matter how much I tried to tell myself it didn't matter, I couldn't hide what my heart wanted.

Eventually I got up and closed the curtains against the night, deliberately avoiding checking the street outside. It was too early to go to bed so I made myself a coffee and sat on the sofa. My eyes flicked to one of the bookshelves and focused on *Of Mice and Men*. I got up and removed the book, taking it back with me to the sofa. Once more, it made me think of Ben, but that did little to comfort me. I liked him, but he wasn't Julian.

I began reading and had only managed a few lines when the buzzer chimed. Rushing to the window, I peered out, and there was Julian, pacing up and down, rubbing his hands together.

'I'm so sorry,' he said, when I opened the door. 'I was on my way back when my brother called. He's having some trouble with his girlfriend and needed me to…mediate, I suppose. I've been on your doorstep this whole time. Didn't you hear me?'

And then I laughed. Whether from relief or the thought of how paranoid I'd become, I wasn't sure, but it felt good.

Julian frowned but didn't question my reaction. Instead, he followed me inside and headed straight to the kitchen to open the wine. 'Are you sure you don't want a glass?'

'No, I just made some coffee. I've got a sore throat coming so thought a hot drink might help.'

Again, if he thought me strange he didn't say a word. Perhaps when you were with someone you felt strongly about you just accepted their weirdness. Isn't that what I had done with Adam?

It was happening again: my mind drifting to Adam when I wanted to be fully present with Julian. Although I had never acknowledged it, perhaps this was why I had avoided men for so long. Subconsciously I must have known any contact would remind me of him.

'Shall we sit on the sofa?' he asked, glancing at my tiny kitchen table.

I shrugged and led the way, knowing I must seem nonchalant, when inside I felt my stomach twisting itself in knots. Sitting with Julian on the sofa was a risk; it had got strange last time and I didn't need a repeat performance. I didn't know what I needed.

'I like you, Leah,' he said, as soon as we sat down. 'I know I'm being direct but…there's something about you.' He looked down at his shoes and I preferred it that way. This was new territory for me. Even Adam hadn't been as forthcoming about his feelings.

'I do too,' I forced myself to say. Although it was the truth, the words didn't come easily.

Julian's kiss took me by surprise. His mouth was cold and he tasted of wine, but somehow it warmed me up. It felt right.

What was even more surprising was that I didn't think of Adam when Julian pulled me up and led me to my bedroom. We didn't turn the light on, but even in the darkness, as we shed our clothes, Julian felt nothing like him. None of it was the same. So I let myself get lost, enjoying the forgotten sensation of a naked body against my skin, feeling as if this was my first time, and nothing had gone before.

Feeling healed.

Afterwards, I couldn't wipe the smile from my face. What had started as a horrible day – with Sam delivering the news that I had no chance of promotion – had completely turned around. I hardly dared believe it was real, that there was a man I liked in my bed, but there he was. People always said it was easier to deal with things with someone by your side, but until now I had dismissed that idea.

I turned to Julian and he was smiling too, watching me intently. But my happiness quickly faded. Any moment now he would become distant and move away from me. He'd probably tell me he had to go. I would get no explanation but would be left here wondering what I had done wrong.

But half an hour later we still lay together, talking about the TV programmes we both loved as kids, Julian clutching my hand. It was comfortable. It was right. Even the headache I felt coming on couldn't dampen the moment.

CHAPTER EIGHTEEN
2000

All day I've waited for the bell to ring, wanting lessons to be over so I can see Adam. I need to know everything's okay after what we did yesterday. I need to know he still wants me. I knew he'd be playing football at lunchtime so there'd be no chance to catch him then, which left me no choice but to thrust a piece of paper into Corey's hand this morning, urging him to give it to Adam.

I smile now to remember ripping out the back page of my maths book, writing that I needed him to meet me after school by the art block. I didn't want to sound desperate so I added an extra line. *I'll understand if you don't want to.* This way he has a get-out clause, the option to put it behind us, just one of those things, fun while it lasted. I am hoping he won't take me up on this.

Finally the bell rings out across the school and there is an urgent flurry as everyone flocks to the gates, relishing the promise of freedom for another evening. Not me. I head in the opposite direction, a mixture of excitement and anxiety causing my stomach to churn.

I spot Imogen heading out of the English block and sprint over to her, shouting at her to wait. She spins around and when she sees it's me her face lights up and she wraps me in a hug. She always does this, even when I've seen her less than a couple of hours ago.

'Did Corey give Adam my note?' I am out of breath and my words barely make sense.

Imogen thinks about this for a moment. 'Oh, yeah, course he did. They had history this morning and he gave it to him then.'

Relief floods though me; this is one less thing to worry about. Now I just have to hope he turns up.

'So,' Imogen says. 'Do you feel different? Kind of grown up? Like a real *woman*?' She exaggerates the last word so that it sounds comical, not like a real word at all. I'd told her this morning as we walked to school, but am already regretting it. She's reducing it to something trivial, when to me it is huge. The most important thing I've ever done.

'No,' I say, not smiling so she'll realise what Adam and I have done is serious. 'Not really. I just…need to see him.'

Imogen tuts and flicks her eyes upwards. 'You're not worried he's gone off you now he's had his way with you, are you? That's silly. You guys have been together ages so why—'

'No, course not. I just need to tell him something.' I stare at my feet. I hadn't noticed before now that my shoes are starting to peel at the tips. I'll have to remember to tell Mum I need a new pair.

She sucks in her breath. 'You're not…pregnant are you?' Her face breaks into a smile.

'Don't be stupid, Imogen.' I have no time for this today. Why can't she take this seriously? 'I just need to speak to him. It's not about anything.'

'Okay. Well, catch you later.' We hug goodbye, even though we will see each other tomorrow morning, and I watch her trot off, probably to meet Corey. Neither of their parents have a problem with their relationship so they are allowed this luxury.

There is no sign of Adam when I turn the corner to the art block, and the only people I can see are Charlie Woods and Richard Seymour. They're messing around play fighting and don't look in any rush to get home. They're always hanging around the school, long after everyone else has gone, and I have no idea what they're up to. Please don't let them speak to me.

I slow my pace, wishing – not for the first time since I started at this school – that I could disappear into the ground. What if they know? What if somehow they have found out what I did with Adam last night? I cringe inside. When Tommy Scott slept with Anna Proctor it was all over the school within hours. Even now I can't look at her without picturing it.

But the moment they see me they head off, no doubt assuming I will get them into trouble for whatever it is they're doing. As soon as they disappear I sit on the step and pull out my book. Our coursework is due in a couple of weeks and I want to read *The Crucible* one more time, just to make sure I haven't missed anything.

Ten minutes pass and there is still no sign of Adam. I'm beginning to get a gut ache. I know he isn't coming, I just know it. I will give him another half hour, though, just in case he's been delayed. The football crowd is always trying to get him to take it more seriously and join them for after-school matches. When will they realise he's just not interested? He plays for fun some lunchtimes but that's as far as he wants to take it. 'I'm not even that good,' he told me once. 'They just seem to want me anyway.' I didn't tell him that I know why this is. *Everyone* wants to be around him, they feel privileged if he chooses their company.

But none of them really get Adam.

And now, sitting here, waiting, I'm beginning to feel as if I don't either.

It takes me another half hour to admit defeat. To acknowledge that he's not showing up. He's made a choice and I'm not what he wants. Slowly I rise, feeling as if my body will crumble if

I move too quickly. Feeling as if I will throw up. The walk to the school gates is like walking the plank; how will things be without Adam? He was my friend as well as anything else. Everything else. Now I've lost it all.

At the dinner table, Mum and Dad stare at me while I push food around my plate. Food always looks lovely when it's first served, but it quickly becomes a sickening mess. Mum has cooked my favourite tonight: roast chicken and mashed potato, but I can't stomach any of it.

'Aren't you hungry?' she asks, delicately placing her fork in her mouth, as if I will be tempted by seeing her enjoy hers.

I shake my head. 'Sorry, I think I ate too much for lunch. I'm still full.'

She won't believe this. I may as well tell them Adam has dumped me because it will make their day. Of course I wouldn't add the reason why he has done this; they can't know that. But in the end I can't bring myself to say anything. Thinking it is hard enough.

For the sake of peace, I make an effort to shovel in as much food as I can, but it's still not enough for Mum. Afterwards, when she's clearing up, I hear her moaning as she scrapes my leftovers into the bin.

'People are starving in third-world countries,' she says to Dad. 'What a waste.'

I can't see either of them because I'm on the stairs, but no doubt he is nodding his agreement.

I tell them I've got studying to do and retreat to my bedroom, shutting the door on the day that's turned out to be the worst of my life.

Only now do I cry, letting my tears flood out and hating myself for not wanting to control them. I have become one of those girls I despise, the ones who only care about boys and when their boyfriend leaves them they fall apart.

This isn't just someone, though, this is Adam.

I can't sleep tonight. I turn on my bedside lamp and lie on my back, staring at the textured ceiling. Whoever thought of creating swirls in paint? It's a ridiculous idea, and staring at the misshapen circles is making my head hurt. It's past midnight, my eyes are sore from the river of tears that's escaped them for the last few hours, and there is barely a dry patch on my pillow. I lean over the bed and scramble around in my school bag for *The Crucible*, hoping that getting lost in John Proctor's problems will help me escape my own.

Just as I begin reading, something smacks against my window with a sharp crack. I freeze, waiting to see if it will happen again. It does. A harder thwack this time, followed by another.

The curtains are closed so I have no idea what it is, but I slide off my duvet and tiptoe to the window, pulling the edge of the curtain aside slightly to make a slim gap.

Adam is there.

He's standing on the pavement with his hand outstretched, ready to hurl another stone or whatever it is he's lobbing at the window. He stops when he sees me, smiles and lowers his arm before striding into the garden.

With my heart feeling like it's in my mouth, I check to make sure I can't hear my parents waking up, and then I open the window, careful not to make any noise.

'What are you doing?' I have to keep my voice low, but the night is so silent he has no trouble hearing me.

'Leah, let me in, we need to talk.'

I stick my head out of the window and lean down as far as I can, feeling like Juliet on the balcony. 'I can't, Mum and Dad will wake up. What are you doing here?'

'Well, if you won't let me in then I'm coming up.' Before I can stop him, he hauls himself onto the porch roof, and once he's up, reaches for my windowsill. 'Open the window, will you? Wide as you can.'

Excitement courses through me. Adam is here and I'm sneaking him into my bedroom. I've never done anything like this before and it feels wrong but right at the same time.

He makes far too much noise clambering in and I press my finger to my lips, urging him not to speak for a moment. I head to my bedroom door and stick my ear against it, listening out for any sounds in the hall. There is nothing. We are safe.

I turn back to Adam, who is now pacing my room. 'Why are you here?' I ask again, trying to sound annoyed, when really I don't care what's brought him here, I just want to rush over and hug him.

'Leah, listen. I wanted to come and meet you after school. I was on my way but then Hollis stopped me.' He takes a deep breath, sucking in as much air as he can. 'She said I owed her a detention for not turning up to one she gave me last week, and that I had to do it right then.' He shakes his head, as if he's trying to erase the memory. 'Can you believe that? I told her she couldn't make me do it, that she had to let my parents know in advance and guess what she said?' He looks at me, nodding his head as if he is expecting me to have a go at guessing.

'I...um...'

'She said she'd already called them. What the hell? The sneaky bitch had planned it all with my mum. I could fucking—'

'Shhhhh. Keep your voice down.' Even Adam's whisper is too loud.

He ignores me and makes no effort to lower his voice. 'She kept me there for an hour, Leah. An *hour*. What other teacher does detentions for that long? I swear…' He trails off and gets lost in his thoughts before finally calming down. Grabbing my hand, he leads me over to the bed and we sit cross-legged, facing each other with our knees touching.

'What's wrong with your eyes? Have you been…?' I'm glad he doesn't finish his sentence.

'I'm fine,' I say, swiping at my eyes, probably making them worse.

'It's all her fault, Leah. She's the one who's done this to you. Made you think I wasn't coming. That I didn't want to know you any more. Can you see that?'

I nod and smile, even though it is nonsense. He got himself that detention, after all. I think about asking him what he did in the first place, but think better of it. The sooner I get him off this topic the better.

'Kiss me,' he says suddenly. 'Make it all better.'

So I do.

And then we are naked in my bed. Adam's body feels cold against my skin, probably because he's been outside, and I move closer against him to warm him up.

It feels different this time, better because we have already done it once, so this should be easier. Less pressure. I just have to let myself go. At first I think I won't be able to; I'm thinking too much when I should be relaxing and going with it, but then I feel Adam getting excited and that makes me feel good.

I give in to him. He is mine and I am his in this moment. Nobody else exists.

When it is over I can't wipe the smile from my face. I have forgotten all about Adam not turning up, and the fact that my parents are across the hall. He, I am sure, has also left all his troubles behind. His detention. Miss Hollis. None of it matters any more.

But even though he smiles at first, it's soon replaced with a frown and that familiar distant look is right back on his face. We lie still and silent. I want to ask him so many questions but I don't dare. Imogen has told me Corey's usually too tired afterwards and doesn't like to talk much for a while.

'I better go,' Adam says, eventually. 'I don't want your parents catching me.' He pulls the duvet from him and hunts around for his clothes. 'But I'll see you tomorrow. Let's meet at lunchtime. At the art block?'

I agree, thinking how lucky adults are that they don't have to sneak stolen moments together. Their time is their own to spend how they please. But one day that will be us too. One day soon.

Even though I'm disappointed that Adam has to leave, I can't complain. There is no way he could stay much longer. Rather than making him climb back out of the window, I risk sneaking downstairs and opening the front door. I don't know how it's possible Mum and Dad don't hear the click as it closes, but nobody stirs. We have got away with it.

When I'm back in bed, I roll onto my front to breathe in Adam's lingering scent, a mixture of sweat and deodorant that can only belong to him. And I try to forget that he was distracted again tonight. That I couldn't take his mind off Miss Hollis for long.

CHAPTER NINETEEN
2014

Spending the night with Julian had lifted my spirits. Walking to work the next morning, I could feel the smile still plastered to my face. I had transformed into a lovesick teenager, a feeling that was haunting me at the same time as it left me elated.

But even in the midst of that, I warned myself to calm down, that if I got carried away I would only be heading for a fall. Planning for a more fulfilling life was not without huge risks. I may have been telling myself this, but my stubborn smile remained, until I arrived at the library and crashed back down to earth.

'Leah! Where have you been? You were due in at eight today to help with the reorganisation.' Sam stood before me, her hands resting on her hips as she fired her words at me.

I checked my watch. It was nearly ten to nine but I wasn't due in until nine. I told Sam this but she snorted and raised her eyebrows.

'You were due in at eight. I've been trying to call your mobile since ten past. This isn't acceptable, Leah. Maria's not in until twelve so I've been on my own down here, trying to get everything ready before we open. I'm going to have to give you an official warning for this.'

Worse than the way she spat her words at me was the mistrust emanating from her narrowed eyes. It was more than mistrust, though, it was dislike. I was sure of this. Until recently we had always got on well so I considered asking her if I'd done anything wrong. But now was not the time. All I could do for the moment was prove I wasn't late, that I was due in at nine, not eight.

That morning I had found an old bag in the back of my wardrobe I'd forgotten I owned and I rustled in it, searching for my diary. I was meticulous about writing down my schedule for each week and wanted to show it to Sam.

But she didn't wait for my evidence or any explanation. She had already stormed off and I was left staring at her back.

Finally finding my diary, I flicked through the pages until I found today's date. Nine o'clock. I knew it. I had never made a mistake with my rota before. I considered going after Sam to thrust the diary at her, but I needed to check the online schedule first. Just in case.

Minutes later I was logged on to the front desk computer, scrolling through the spreadsheet until I came to my name. I found today's date but when I checked my name, the time next to it clearly said eight o'clock. Not nine. I checked my diary again but there was no refuting it. I had written down the wrong time. Confused, I tried to think how I could have done that when I was always so careful. No answer came to me.

An elderly man shuffled up to the desk with a pile of books to return, so I closed down the spreadsheet and tried my best to focus on him. He asked if we had a book in stock, but I struggled to hear the name of the author. I was too engrossed in wondering how to make my error up to Sam, and all I could come up with was working extra hard for the rest of the day and staying late. But given her attitude towards me lately, I was sure my efforts would go unnoticed.

Shortly after Maria arrived, Sam sent me an email to say I was needed up in the study room for the afternoon. It would have been easy for her to tell me face-to-face, but she'd chosen this impersonal method of communicating her wish. Something wasn't right. And now there was no chance to apologise for my mistake today; I would be stuck up there in the monotonous silence, with nothing to do but watch people studying.

At four o'clock, when I could take no more of the silence and intermittent rustling paper, Maria finally came to relieve me. I tried to question her about Sam, to find out if she was being off with Maria too, but she brushed me aside, reminding me to be quiet in the study room. The cold look she gave me warned me not to push it.

To make up for being late I stayed an extra hour, but when five o'clock came, I rushed out into the cold, relieved to be outside, wondering what the hell was going on with Sam and Maria.

Only when a man brushed past me, heading into the library, did I remember I needed to be alert. And that's when it hit me how alone I was. Things might have gone well with Julian last night but I couldn't drag him into this. It was too soon. He needed to get to know me first before he learned what a mess my life was. Sinking onto the steps, I hugged my knees to my chin to shield my face from the wind and called Ben.

'Thanks for meeting me,' I said, as soon as Ben reached my table. We were in the café near the library and I sat in my usual seat at the back, facing the entrance.

He peeled off his coat and unwrapped his scarf, draping them both over his chair. 'It's okay. Sorry you had to wait so long. I just couldn't get off any earlier.'

I had already had three teas and couldn't stomach another, but I offered to buy Ben a coffee. Now that he was there I began to doubt whether I could actually open up to him. I'd known him such a short time so how could I expect him to understand? To help me? And I hardly knew where to begin.

Sam and Maria's behaviour today had got to me and I was finding it hard to deal with. Work was the one place where everything was okay, something I could rely on, but now everything was being shaken up.

'No, I'll get it, you sit tight,' Ben said, heading off to the counter before I could object. I watched him walk away and tried to compose myself. Perhaps all I needed was some company. Maybe I didn't need to talk about anything at all. As long as I wasn't alone. How ironic, when all I'd done for years was crave isolation.

'How's Pippa?' I asked, when Ben came back. In his hand was a huge mug of cappuccino, filled so high to the brim that chocolate-sprinkled froth pooled over the sides. He took a sip before sitting down.

'She's ill at the moment. Nasty bug. But she'll be fine in a day or two.' He smiled, but his lips remained tight and I wondered if her illness was more serious than he was letting on. And only then did it occur to me that he might not want to open up to me about personal things. I decided not to push it.

Nodding, I wondered what else I could talk about to stall for time. Opening up to Ben was going to be harder than I'd imagined and I had no clue where to begin. But now I had dragged him here I owed him some conversation. But all I could think of was to ask him about his work.

He humoured me for a while but he wasn't fooled. 'Are you okay?' he said, taking another sip of his cappuccino. 'It's just that on the phone you sounded kind of upset. Has something happened?'

He watched me and I knew it was pointless trying to deny it, but how did I even begin to explain what had been going on?

Especially without mentioning I knew exactly why it was happening. I placed my hands on my legs, out of Ben's view because they had started to shake. I hadn't even opened my mouth and yet I was already terrified of talking to him.

The room began to crowd in on me and I suddenly felt desperate for fresh, cold air. I glanced towards the door, already picturing running out of it. But it was better to talk in here where I could see whoever came in.

I turned back to Ben. 'I'm okay, just… it's not been a good week, I suppose.'

He offered me his kind smile. 'I can tell. Can I do anything?'

That was my opportunity. He was offering me help, all I needed to do was take it, be willing to open up to someone for the first time.

But I couldn't.

If I told him anything about what I'd done, his seat would be empty within seconds, as if he'd never sat there. 'I'll be okay,' I said, checking how my hands were doing. The shaking had subsided so I reached for my mug. 'But thanks for caring.'

Looking across at him, I could see he was disappointed. He made a show of brushing it off, sipping his drink and telling me how good it tasted, but it was too late. I had seen what was there. He was trying to form a friendship with me and I was pushing him away.

After a few minutes he tried again. 'Look, Leah, I know we've only just met. But I do like you. As a friend, I mean. I've got Pippa, of course. But if you need to talk then I'm here. I want you to know that. No matter what it is.'

'Can we go for a walk?' I hadn't planned to ask this, the words just formed themselves and left my mouth.

He seemed surprised at my request, but agreed, quickly finishing his drink. As we stood up I noticed half of it remained in his cup and I felt both comforted by, and envious of his selfless-ness. He had put me – a virtual stranger – first and that made him a better person than I was.

Once outside, I immediately felt better. I still didn't think I could open up to Ben, but I wasn't yet ready to be alone. Both of us were silent as we trudged through the fresh snow, trying to avoid patches of old ice.

He soon filled the gap, and I was grateful just to hear his voice. It didn't matter at first what he was saying. 'When I first met Pippa, I was worried what she'd think of me if she knew all about my past relationships. But she couldn't let it go. She had a desperate need to know. I couldn't understand that, I mean, I didn't want to know any details of what she'd done before.'

I didn't know what to say to this. I had so little experience of what he was talking about that I didn't feel I could make a fair comment. As well as that, I was shocked he was telling me per-sonal things about his girlfriend when only moments ago I had been worried about pushing him to talk about her illness.

'So…was there anything that bad that you couldn't tell her?' As soon as the words left my mouth I regretted them.

'Oh no, nothing bad. Just that I'd…really loved someone be-fore and didn't want her comparing my feelings.'

Relief spread through me. With everything that had hap-pened lately, I wasn't ready to hear that Ben wasn't the man I had taken him to be. I still had my guard up, of course, but I had a modicum of trust for him.

'So what did you tell her?'

'Just that I'd been in love before and…well, it sounds corny, but had my heart trampled on. That's exactly how I put it, too. Pippa didn't like that. She was a bit distant for a while, but we're fine now. This was all years ago. But my point is, I trusted my instinct and did the right thing. Being open often helps.'

I hadn't noticed we'd come to a break in the pavement and I stepped out onto the road. Suddenly Ben was pulling me back, less than a second before a car screeched to a stop, inches from where I had just stood.

'Are you okay?' he said, still clutching my arm.

'I…I'm okay.' But I wasn't. Everything was a mess, I couldn't even concentrate on crossing the road. I needed help.

Ben let go of my arm and we began to cross. 'Leah, I think you better tell me what's going on.'

I looked at him then and knew I had to ask him for help. But it was only when we were safely across the road and continuing our walk that I began to speak. 'I think I'm being stalked. Well, I don't know exactly what it is, but someone is …doing stuff. Kind of tormenting me.' Saying it aloud felt strange, trivialised it, made it seem it was no big deal. I expected Ben to burst into laughter.

Instead, he stopped and pulled me to the side of the pavement. 'Say that again. And tell me everything.'

So I did. I explained about the card, the emails and the fake acid attack. All of it. And all the while, Ben listened, never interrupting me, his eyes fixed on me, even though what I was telling him must have sounded far-fetched. We'd only known each other a short time so how did he know I wasn't some crazy woman, trying to get attention? I wished it were as simple as that.

When I'd finished speaking, telling him everything except the most important part – that I knew exactly why I was being targeted – he grabbed my hand.

'This is awful. Why didn't you tell me before? I can't believe this is happening to you. You're just so…nice.' But I was far from that, my deceitfulness at that moment further evidence it was a false description.

Trying to push that aside, I stayed silent. What could I say without revealing too much of myself? I couldn't pretend it was okay, that I was handling it because it was obvious I wasn't. And now opening up to Ben felt like I'd bared my soul. But also that I'd shared my burden.

'A small mercy is that you haven't been hurt. But something has to be done about this person.'

And then I remembered the mugging. So far I had wanted to believe it was a random act, but what if my emailer had been responsible for that too? It seemed far-fetched but I couldn't discount the possibility.

I hadn't planned to, but I began to tell Ben about the mugging. While I spoke he seemed upset, shaking his head while his cheeks reddened. I wondered if he was more upset that I hadn't told him, especially as it had happened on the day we'd met up, but I didn't want to ask. It wasn't important.

When I finished, he mulled over what I'd said, then nodded. 'It's too much of a coincidence to be a random mugging, surely? Look, Leah, we need to go to the police. Now.'

My phone vibrated in my pocket but I ignored it. I had to think of a logical reason for not wanting to report my harassment, one that Ben would buy into.

'I just want to wait. To have more evidence to give them. I mean, so far it's quite flimsy, isn't it? And I didn't report the mugging or the water incident.'

Ben looked around then said we should start walking again. 'Are you hungry? We could get a burger or something? My treat.' He pointed across the road at a Burger King. 'I know it's junk food but there's nothing else around here and at least we'd be out of the cold.'

I nodded. 'Only if you let me pay, though. To say thank you for listening.'

Ben opened his mouth, probably to protest, but let it go. 'We'll see.'

We crossed the road, both of us being careful to walk only when there was a large gap in the traffic. I had no doubt that the minute we sat down, Ben would try to convince me to report the harassment, but listening to that was preferable to going home to my empty flat. Why I suddenly felt this way after so many years was obvious. I knew something else was going to happen, and didn't want to be alone when it did. Even though I couldn't be with Ben all the time, at least I'd have an hour or two without facing it alone.

We ordered far too much food and took it on a tray to a table by the window. Ben unwrapped his cheeseburger and bit into it, watching me while he did so. 'I can't force you, but I really think you should report it, Leah. At least just think about it.'

There was no point protesting, it would only make him suspicious, so I nodded, dipping some chips in Ben's ketchup. My phone beeped in my pocket but I ignored it, I would check it after I'd eaten.

We finished our food in silence, my hunger surprising me. When Ben got up to use the bathroom, I thought about how I could deflect him from focusing on the police. Of course he was right, and most people would report what had happened, but he didn't know that it was impossible for me to face any police again. I just couldn't do that to myself. Instead, I needed to convince him to help me track down my emailer, but that would be no easy task when I couldn't be honest with him.

My phone rang then, reminding me I'd received a message a few minutes ago. I pulled it from my pocket and Dr Redfield's name flashed on the screen. I couldn't talk to her now, I would have to call her back. Leaving the phone to ring out, when it finally stopped I checked my message. It was an email. My stomach sank. As I always did, I knew before I even scrolled to my inbox that it was from him. It was funny how I still thought of the person as male when they could just as easily be a woman.

I didn't want to look this time. Didn't want to deal with whatever words I would be faced with. But then Ben appeared and headed back to the table, smiling reassurance. I clicked on my inbox and opened the email. The words were different this time, but the message was clear.

An eye for an eye, a life for a life.

CHAPTER TWENTY
2000

There is no greater feeling than this. Our exams are over and we are free for six weeks. Plus, now I am sixteen, no longer a child, no longer beholden to my parents. Dad can't stop me seeing Adam; I'm even old enough to marry him if I want to.

I've arranged to meet everyone at the corner of my road and I make my way there now, with the sun warming my skin. It is best to meet away from the house because Dad is there as usual, and even though he can't stop me seeing Adam now our exams are over, he still won't welcome him into the house. I don't know what he thinks we'll get up to with Imogen and Corey there; he's overreacting as usual.

All these months of Adam not being able to come over have put a strain on our relationship, but I haven't let Dad stop me seeing him. We've just learnt to steal every moment we can, and laugh behind my parents' backs because they can't keep us apart. And we have survived. We can survive anything.

Adam has promised me things will be better now, that he won't be distant now that some of the pressure is off. Please let this be true.

Imogen and Corey are already there when I get to the corner, their arms wrapped around each other so they look as if they're one person. Perhaps in some ways they are. I feel a pang of envy because it is so easy for them. It always has been.

There is no sign of Adam. This is strange because he was the one who called last night saying we all had to meet him this afternoon and couldn't be late. It sounded so mysterious and I've hardly slept from wondering what he's planned. At first I thought it could be a surprise for me, but if that were the case surely he wouldn't want Imogen and Corey to come too? Unlike those two, Adam doesn't do public displays of affection.

'I thought Adam was with you,' Corey says, as I bounce up to them and wrap Imogen in a hug. She smells of perfume and up close I can see she has make-up on. Her foundation is too dark for her, making her look as if she's been under a sunbed, but I don't say anything. She is happy and I'm not going to take that from her.

'No,' I say. 'I thought he'd be here by now.' I check my watch and it's exactly two o'clock. The time Adam said we needed to be here.

The house we're standing outside has a low wall bordering the garden, and Imogen and Corey are sitting on it, not at all bothered that they are trespassing on someone else's property.

'Come on, Leah, sit down,' Imogen says, patting the wall beside her. 'He could be ages.'

I hesitate for a moment but then join them on the wall. I only sit lightly, though, ready to jump up if the owner of the house appears.

While we wait, Corey starts talking about his plans for the summer. His mum owns a timeshare apartment in Spain and she has invited Imogen to go with them this year. 'She loves me!' she says, nudging Corey. I'm not surprised that Mrs Bannerman is letting Imogen go. She's a flexible mum, after all, unlike mine. Even though I'm sixteen now I would never be allowed to go anywhere with Adam, even just for a night.

At least Adam isn't going to America now. I shouldn't feel good about this – he wanted it so much – but I'm glad he'll be here with me. I've already written a list of things we can do, but haven't shown it to him yet. I'm too worried he won't like any of my ideas, or that he'll think I'm enjoying the fact he's not going away too much.

He turns up half an hour late, strolling towards us as if he's in no hurry, as if it's no concern that we've been waiting this long for him, even though he was the one who dictated the time we should meet.

'Sorry!' he says. 'But it will be worth it, you'll see.' He leans down and gives me a quick peck on the cheek. It's nice to see the clownish smile on his face; he must be having a good day. 'Come on. Let's go.'

None of us ask where we are going but we jump up and follow him, almost able to touch the inexplicable excitement that being around Adam brings us. I know it's not just me and that we are all captivated by him.

We walk for some time, passing Imogen's old primary school and unfamiliar roads. Adam and Corey walk ahead of us, giving Imogen and me a chance to catch up. We've not seen much of each other since our exams began so there is a lot to talk about.

'So,' she says, 'Are you and Adam okay? I really hope you are.'

I wonder how much to tell her. If this was months ago then I would have spared no detail, but things have changed. I don't know whether it's because she spends more time with Corey now, or whether I'm just distracted by Adam, but we aren't as close and I can't pretend otherwise.

'It's great. At least it will be now I can see him more. Dad can't stop me any more. Not that he really did. But I'm sick of hiding away.'

She leans closer towards me and lowers her voice. 'Is it true about his maths exam? He must be fuming!'

I've been expecting Imogen to ask me about this; she tried to the last time we spoke on the phone but I brushed it off. And now I look at Adam and wonder if he would mind me talking about it. He was devastated at the time but seems to be okay about it now, so I make a quick decision and tell her what happened. She listens wide-eyed as I explain how he was only five minutes late for his maths exam, but Miss Hollis, who'd been invigilating, refused to let him in. And how she then told everyone that he had been much later than that so she couldn't let him sit the exam, and now he has to take it in November, along with his A-levels. It was his last exam too, so it should have been over for him now, as it is for us, but instead it's still hanging over his head.

'Wow, what a bitch. He must hate her guts even more.'

I don't answer. I've heard enough about Miss Hollis to last me a lifetime.

Up ahead, the boys duck into a newsagent and once we catch up with them we join them inside. I spot them by the pick and mix counter, shovelling sweets into paper bags. Beside me, Imogen squeals and rushes up to them, grabbing an empty bag to fill.

'Come on!' Adam says. 'We need to stock up with food for this afternoon.'

I open my mouth to ask him why but quickly close it again. There is no point pushing him; we'll find out soon enough. When he wants us to. I look around the shop and start picking out snacks to buy. Watching Adam do the same, the excitement on his face is infectious and I decide to go with it. I don't like surprises, but what the hell? It's summer and we're free for six weeks, I've got to get in the spirit of things.

With each of us carrying a bag crammed with snacks, we head back outside, once again letting Adam lead us. We all walk together this time, blocking the pavement but not caring because we have each other. We are invincible.

Without warning, Adam stops and points at the road to the left of us. 'Here we are,' he says, a triumphant smile on his face.

I look at the road sign. Kytes Drive. It means nothing to me and judging by the frowns on Imogen and Corey's faces they are just as flummoxed as I am.

'But what's here?' Corey asks, trying to get a closer look at the road. 'There's nothing but houses.'

Still smiling, Adam begins walking again, turning into the road that has no meaning. 'All in good time, my friends,' he says, and for the first time today I realise I don't like the sound of this.

The road is almost circular, with a huge grassy area in the middle, and Adam leads us halfway around it before he stops outside a large bungalow. He studies the house through narrowed eyes and, with no explanation, crosses the road to the green and sits on the kerb, waiting for us to do the same.

'Better get comfy,' he says. 'We could be here a while.'

Imogen, Corey and I look at each other, silently asking each other what Adam is playing at. But when neither of them speaks, it is left to me to question him. I cross the road and sit down next to him, the other two following my lead.

'What's going on? What are we doing here, Adam?' I try to keep my voice upbeat and not show the concern I feel in the pit of my stomach.

He digs in his carrier bag and pulls out a can of Coke. 'Let's just call it a stakeout,' he says, a huge grin spreading across his face.

And then I know with certainty what we're doing here. That the house across from where we sit belongs to Miss Hollis. And that Adam has no intention of leaving here until he has seen her.

'Miss Hollis,' I say, my stomach sinking.

'What? Seriously? That's Hollis's house?' Corey chimes in. He and Imogen are still standing up, and both of them spin around and stare at the house.

'That's right,' Adam says, taking a sip of Coke.

Corey turns back to him. 'But how? Where did you—'

'I can't give away my secrets, can I?' Adam chuckles, and I try to think of a time I've seen him this at ease, but can't. He is always stressed about something and it's usually the woman whose house we're standing opposite.

I reach across and lay my hand on his arm. His skin is warm from the sun and feels nice. 'But you're not planning to do anything, are you? We'll get in trouble, Adam. Serious trouble. We shouldn't be here.' One of us has to point this out, and looking at the smiles on Imogen and Corey's faces, I doubt it will be either of them.

Adam turns to me, the grin dropping from his face. 'Course I'm not going to do anything. We're just gonna sit here. Freak her out a bit just by being outside her house. There's nothing she can do about it, and we can't get in trouble because it's not private property on this grass, is it?'

He's clearly thought about this, and whatever I say he'll have his justification already planned. I turn away from him and rifle through my bag for something to distract me. I don't feel good about being here, but I can't tell Adam this. Instead, I convince myself it can't do any real harm just being here. Can it?

Hours pass and we tuck into our snacks, chatting away about our dreams for the future. I almost forget where we are until a blue Toyota pulls into Miss Hollis's drive.

We all freeze except for Adam, who continues munching his crisps. Each crunch seems magnified because the rest of us are holding our breath, trying to keep quiet and remain unnoticed.

A tall man steps out of the car and I immediately recognise him; he was with Miss Hollis when we went ice-skating last year. His hair is shorter but it is definitely him. Beside me, Adam's expression changes and he stops eating, shoving his half-empty crisp packet in his bag. It's not hard to tell that he is seething because he stays silent, his forehead creasing.

The man knocks on the front door and within seconds it is open and he steps inside. We all lean forward to get a closer look but cannot see who's letting him in. A few minutes later he reappears, carrying a huge suitcase, which he loads into his car.

Adam smiles. 'Come to his senses finally,' he says, thinking the same thing I am: that Miss Hollis has been dumped.

But seconds later, she appears at the door and steps outside. She is wearing a huge floppy sunhat, shorts and sandals, and smiles at the man before locking her door. When she walks to the car he is standing by the passenger side, holding the door open for her, beaming back at her. He kisses her on the lips before she gets in, and they drive off, to whatever country they're flying off to for their holiday. Thankfully, neither of them has noticed us out here, and I let out a deep sigh.

Corey turns to Adam. 'Teachers have such an easy life, don't they? Did you see her? With her stupid *boyfriend*. She's not bothered at all about what she's done to you.'

Imogen slaps him on the arm. 'What's she supposed to do? Cry about it? She's too much of a bitch. Adam's the last thing she's thinking of...' She trails off, grabbing Corey's arm when Adam looks up at her.

I am expecting him to say something. Anything. But he doesn't. Silently, he stands up and, leaving his carrier bag on the floor, walks away from us. Crossing the road, he stops outside Miss Hollis's house again, staring at it as if he's a building surveyor making an assessment. For a horrifying moment I think he will do something like smash one of her windows, but he doesn't. All he does is walk off, leaving us on the green, wondering what to do.

'Come on,' Corey says, jumping up. 'We should go after him.'

But Imogen shakes her head. 'No, leave him.'

He's about to protest, but then, like us, realises it's better to give Adam space.

When I try to call him that night his mum answers and tells me he's busy. She doesn't say it unkindly, but with pity, so I know he has told her he doesn't want to speak to me. I hang up, feeling as if I can't breathe, and see Dad is here watching me. He doesn't say anything but shakes his head sadly. *I told you so*, his eyes say.

CHAPTER TWENTY-ONE
2014

Ben called the next day and tried his best to convince me to go to the police. He offered to come with me, saying he would stay with me for as long as I needed him. When I protested, telling him he had his own life to get on with, he assured me that Pippa wouldn't mind; he had told her I was being harassed and she had agreed he should help me in any way. 'She wants to meet you,' he said, and I shuddered at the thought. Would she be jealous of the attention Ben was giving me? I couldn't blame her if this were the case; in her shoes I'm sure I would feel the same.

I put him off both these things, assuring him I would wait to see if anything else happened, then consider going to the police. He seemed only slightly appeased by this, but let it go.

'Well, if you won't go, then give me the email address this person is using. I know some tech guys and they may just be able to trace it. I can't promise anything, but I'll try.'

I repeated the address, memorised by now, and heard him scribbling it down. 'Thanks, Ben. I really appreciate what you're doing for me.'

I thought about the last message I'd received:

An eye for an eye, a life for a life.

I had held back from mentioning this one to Ben. He would know immediately this was a direct threat, and he would push me until he got more answers. Even though he didn't know me well, anyone would be able to see I was not being targeted randomly. That I must have done something to invite this harassment.

I hadn't heard from Julian since we had spent the night together. That had been Monday and it was now Wednesday so it didn't look good. I may have been new to this, but it was common sense that if someone didn't call you after you'd slept with them then they probably weren't interested.

Although I knew this, I didn't want to believe it. I kept replaying that night in my head, remembering how loving he had been afterwards. Completely different to Adam. There had to be an explanation. He had lost my number and hadn't had a chance to come to the library or my flat. It wasn't as if I lived nearby.

Ignoring the doubts, I called him, only to find his phone was switched off. There was only one thing I could do then, and even though it would take all my strength, I needed to see him. If it was over, if it had only ever been about one night, then he could tell me to my face.

Somehow I made it to Bethnal Green. I fought against the fear that was crushing me and tried to ignore the feeling I was being watched. Julian had mentioned that he lived in a flat on Broadway Market, and although I found the road easily enough, I couldn't remember which number it was. His flat number was 6b but I had no idea of the building number. After a quick scan of the street, I narrowed it down to two possibilities; only two of the buildings had flats numbered six.

Outside the first building, I pressed the doorbell and waited, my heart thumping in my chest. I hadn't felt like this since Adam and I didn't like feeling so out of control. I could have walked away, before anyone answered, and put it down to experience. That's what I should have done. But I knew I had to see this through. It was easier to do this when I thought of Julian turning up at the library twice. I was only doing the same for him.

I held my breath as the door opened and a man's face appeared. For a second I thought it was him, but it was only a cruel trick my mind was playing. This wasn't Julian. The man staring at me was taller, older, his expression stern and unfriendly. It must be the wrong flat.

'Yes?' he said.

'Sorry...sorry to disturb you. I was looking for a friend of mine and thought this was his address. Julian Greene?'

He continued staring but didn't say anything. Instead, he started to close the door but then changed his mind and swung it back open again. 'Who are you?' he asked.

This man was beginning to worry me. He hadn't said he knew Julian so why was he suddenly asking who I was? I repeated my story, that I was a friend of Julian's and needed to find him.

He listened, then screwed up his face. 'You're Leah, aren't you?'

Something wasn't right. How did he know my name? What was going on?

'I'm...I...'

'You are, aren't you? You're that sick psycho bitch Julian told me about. Don't fucking come back here and stay the hell away from my brother.'

And then the door slammed, so close to my face that I could feel a draught on my skin.

Back at home, safely cocooned in my flat once more, I tried to make sense of what had happened. The man who had answered the door was Julian's brother and he had told me to stay away from him. It didn't make sense. I hadn't done anything to him, and the last time I'd seen him things had been fine between us. Better than fine. But perhaps I'd been wrong to assume that. Maybe I had misjudged the situation so badly, like I'd done with Adam, and couldn't tell that Julian hadn't been interested. Somehow I had come across as a stalker and scared him off.

But the more I thought about this, the more convinced I became that it wasn't that. Julian had clung to me that night as we'd slept, there was no mistaking that. He had been so different to Adam afterwards, there was no way I could have misread things.

In the kitchen, I boiled the kettle to make some tea. Although I didn't feel like a drink I hoped it would comfort me. Just the routine of making it was familiar and secure, but it did nothing to alleviate the emptiness inside me. It was far worse to have had that moment with Julian, only for it to be snatched away. I was fine before. Now I didn't know what I was.

I took my mug to the living room and sank onto the sofa. It was almost as if I was in a trance until my phone vibrated on the coffee table, snapping me alert. Picking it up, I noticed I had a voicemail message. I hadn't heard the phone ring but I'd had the kettle on so wouldn't have heard it. It had to be Julian, calling to tell me his brother had played a cruel trick on me and that he was sorry.

Ready to give him hell for messing me around, I pressed the phone to my ear and waited for the message to kick in. I was so desperate to hear his voice that it took me a moment to realise it wasn't him. The voice I was hearing was deep and unfamiliar, delivering another message that was meant to pierce me in the gut:

How does it feel to have everything taken away from you? Tick tock, tick tock.

I'd held it together until that moment but now my defences came crashing down and I collapsed to the floor. This was it. I could no longer ignore that I was being threatened. That my life was in jeopardy. Karma was calling and there was no way to escape.

It took me too long to compose myself, and minutes flicked past in a blur. Then, slowly I began to realise I didn't have to let this defeat me. I would fight back, deal with it head on, take my life back.

And there was only one person who could help me.

'Are you okay? I've been so worried, Leah. Why wouldn't you tell me on the phone what's going on?'

I sighed, hoping I hadn't made a mistake. This was not going to be easy. 'Can I at least come in first?'

Mum stood aside to let me past, closing the door behind us. 'Well, I can see you're in one piece at least. Now, would you like tea or coffee?'

I told her I'd just have a glass of water and she seemed disappointed. Perhaps she didn't feel she was being hospitable enough unless she could make me a hot drink.

In the kitchen, she watched me sip my water, her eyebrows arched as she waited for me to speak. There was no way I could tell her everything. She would only drag me to the police station and insist I stayed at the house with her until it had all been sorted out. That was the trouble with Mum: even after everything I had put her through, she still believed things worked out in the end, tidied themselves away, never to be a bother again. But I had to say *something*; I needed her help.

'Mum, I know you don't like talking about it but I need to ask you something. About that night.'

Her skin paled and she turned away from me. 'Now why would you want to drag all that up again?'

'I just need to ask you one thing. That's all, I promise.'

Mum frowned and pulled out a kitchen chair. She made no move to sit on it, but gripped the top of it as if it was a Zimmer frame. Clearly she felt uncomfortable and I hated doing this to her, but I had no choice.

'What is it?' she asked, her voice thick with apprehension.

I took a deep breath. It was never easy discussing anything to do with that night. 'Is there anyone you can think of who might know about me? Apart from her family? Anyone at all?'

She digested what I was saying before answering, her eyes glazing as she relived her side of it. 'Well, no. Your name was kept confidential. How would anyone know? And why are you asking this?' She stared at me, seeming to search my face for something. Probably the truth.

'It's just…I just want to be sure. I've been having bad dreams about it, that's all.' It was a feeble lie; I should have been better prepared for her questions.

'Well, that's probably because of the anniversary, isn't it? It's bound to…When was the last time you saw Dr Redfield? You've cancelled so many appointments and I can't understand why. She's a lovely woman. And you…' She didn't bother finishing her sentence, and I wondered what the ending would have been. I'm a mess? I clearly need help? I'm always alone and it's not normal?

'I went recently. And I'm fine. I just wondered if there was someone I might have overlooked who was…affected. Or someone you might have told without—'

Mum slammed her mug down on the table. 'Leah, really! What do you take me for? Why would you think I'd go blabbing to people when I've spent all these years pretending nothing happened?'

She stood up and took her mug to the sink, leaving me to feel guilty for even thinking she might have talked about it. I should have known; she didn't even want to mention it to me so why would she discuss it with anyone else? But still I'd needed to be sure.

She turned on the tap too fully, releasing water with a violent spatter, making a point of demonstrating how upset she was. I didn't need that, on top of everything else, so got up to join her, taking my glass with me. She didn't look up but took my glass and began washing up.

'I'm sorry, Mum. I didn't mean to upset you.'

'Look, Leah, I don't know what's going on but I don't believe this is all just about some stupid dream. But I won't push you to tell me. You'll do that if you ever decide I deserve to be part of your life.' Still not looking at me, she walked to the fridge and pulled out a bag of carrots, bringing them back to the sink to peel. 'Anyway, did it occur to you that she could have told people? What was to stop her? And there's nothing you can do about that.'

I had thought about this, of course I had. But I knew she wouldn't have told anyone. I had no rational reason for believing this, but something in my gut was telling me she had buried it as soon as it had happened. But I needed to keep an open mind and explore all the alternatives.

It was time to change the subject. I had got as much as I could out of Mum and didn't want to cause her any more stress. 'Can I stay the night?' Until that moment I'd had no idea how long I was planning to be in Watford, but I needed to be there, close by. Plus, it felt safer than being alone at home.

Mum spun around then and reached for my arm. 'Of course you can. This is your home.'

Upstairs in my old bedroom, I was grateful that Mum had changed it so drastically. The whole room felt as if it had never belonged to me, like it had never been my sanctuary. I had left my shoes downstairs because Mum didn't want the carpet to get dirty and I sat on the floor with my legs stretched out, rubbing my hands over it and breathing in the new scent, feeling as if I were in a carpet showroom.

Mum had actually let me take a mug of hot chocolate up with me, although she'd insisted I use a coaster and hold the mug tightly so I wouldn't spill any. It was like being a child again. Just another reason my visits back to Watford were so irregular.

I had borrowed a notebook and pen and I opened it on the floor and began writing a list of everyone connected with what had happened. It had spread far beyond five people and had to include family members. Imogen only had her parents around but what if there were cousins? Aunts or uncles? I couldn't rule any of these distant relatives out without extensive research. I wrote a question mark beside Imogen's underlined name.

Then there was Corey. I remembered he had three sisters, who were all a lot older than him, so I would need to check them all out. His mum was a single mother and he'd barely known his dad, so I didn't think it likely this stranger could be responsible. Also, it didn't seem possible a parent would be doing this to me. Even after what I had done.

Adam had his parents and an older brother, but had never mentioned anyone else. I wrote another question mark by his name.

So that just left one more person. Miss Hollis. I knew nothing about her family or the boyfriend we had seen her with. I wrote two question marks next to her name. That one would not be easy.

By the time I'd finished compiling my list, my head was pounding and a revolting layer of skin had formed on the top of my hot chocolate. I put the mug on the bedside table, leaving it to go cold. I was exhausted and needed to sleep. The day had seemed endless, and I couldn't believe it was only a few hours ago I had stood on Julian's doorstep, being shouted at by his brother.

I pulled my mobile from my pocket and scrolled to his name, pressing it before it was too late to change my mind. This time it didn't go to his voicemail; instead a message told me that the number had not been recognised.

Climbing into bed, I turned onto my side and closed my eyes. I hadn't brought nightclothes or anything with me so would just have to sleep in my jeans. At that moment I didn't care, I just needed to rest. Tomorrow the hard work would begin.

I would find out who was threatening me. I had no idea what I would do once I knew, but I wanted my life back. Or rather, the new life I could now see myself living.

All punishments eventually had to come to an end.

CHAPTER TWENTY-TWO
2000

I've moped around the house for two weeks now, not knowing what to do with myself. Mum has given up asking if I'm okay and why I'm not out with my friends. She knows Imogen is away with Corey and that Adam has just fobbed me off with another excuse for not being able to see me today. This time it's because he's snowed under with maths revision for his exam in November. But I know this isn't true. Firstly, Adam doesn't need to revise; he could pass his GCSE without even reading the questions. And secondly, the exam is months away, so why would he give up his summer like this?

As usual, Dad is working from home today, sitting opposite me at the table, peering over the top of his newspaper while I push soggy cornflakes around my bowl.

'No Adam today?' he asks.

I am surprised at his question, both of us having developed a silent agreement not to mention him, and I stare at him, wondering how to answer.

'He's busy,' I say eventually. 'Studying.'

No matter how distant Adam has become lately I still want him to look good in Dad's eyes. I still want Dad to accept Adam as my boyfriend. Recently he has begun to come around to the idea that we are together, so I don't want anything to set back this progress.

He puts down his newspaper, folding it carefully, as if it's a shirt that's just been ironed. 'Look, Leah, I know it's difficult…but you're so young. Both of you. There are so many more important things to concentrate on. You shouldn't be sitting around waiting for a boy to call. You should be out there living your life.'

I don't know where this lecture has come from but I'll scream if he adds that I should be meeting other boys. He doesn't, so I let him off. Clearly he's given this a lot of thought. As much as I want to, I can't be angry with him; he's just looking out for me. I see that now.

'I…I love him, Dad.' I say this as if it is the solution to everything, as if nothing else matters provided love is involved.

'Yes, you may think—'

'Dad! Not everyone meets the right person when they're conveniently older. You and Mum didn't! Just because we're young it doesn't mean Adam's not the one for me.' I don't mean to raise my voice but I need to defend us.

He sighs and then slowly nods. 'I know…I know. And the heart wants what it wants. But is he good to you? Is he treating you right? Because all I've seen lately is you hanging around the house waiting for him to call.'

I open my mouth to argue but he is right about this. Instead I say, 'I love him. That's all that matters. Look at you and Mum. Neither of you are perfect but you overlook that because you love each other.' Even as I say this I am astonished that I'm speaking this way to Dad.

He doesn't reply, but smiles, so I know he agrees with me. Picking up his newspaper, he unfolds it just as carefully as he folded it and continues reading.

To avoid another lecture, I force myself to eat a couple more mouthfuls of cornflakes and then jump up.

'Anyway, I won't be hanging around the house today, I'm meeting Adam.'

It's only just occurred to me that I don't need to wait for an invitation. After all, I've got to follow my heart and it's telling me I need to see him. Now.

Dad seems surprised but tells me to enjoy myself. For once he doesn't ask what time I'll be home.

I can count on one hand the number of times I've been to Adam's house. It's at least a forty-five minute walk from mine and is twice the size. He's very vague about what his parents do but they must have great jobs to afford to live in such a huge house.

I think Mr and Mrs Bowden like me, but it's hard to tell whether they care one way or the other. Don't they say that indifference is the worst of all? It has crossed my mind that they think I'm just a friend, like Imogen and Corey, but it's probably best they think this. This way they leave us alone. Why does everything have to be so complicated?

I pass a Costcutter and decide to get Adam some chocolate. He loves Maltesers so I buy him a family size bag for us to share. The man behind the counter gives me a strange look, probably because I'm grinning like a demented clown.

When I turn onto his road, nervousness replaces my excitement. I've never turned up here unexpected before and don't know how he'll react. I still fear being one of those needy, desperate girls like Anna Proctor, who practically stalks her boyfriend, but I want to see Adam. I want us to make the most of the summer holiday before it's over and we're swamped with our A-levels.

I am in the middle of planning an excuse for turning up unannounced when I notice him coming out of his house. I'm still quite a distance away so he doesn't see me, but turns in the other direction, walking slowly as usual. He's never in a hurry to get anywhere. I stop for a moment and try to organise my thoughts. Even though I didn't think he would be studying, I am shocked to see him leaving his house. I shouldn't be; he is free to come and go as he pleases and doesn't have to update me on his every move, but if he was going out somewhere then why didn't he want me with him? Turning around, I resign myself to going home without seeing him, until an idea occurs to me.

It feels wrong following Adam but this is what I do. My head screams at me to turn back and go home, but my legs keep walking, heading in his direction. At first I tell myself he's only going to the shop and there is nothing for me to worry about, but the closest one is the Costcutter I've just been in. Imogen and Corey are away and there's no one else Adam bothers to hang around with. Loads of kids at our school have tried to become his friend, but he only has time for us.

As we keep walking I become plagued with doubt. Something isn't right. He's meeting a girl. Someone from school, it has to be. My heart pounds in my chest and I walk faster, ensuring I keep a safe distance between us. At least I will know one way or the other. Isn't it better to know? If Adam doesn't want me then I won't force him. Like Dad says, I am young. There will be other people out there for me.

For twenty minutes I keep repeating this, whispering the words to myself, while I watch Adam's back. And then I realise the road he is turning into looks familiar. But I have no sense of direction so can't be sure. Until we pass a shop I've been in before.

And then I know with certainty that Adam isn't cheating on me. This is much, much worse.

Even though I now know where he's going, I still follow him, just to be sure. And to see exactly what he will do this time. Miss

Hollis and her boyfriend must be back from their holiday by now.

My suspicions are confirmed when Adam turns into Kytes Drive and follows the road around to her house. And then, like last time, he stops right outside and inspects the property. I stop where I am; any closer and he will surely see me. There is no way I can explain what I'd doing here, following him, being a stalker like Anna Proctor.

He sits down on the grass, in exactly the same spot we all sat last time, and pulls a book from his pocket. I can't see the cover, but it looks too small to be a maths textbook.

I lean against a tree, hoping it's hiding me enough, and watch him sit there. Nobody comes out of the house, but every few minutes he glances up, just to make sure. I don't know how long he's planning to stay there but I can't be part of this. No good can come of whatever it is he's doing.

CHAPTER TWENTY-THREE
2014

Standing outside Adam's house caused a flood of memories to overwhelm me. Just like mine, his had barely changed, as if time had stopped. I wasn't even sure the Bowdens still lived there. When I'd questioned Mum about it that morning, she'd told me she had no idea where they might be. That she had kept away from them, and vice versa.

So there I was, taking a leap into the unknown, not prepared at all, but knowing I had little option but to confront the Bowdens. Standing on people's doorsteps had become a regular occurrence but I needed to get used to it; there would be more to come.

The woman who answered the door was not Adam's mother. She looked around the same age that Mrs Bowden would be now, but there was nothing else similar about them. This woman had a kind face, soft and oval rather than the harsh angles of Mrs Bowden's.

'Can I help you?' she said, her voice as warm as her face. It was a strange thing to say: old fashioned and out of place.

'Hi, sorry to bother you. I was looking for the Bowdens but I'm guessing they don't live here any more?'

She smiled then. 'That's right. We moved here a couple of years ago. Lovely house, isn't it?'

'Yes.' Memories of being inside it tried to invade my head, but I forced them aside. 'Um, do you happen to have a forwarding address for them?'

Shaking her head, she folded her arms. 'Sorry, they didn't leave one. They moved to America. I suppose we should have asked them for it, I mean mail for them still arrives here and we just have to chuck it. Sorry.'

'Never mind, thanks anyway.' I turned away. Although I was disappointed, at least I had been spared having to confront the Bowdens.

'They do have a son in London, though. Maybe you could try him?'

My chest tightened and I began to feel faint but I forced myself to turn back to her.

'Jeremy, I think his name is. Trouble is I don't have an address for him either and don't know where he works. I think they said he was a lawyer, though.'

Thanking her, I walked back to Mum's, taking my time so I would have a chance to think about my next move before she interrogated me about where I'd been. So Adam's brother was in London. I wondered why he hadn't gone to America with them. When I'd first met Adam his brother had been studying there on a basketball scholarship, so I was surprised he was back here. But that didn't matter. Finally I had somewhere to start.

Mum was in the kitchen making lunch when I got back. I could smell salmon and it made my mouth water, even though I didn't want to waste time sitting down to eat. I had borrowed the spare key and handed it back to her, watching her face drop as I did so. It was a look I'd seen a hundred times before: the one that begged me to explain why I wouldn't keep it. 'What if I have an accident and you need to get in urgently?' she always said. My constant excuse was that I was too worried I'd lose it. Of course

I couldn't tell her the truth: that I didn't want any piece of this house. The key would just sit in my flat, reminding me of the life I'd tried so hard to put behind me.

The truth was nothing that had happened had anything to do with this house, not really. But to me it would always be linked.

Mum stayed quiet this time and taking the key from me, hung it on one of the key hooks by the kitchen door.

'Can I use your computer?' I asked, before she could question me about where I'd been. I'd told her I was going for a long walk but knew she didn't believe me. 'I just need to check something for work.'

'Of course. Just be quick, lunch will be ready in fifteen minutes.'

It was strange being in Dad's office again. Unlike my bedroom, nothing had changed in there and all his books still lined the floor-to-ceiling shelves. It was no wonder I was such a bookworm when Dad had been the same. But my habit had come on much stronger later. A way for me to escape.

I browsed the shelves for a few minutes, picturing Dad reading on the sofa, but then the memory got too painful and I pushed it away.

The computer took a while to load up and by the time I was typing *Jeremy Bowden, lawyer* into Google, I only had five minutes left before Mum would call me for lunch. But I was in luck and the top result showed a law firm in London called Slater and Gordon. I clicked on the link and studied the homepage. On it there was a link to a list of staff, and clicking on that, I saw there were pictures next to the names. Scrolling down until I found Jeremy's name, my hand froze. Although much older, he looked identical to Adam and I wasn't prepared for that. To be confronted with the adult Adam could be now.

After copying the address into my phone, I shut down the computer, feeling numb. What if things had been different and Adam and I had made it? What would we be doing at this moment? Perhaps we'd own a house and have children, although I couldn't see Adam becoming that cliché. Or maybe he wouldn't be the same person, we were barely adults the last time I saw him. I needed to stop thinking about this. For years I had successfully avoided the past, but now it was sucking me back in.

Downstairs, Mum and I ate the salmon she'd cooked and, even though I was eager to get going, it tasted delicious. She didn't talk much, but every time I glanced at her she smiled and this was enough for me. She was happy I was there.

'What are your plans this afternoon? You will stay another night I hope?'

I stood up and walked around the table to her, wrapping my arms around her. 'I can't, I'm sorry. I have to work tomorrow. In fact, I have to go in this evening just to check something so I'll have to leave after this. I'm sorry, Mum. I promise I'll make more effort, though. I will.' I released her from my hug and sat back down, searching her face to work out what she was thinking, but it only seemed to fold in on itself.

The truth was I had told Sam I'd had a family emergency and needed a few days off. She'd said she hoped everything was okay but her voice was cold and flat, as if she was forcing herself to be a considerate employer. Maria hadn't bothered texting to see if I was okay but I tried not to let that get to me. I had more important things to deal with before I could focus on the tension at work.

'Okay,' Mum said, looking down at her plate. 'I've got my book club later anyway.'

It didn't feel good lying to her, but I needed to go somewhere after this and she would never have understood. She would have tried to stop me.

After we'd finished eating, I helped Mum clear away, trying not to show that I was itching to leave. She could tell, of course, and it wasn't long before she told me I'd better go and that she'd finish up. 'I don't want you to get in trouble at work,' she said, but I knew she was just setting me free.

Leaving the house, I followed a familiar route, cutting through the small park we had spent our childhood playing in. Everything was the same, the only difference was the heaviness in my chest as I walked.

Then there it was in front of me: Imogen's terraced house. Stuck in the same time warp as Adam's and my own. The minute I saw it I began to wish I'd called instead. But that would give Mrs Bannerman the chance to hang up on me. She could still slam the door in my face now, but it would be a lot harder to ignore me.

I rang the bell and stood on the path, trying to stop my legs shaking. I'd had a break earlier by not having to confront Adam's mum, but I was certain that wouldn't happen this time.

A bearded man I'd never seen before answered the door, a scowl on his face. I knew from Mum that Mrs Bannerman had remarried after Imogen's dad had left her, and assumed the man I was seeing now was her new husband.

'Look, whatever it is, we're not interested, okay?' He grabbed the door, ready to shut it in my face.

I took a step forward. 'Oh, I, no…I'm here to see Mrs Bannerman. Silvia.' It was the first time I'd used her first name and it made me uncomfortable. She had only ever been Mrs Bannerman or Imogen's mum, nothing else.

His scowl was quickly replaced with a smile, lighting up his eyes. He already seemed a lot warmer than Imogen's dad had been. 'Oh, okay. She's in the kitchen. Who shall I say is here?'

And that was the problem. If I told him my name he would either slam the door without any more questions, or if he didn't know about me, Mrs Bannerman would soon tell him to get rid of me. But I had no choice. All I could do was try to get away with not revealing my name.

'I'm a friend of her daughter's. I was just visiting friends and wanted to see how Mrs…Silvia is.'

He frowned, as if weighing up whether or not to believe me, but then told me to wait there. He left the door open and headed to the kitchen. Even though that door was shut I could make out muffled voices, growing louder, until the kitchen door opened and Mrs Bannerman appeared. She headed towards me, squinting because even though it was freezing, the sun was bright that day.

She looked different. Plumper than I remembered and far from the glamorous woman she used to be. She wore slouchy trousers and a baggy top, but if she wasn't going out I couldn't blame her for dressing comfortably in her own home.

It took her a moment to register who was standing on her doorstep but the second she did, she stepped back. 'What? What are you doing here?' She turned round, probably wanting to call for her husband. As if I was someone to fear.

'Please, Mrs Bannerman. I'm really sorry, but I just need to talk to you. Just five minutes. Please can I come in? Or if you prefer we could go for a coffee somewhere?' Despite my insides turning to jelly, I had managed to deliver my carefully prepared speech.

She turned back to me, her eyes filled with horror and sadness. I couldn't blame her for that. 'No…no, go away, Leah. You shouldn't be here.'

But now that I was there, I couldn't leave. Not without giving it my best shot to get her to talk to me. 'I promise, just five minutes. That's all I ask.' I hoped she could hear the sincerity in my voice. Or was it desperation?

She began shaking her head, looking around once more for her husband, and I was certain she was about to shut the door. But then she seemed to give in, her whole body sagging from the effort it had taken to refuse me.

'Come in then. Five minutes.'

There was new furniture in the living room: the comfortable fabric sofas I remembered had been replaced with cold, scratchy leather ones and the room felt cold and empty. We both sat down, perching on the edges of our seats, unable to relax.

'So what's this about, Leah? Why are you here?'

I might have prepared my initial speech but had no idea what I would say once she'd let me in. Perhaps I was expecting that she wouldn't, that her door would be just another one slammed in my face.

'I, um, I know this must be hard for you. Seeing me. I just didn't know what else to do.'

I didn't expect sympathy, but Mrs Bannerman's stare cut right through me, turning me cold. 'What is it? Just get to the point and then get out of here. I'm busy.' I knew this was unlikely. Mum had told me that she didn't do much of anything any more.

Taking a deep breath, I began to tell her everything that had happened. I spared no detail; I didn't have to with her because she already knew the worst. She would know why I was being targeted. By the time I'd finished speaking her expression had changed, the icy stare replaced with a smirk.

'Well, what do you expect?' she said. 'Did you think you'd be left alone to live in peace? After what you did?' Her voice was louder now, more confident, and I saw a flash of the strong woman she had once been. The woman I had thought of as a goddess.

'But—'

'But what? You're a poor innocent victim who doesn't deserve this? Is that what you were about to say? Because that's not true at all, is it?'

She was attacking me but how could I have expected anything else? 'You're right,' I said. 'I do deserve to be punished. But, Mrs Bannerman, I *have* been. What kind of life do you think I have? Am I married with kids? Living in a nice house with a good husband? Am I a really successful career woman with money weighing down my pockets?'

'I know exactly how you live, Leah. In your crappy little flat with a job that you're overqualified for and no man interested in you, but do you expect me to feel sorry for you?'

I wondered how she knew all this. I couldn't imagine Mum discussing the state of my flat or the fact I'd not had a boyfriend since Adam. Gossip was rife in the circles Mum moved in, but she was such a private woman I knew she would do her best to keep herself, and me, out of it. Besides, Mrs Bannerman wasn't even part of that group.

'No, I don't expect that, I've accepted that this is how my life should be. But these threats are something else, aren't they? Or are you saying I deserve to die?' I was being over-dramatic but I had to get my point across.

'Yes, Leah, that's exactly what I'm saying. I'd love to know who is doing this to you. Do you know why? Because then I could thank them personally for doing something I wish I could carry out myself.' She stood up then, signalling our time was over, and walked out of the room, leaving me with her cold, hard words.

Before I had time to sort through what she had said, her husband appeared, telling me I needed to leave. Now. His smile from earlier had gone; he must have known by then who I was.

'Don't come back here and bother my wife again,' he said, but before I could reply he slammed the door in my face.

Back at home, I stood looking around my flat. It no longer felt like my sanctuary, a safe place far removed from my previous life. Now the past had encroached upon it and I was sure it wouldn't be long before there was a knock at the door. My emailer was leading up to something and had no intention of sticking to messages and words. The mugging and water attack had just been a warning of things to come.

At least I now knew that Mrs Bannerman had nothing to do with this so I could cross her off my list. But our earlier confrontation had highlighted to me just how many people loathed me. Had I ever thought differently? Tomorrow I would pay a visit to Adam's brother. It wouldn't be easy but at least he shouldn't recognise me. He had been in America the whole time I'd been with Adam and there were no photos of the two of us together that Adam could have shown him.

I tried not to think about Julian. I don't think I'd realised until then the full extent of my feelings for him. But now he was gone from my life, snatched away from me like everything else seemed to be, and I had no clue why.

At least I still had Ben. I decided to call him, hoping he would have news about tracing the emails, but knowing that he'd only try to persuade me to go to the police. Still, I needed to hear a friendly voice. His mobile rang for almost a minute but he didn't answer. When his voicemail finally kicked in, I hung up. He was probably with Pippa, having a normal life, trying to ignore the heavy burden I had become.

Like everyone else, he too had probably slipped away from me.

CHAPTER TWENTY-FOUR
2014

I sat shivering on a bench in front of the Slater and Gordon law offices. The huge modern building was in Holborn, with floor-to-ceiling windows on every level; Jeremy must have been doing well. He, at least, had managed to salvage a life for himself. Adam had wanted to be a lawyer, but I'd never heard him mention that was also his brother's dream. Perhaps it hadn't been then.

It had just gone five o'clock and there was no telling how long I'd have to sit there, slowly turning to ice. When I had called the law firm earlier to check that Jeremy was in the office, the receptionist confirmed that he was. So sooner or later he would have to come out. I assumed that most lawyers didn't leave work this early, but I was prepared to wait. I had to know if Adam's brother was my tormentor.

As I sat there, cradling a large café mocha I'd bought from Starbucks, I watched people walking past. Everyone seemed in a hurry, as if they were scared time would catch up with them if they slowed down even for a moment. And they were all dressed smartly, proving how together they were, how in control of their own lives. But none of us truly were, so they were only fooling themselves. Still, I couldn't help but envy them.

The waiting seemed endless. My book was in my bag but I didn't dare pull it out and risk the chance of missing Jeremy while I got lost in the words. It occurred to me that although I knew what he looked like now, I had no idea what to expect from this man. He might have been Adam's brother, but I knew nothing about him: now or then. And if he was the man behind the threats then surely he would recognise me immediately? What then? I was only now considering this possibility. At least we were in a public place so surely he wouldn't dare do anything with a hundred witnesses around?

Eventually a plan formed in my head. I had no idea if it would work but it had to be worth a try.

I continued scanning faces passing by and when he appeared, a figure in the distance, I immediately knew it was him. I had studied his photo on the law firm's website so carefully that all his features were ingrained in my head. He was walking briskly and would end up passing me any second if I didn't do something.

Summoning all my nerve, I stood up and placed myself in his path, hoping my smile was warm rather than sinister. I only had one chance to get this right.

'Hi, Jeremy Bowden?'

He glanced at me but carried on walking. 'Yeah?'

I searched his face for any hint of recognition but found nothing. He only looked confused, and slightly harried. If he was my emailer – which was still possible – then he was doing it without having any idea what I looked like now, and that didn't seem likely.

I moved on to phase two of my plan. Turning to him, I thrust my hand out. 'My name's Anna Proctor. I went to school with your brother.'

That stopped him in his tracks. 'Oh, right.' Slowly he reached for my hand, shaking it only briefly before pulling away. Again, I saw no hint that he recognised me. Or that he didn't believe me.

'I just wondered if you might have time for a quick chat?' I hoped my voice wasn't betraying how nauseous I felt. I had come this far but still wasn't sure I could see it through.

Jeremy frowned then and I was sure he was about to tell me to go to hell. 'Do you need legal help? Because I'd be happy to help but you'll have to make an appointment in the morning.'

I shook my head. 'No, it's not that. I've been living abroad. In France. And never have a chance to get to London and it's just, well, Adam and I were really close at school.' I continued trying to read his expression, but he seemed distracted. 'Did he ever mention me?'

Finally he focused, eyeing me cautiously, taking in my appearance, trying to work me out. 'Can't say he did. Sorry. But then I lived in America for years and we hardly spoke during that time. Just the usual small talk. You know. Until he…went off the rails I guess.'

Trying to ignore the bile rising to my throat, I forced myself to believe I really was Anna Proctor. If she truly had been friends with Adam then how would she feel talking to his brother now? How would she feel about me?

'Listen, do you have time for a quick coffee?'

Jeremy eyed the coffee cup I still held in my hand, and then glancing at his watch, shook his head. 'Sorry, got to get home or my wife will kill me. I promised her I'd be home early tonight and I need to go to Covent Garden to pick something up. But which way are you heading? You could walk with me if you want to talk for a minute?'

His kindness sent a wave of guilt flooding through me. It was wrong to mislead him this way, but I had to be able to rule him out, and there was no other option I could think of to help me do that.

'Great,' I said. 'I'll get the Tube from there, then.' He didn't need to know there was no way I would head underground again.

Jeremy walked so quickly, towering over me so that I had to take long strides in order to keep up with him. But it felt good to be walking; it took some of the pressure off, left me free to avert my eyes from him.

'You know, none of it was Adam's fault. I blame Leah Mills. If he hadn't met her, it would all have turned out differently.' I swallowed the lump that had lodged in my throat.

Jeremy slowed down a fraction and exhaled a deep breath. 'Thanks for saying that.' He paused. 'That's a name I haven't heard in a long time.'

'I'm so sorry. I didn't mean to—'

'No, no, it's fine. We can't pretend she doesn't exist. As much as we've all tried.'

This was going better than I'd hoped, and the more Jeremy spoke, the more convinced I became that he wasn't behind the threats. But that didn't mean he believed I was Anna Proctor.

'I never liked her at school,' I said. 'She always thought she was better than everyone else. Thought she was something special.' This was so far from the truth, and I hadn't planned to say it, but the words flooded out without me knowing what would come next. I had to be careful.

'Well, my brother liked her. Probably loved her actually. More fool him.'

Hearing these words, I almost froze. They were too painful to hear. Adam had only said it to me once, and he quickly followed it with a warning that he didn't find it easy to say so probably wouldn't make a habit of it. But that I just had to trust that he did. Did I believe him? Time chisels away at memory so I'm not sure now, but I must have believed in him. Only afterwards did I have to convince myself that he didn't. It was easier that way.

Pulling myself together, I nodded, even though Jeremy's eyes were fixed straight ahead so he couldn't see me agreeing. I wondered if he was taking anything in or if all he could do now was picture his brother.

'Do you know what the worst thing is?' I said. I was back to being Anna Proctor. 'That she's probably living a cushty little life now, free from blame and scrutiny, while the others—'

'Do you mind if we change the subject, Anna? I really don't want to talk about her, or think about her. We've all worked hard to put everything behind us so I'd rather not rake it all up now. Is that okay?' He turned to me and his eyes had become glassy. Jeremy wasn't my emailer.

I had further confirmation of this when we reached Covent Garden station and he pulled out a business card from his pocket. 'In case you ever need anything,' he said. Then, reaching inside his suit jacket, he dug out a pen and began writing on the card. 'I'm giving you my mobile number too. In case you want to ask anything… about Adam.'

'Thanks,' I said, taking the card. I watched him walk away and almost ran after him to hand it back. Of all the things I'd done, my lie to him felt like the worst.

Later at home, I studied my notebook and tried to make sense of what I knew so far. Although I was no closer to finding out who was threatening me, I could rule out both Imogen and Adam's families. There was no way to be completely sure, but this was as close as I could get.

I hadn't had a chance to go to Corey's old house, and Mum didn't seem to know if his family still lived there, but somehow, even after all these years, I thought I could still remember his phone number. Of course I still remembered Imogen's and Adam's, but I'd hardly ever called Corey. But there were some things my brain wouldn't let me forget. The chances of it still being in use were slim, but once again, I had to try everything I could.

A woman answered the phone, sounding as if she was being hugely inconvenienced by the interruption to whatever she was doing.

'Yes?' she said.

I told her I was trying to reach Juliette Pierce, and she huffed down the phone. 'Really? She hasn't lived here for years.'

'Oh,' I said, unable to hide my disappointment. 'Do you happen to know where she moved to? It's really important that I speak to her.'

'Yes, I know where she is. But who are you?'

'I'm a friend of hers but we lost touch.'

There was a pause and I wondered if she would hang up. 'Well, she's in Ireland now, with family. I don't know her number or address.'

I was about to thank her but she had already gone, leaving the dial tone sounding in my ear.

Writing down what I had learnt in my notebook, I thought it unlikely that if Corey's family were in Ireland they would be responsible for the threats. How would they have got someone to carry out the mugging? It wasn't impossible, but I had to make a decision so I crossed out their names.

That just left Miss Hollis. I'd left her until last because it would be the hardest to investigate. I knew nothing about what she had done afterwards, or any family she might have had. As well as that, I didn't want to remember how she looked that night, how her eyes widened like a frightened animal as she begged and pleaded. No, it would not be easy at all.

As I sat there, once again in the dark because I couldn't face harsh lights, I thought about Julian. I had done nothing to offend him, or make him think I was a psycho, as his brother had called me. Julian knew nothing about my past, yet the words his brother had used were too close to home. But that didn't make sense. None of this did and I was starting to feel defeated.

I pulled myself off the sofa and fetched my laptop from the kitchen table. It never seemed to have a permanent home; it was always just wherever I had last used it. I logged on to Two Become One and clicked on my inbox, looking for my old messages from Julian. Opening the latest one, I began typing a reply, just asking how he was, but when I clicked send, a notification flashed on the screen: *Unidentified User.*

Now I felt even more deflated, as if my blood had been drained and I was just a sack of skin. By being with Julian I had tried to live again, and it had been ripped away from me. It was worse than if I had never met him because I wouldn't have known how good it was to have feelings for someone again.

Clicking on my inbox, I reread all of our correspondence, searching for clues that he had never truly liked me. But I found nothing. Nothing but the beginnings of something that felt like it had been going somewhere.

I thought of Maria then, how she would be able to help me make sense of Julian's disappearing act.

Dialling her number, I kept the phone clamped to my ear, but after a few moments knew she wouldn't answer. My name would be flashing on her screen and she would only turn away from it and wait for the ring tone to stop. I knew this with certainty.

Desperate for human contact – to share my fears, for someone to tell me I'd be okay – I tried Ben's mobile next. He hadn't answered earlier but maybe he would now.

'Leah? Hi.' His voice was warm and friendly, just what I needed to hear. 'You okay?'

I wanted to say yes. To pretend I was absolutely fine and that I didn't need anything from anyone, but I couldn't pull it off.

'Just…you know…still worried.'

'Has anything else happened?'

'No, no. Nothing. 'Are you doing anything?'

'I promised I'd take Pippa for a meal. But I could tell her something's come up, if you need me?'

'No, don't do that. Please. I'll be fine.'

'I contacted a friend of mine about tracing the email address, and he's going to have a go, but it could take a while. Have you thought any more about going to the police?'

'I'm thinking about it all,' I lied. 'I'm just making a record of everything that's happened. You know, times and dates. They'll need all that won't they?'

It was a good excuse but he didn't sound convinced. 'Yes, but you shouldn't put it off.'

'I know, I know. I won't.'

'Listen, I better go, but I'll call you tomorrow, okay? Are you working?'

My plan had been to take another day off to do more research, but now Ben was mentioning it, I realised I missed the routine of being at the library. Perhaps it would be better to be there. At least I would be safe. I told him I would be working the next day and he promised to call in the evening.

After we'd hung up, I made a peanut butter sandwich and ate it on the sofa while I tried to read. It was hopeless. For the first time I couldn't take in the words, they just blurred into each other. It didn't help that my pounding head ensured I got no peace, so I shut my eyes and hoped for the pain to ease quickly.

Then my mobile phone rang, shattering the silence, forcing my eyes open. I didn't recognise the number so this couldn't be good news. I hesitated at first, but then, as it always did, my curiosity took over. I grabbed the phone and waited to hear someone speak.

CHAPTER TWENTY-FIVE
2000

It's approaching the end of summer and I still haven't told Adam that I followed him a few weeks ago. That I saw him sitting outside Miss Hollis's house again. Waiting. I daren't think about what he was doing, what he was waiting for.

Imogen, Corey and I sit in Imogen's back garden, waiting for Adam to turn up. He's late once again, but I seem to be the only one who's bothered about this. His parents are away tonight and are leaving him alone in the house, so of course Adam has arranged a party and invited everyone from school. He doesn't even like most of them, but when I questioned him on the phone last night he said that didn't matter. 'It's time to celebrate the beginning of our freedom, Leah.'

I didn't point out that we have only gained freedom from one thing, and that we will be tied to our A-level studies and then university for the next few years, because I know what he means. He might think I don't get him half the time but I do. I really do.

Imogen and Corey are sitting on a large beach towel on the grass, their legs draped over each other, while I have chosen to sit on a deck chair with my book, a few feet away from them. This says it all. How things have changed. How I feel isolated and separate from the others, even Adam.

'Come and sit with us,' Imogen says. 'There's plenty of room. Reading's not very sociable, is it? And where's Adam? It's too quiet without him here. We're ready to have some fun, aren't we, Corey?' She nudges him and he nods his agreement.

'I don't know where he is,' I say. Imogen should know by now that I am the last person who will know where Adam is at any given time. I stay where I am but offer her a smile so she doesn't think anything is wrong. I need her to think I am the same Leah I've always been.

When Adam still hasn't shown up after another half hour, Corey tells us he will go for a walk and look for him. 'I'll head in the direction of his house,' he says. 'That way I'll probably bump into him.'

I don't bother mentioning that there is no telling what direction Adam will be coming from because he probably hasn't even been at home.

Once he's gone, I get up and sit with Imogen on the beach towel. She grabs hold of my arm and her hands are warm and sticky. 'I feel like I haven't seen you for ages,' she says. 'Not alone at least. We never seem to get time to ourselves any more, do we?'

Again I keep quiet and don't tell her this is because she spends all her time with Corey. I'm not bitter about it; I'm happy she has him to share things with, but why does having a boyfriend have to come at the expense of friendship? Perhaps she thinks I do the same with Adam, although I can count on one hand the number of times I've seen him since we broke up from school.

But the more I think about it, the more I realise it is not Imogen's fault at all. Or Corey's. Or Adam's. It is mine. I am the one who is drifting away, as if I am being pulled by a strong current and can't swim back to them.

'I'm sorry,' I say to her. 'Things are changing, aren't they?'

She frowns and lets go of my arm. 'What do you mean? What's changing?'

It's hard to put into words the jumbled up thoughts that float around my head all day, but I have to take this opportunity, while we are alone, to try and talk to her. 'Us. All four of us. Don't you think?'

She scrunches up her face, contemplating what I've just said, and looks like a small child. 'I don't think so,' she says eventually. 'What do you mean?'

And then before I know what I'm saying, it all comes flooding out, like a river bursting its banks, and I am powerless to stop talking. 'We just don't seem to talk much any more. I mean, we talk, like on the phone, but we don't *talk*, if you know what I mean.'

Imogen shakes her head. 'Of course we talk. We're talking now. What's going on, Leah?'

'Oh, sorry, it's nothing. I'm just worried about Adam, that's all.' I wasn't going to bring him up but the heat I feel talking about my friendship with Imogen is burning me up.

'Why? What's happened? Are you two okay?'

She fires her questions at me and I don't know which one to answer first. I picture Adam sitting on the grass opposite Miss Hollis's house and debate whether to tell Imogen that I followed him that day. What will she think of me? But I have little choice, because dealing with this on my own is eating me up. So I tell her. Everything. Things about Adam's behaviour I haven't even admitted to myself until now.

When I've finished talking, she twists her mouth as if to say *what's all the big fuss about?* So I know before she speaks that she doesn't understand.

'Leah, Adam's fine. I think you're worrying about nothing. So he hates that bitch, Hollis. We all do, don't we? That doesn't mean there's something up with Adam. He's the most together person we know. I look at him and I think, no, I *know* that he's going far in life. Just trust him, he knows what he's doing.'

I stare at my friend, shocked she doesn't get what I'm saying. 'But…we've finished school now, and he's not taking A-level history, so why does he still care? He doesn't need to have anything to do with her again.' Why can't Imogen see this? That it's all so pointless?

Now it is her turn to look bemused, as if she can't understand why *I* don't get it. And then her head creases into a frown, reminding me of how Mum looks when she's about to lecture me. 'Leah, he's your boyfriend. You have to support him however he feels. Otherwise, what do you think he's going to do? Surely I don't need to remind you that bloody Anna Proctor's been after him for months.' She sees my face drop. 'Not that he'd be interested in her, but you've got to stand by him. Like I do with Corey.'

I don't know where all this is coming from, where she's picked up these 1950s housewife notions, but I want no part of it. 'Maybe,' I say, as a holding position until I can figure out what to do. And then I tell her I need to finish reading my book.

'Just don't bring it to the party,' she says, rolling onto her back to bask in the sun.

By evening, I have almost forgotten how I felt earlier. The music has blanked it out and I'm dancing with Imogen in Adam's front room. Christina Aguilera is playing and we're trying to copy her moves from the video, but not very successfully. We spend more time bent double from laughter than dancing.

Imogen whispers to me that someone has spiked all the lemonade and Coke but I only half-believe her. I've never had alcohol so don't know what being tipsy feels like, but I'm sure I'm just excited because of the music. There are hundreds of people here and half of them aren't even from school so I don't know how they found out about the party. No doubt they are here just to say they came to Adam Bowden's party. But still, nobody is causing any problems and there's a great atmosphere.

'This is fun, isn't it?' Imogen shouts into my ear, and I nod because she is right. It's impossible not to enjoy yourself when music is pounding and everyone is having a good time. Everyone, that is, except Adam. I've caught sight of him a few times and on each occasion he rushes past, telling me he has to do something or other and can't stop now. I make up my mind then and there never to host my own party; it's impossible to enjoy it when you have to stress about everyone else. I reach down and pick up my glass from the floor, taking a long sip of Coke. I sniff it but can't detect anything unusual. I'm sure Imogen has got it wrong.

Later, I find Adam sitting at the top of the stairs, staring straight ahead of him. At nothing. He looks sad rather than stressed now, and I feel sorry for him. He's gone to all this trouble and can't even enjoy his own party.

'Are you okay?' I ask, flopping down next to him.

He shuffles closer to the wall, pulling me with him so that people can get past us to the bathroom. There's a downstairs toilet but he's letting people use the upstairs one too. I would never let strangers, or even people I know from school, traipse through my parents' house, but I can't help feeling Adam is punishing them for not taking him to America this summer.

He kisses me on the head, then the cheek, then quickly on the mouth before telling me he's fine. But *fine* is not good is it? It doesn't mean happy, or content. Any of the things I want him to be.

'Are you sure?' I ask.

Nodding slowly, he turns to me and then a huge grin appears on his face. 'Help me find Corey and Imogen. I need to talk to you all together. You get Imogen and I'll hunt down Corey. I think he's in the garden. Meet us out there.'

Adam's enthusiasm spreads through me like an infection. I have no clue what's brought on this sudden change of mood, or what he's planning, but if it's got Adam smiling then I won't complain.

The Bowdens' garden is huge; twice the size of ours and in better condition too. Adam says his mum likes gardening but I've never seen her out there and can't imagine her getting grubby in the dirt. I have my suspicions that they have a gardener, but he's just too embarrassed to admit it. It's a funny world, I think, when people are ashamed of being well off.

Imogen and I rush to the end, where there is a low fence separating the garden from the extensive fields beyond. I've never noticed before how lucky Adam is to live here and I feel a sudden urge to jump over the fence and run as fast as I can through the fields, just to see how far they go on for. Maybe that Coke was spiked after all.

'There they are,' Imogen squeals, pointing at Adam and Corey, who are sitting on the ground by the fence.

'What took you so long?' Adam says, but he is grinning so I know he's not annoyed.

Imogen plonks herself down on the ground and the short skirt she's wearing rides up even higher. 'So what's with all the secrecy?' she asks, grabbing Corey's hand.

Adam throws his head back and laughs. 'Just the plan of the century, that's all.'

Beside him, Corey nods his head, his grin matching Adam's. He's holding a glass of lemonade and I wonder again if it has been laced with something. 'Adam's going to—'

'Wait, let me tell them.' He turns to Imogen and me. 'Listen, you know I've been a bit…kind of stressed lately? Well, firstly, I'm sorry about that.'

I glance at Imogen but her attention is fixed on Adam.

'Anyway,' he continues. 'That Hollis bitch has really had it in for me, and I feel like she's gone too far not letting me into my maths exam. It's bad enough I've let her get away with bullying me for years, but that was the final straw. That's kind of why I've been a bit…absent lately.'

I'm surprised by what Adam is saying. Not that he's talking about Miss Hollis – that's nothing unusual – but the fact that he has recognised his behaviour has been off lately. This is what I've longed for him to say, but I'm confused why he's telling it to all of us like this. Surely he should have waited until we're alone?

Imogen speaks before I do. 'Well, course you've been stressed when she's such a fucking bitch.'

Adam nods. 'Yeah, well, anyway, I know I need to put it all behind me and move on, but there's one thing I have to do first, to help me do that. And I need all of your help.'

We all look at each other. Adam has always been good at creating intrigue.

'You know I've been watching her house?' He says this with no hint of shame, as if it's perfectly reasonable behaviour for someone to stalk their teacher. 'Well, I've found out she's away all this weekend. That idiot boyfriend is taking her to the Lake District or somewhere like that. So…I'm going to break into her house. Tomorrow night.'

Imogen gasps, but she's still smiling. She must think he's joking. 'Very funny,' she says, then seeing the look on Adam's face adds, 'Oh, you're serious.'

'Course I'm serious, why wouldn't I be?'

'But you can't break into her house!' I say. It's the first I've spoken since we came out here and everyone turns to stare at me. There are so many thoughts racing through my head: how does he know she's going to the Lake District? Just how many times has he gone to her house?

Adam takes my hand and I immediately soften, forgetting everything I want to ask him. 'Listen, I'm not going to take anything, just trash the place, freak her out a bit when she gets back and finds the mess. That's all it will be.'

'Yeah, it's not bad,' Corey adds. 'We'll be in and out quickly so nobody will see us.'

Imogen leans forward. 'She does deserve it. And if it will help you put it all behind you, Adam, then I'm in. Actually it's kind of exciting!'

I know Imogen is talking but surely the words can't be hers? How is it possible we've grown so far apart that we feel so differently about what Adam is suggesting?

'No! It's a crazy idea!' I say, letting go of Adam's hand. I am astounded that I seem to be the only one who thinks this. I turn to Adam. 'You have to just let it go now. She's not your teacher any more, is she? You don't need to have anything to do with her.'

'But she'll still be there at school, won't she? Smirking at me when I pass her in the corridor. Knowing she's won.'

I stand up now. 'Won what? There's nothing to win or lose. What are you talking about?'

The way Adam looks at me turns my insides cold. His eyes shoot disappointment at me, but it's more than that. There is something else and I don't want to acknowledge what it is. 'Really?' he says. 'You don't get it? You don't get me?'

I turn and walk away then, because if I don't I will say something I can't take back.

CHAPTER TWENTY-SIX
2014

'Leah, it's me. Maria. You called me.' It wasn't a question, but a flat statement, delivered in a cold, emotionless voice.

At first I was confused, unsure what she was talking about. She was the last person I was expecting to hear from. When she'd ignored my call, I'd taken it to be a sign that whatever friendship we'd been forming was over, before it had even started. At least it wasn't my emailer. I wasn't ready to hear his voice, not without being prepared.

I thanked her for calling back and she responded with a grunt. Now that she was on the other end of the phone I had no idea what to say to her. I'd hoped to get her advice about Julian, but given the mood she seemed to be in, how could I bring him up now? Deciding to talk about work instead, I opened my mouth to speak, but she beat me to it.

'Actually, I'm glad you called. I want to talk to you. But not on the phone.' She paused for a moment, rustling something that could have been her bag. 'I'll come over to you. I just need half an hour.'

This was all wrong. She hadn't spoken to me for days and now she was inviting herself to my flat. Again.

'No,' I said, still in shock. 'But I can come to you.'

When she didn't respond, I quickly added that I was redecorating the flat and it was in no state for visitors. We both knew it was a lie but she didn't waste time challenging me.

'Okay,' she said, making no attempt to hide her annoyance. 'I'll text you my address. Half an hour. Please come, it's important.'

When she hung up, I stared at my phone, wondering if I was going crazy and had imagined the whole conversation. I checked my watch and it was eight-forty-five. That meant it would be after nine before I made it to Maria's. I wondered if she was in some kind of trouble and needed my help; but what assistance could I be when I couldn't even straighten out my own life?

Her text came through with an address I'd never heard of. Heathfield Gardens. I checked Google Maps on my phone and saw that it was close to Wandsworth Common. If I attempted to walk it would be nearer ten p.m. by the time I got there, so I called a cab, the woman who answered telling me it would be at least ten minutes before it got to me.

I threw on my coat and scarf and grabbed my bag, choosing to wait downstairs in the hallway rather than outside. At least that way there was a barrier between me and whoever was out there, watching me.

As I sat in the taxi I felt like a puppet, being moved about by someone else. I didn't want to go to Maria's house with no clue why I was going there. I also didn't want to hunt down a person who had taken it upon themselves to torment me, to infiltrate my life. I just wanted to be left alone.

Half an hour later I stood outside Maria's huge house, wondering how she could afford such a lovely home on our salary. At first I'd assumed the house must be converted into flats, but it was number ten, and as far as I could tell it was just one property. I shouldn't have been surprised; there was so little I knew about her other than the fact she was looking for the right man. Maybe she had already found him and fate had conspired to keep them apart. Nobody wanted to consider that possibility. Only I had no choice but to think about it.

She answered the door in jeans and a hooded top, and it was strange to see her dressed so casually. Her mouth turned up at the corner, but it wasn't a smile. I didn't know what it was, but once again I questioned what I was doing there. Not speaking, she moved aside to let me in and I stepped into her hall. It didn't feel much warmer inside than it was on the other side of the door so I made no move to take off my coat or scarf, and neither did she suggest it.

'Coffee?' she said, heading to the end of the hall.

I followed her into the kitchen, which was smaller than I'd have expected for a house like this, and looked as if it had only recently been fitted.

'Have a seat.' She flicked the kettle switch and grabbed two mugs from a cupboard.

Her words weren't delivered in a kind way, as if she'd been thinking of me and was doing something nice. Instead, they were tinged with resentment. I still wasn't sure what I'd done to cause this tension between us.

The white kitchen table was too big for the room and had enough space for six chairs. I wondered why Maria, who as far as I knew lived on her own, needed all that space, but I kept quiet. Now was not the time for personal questions. I pulled out one of the chairs but perched on the end, unable to make myself too comfortable. Something didn't feel right, and until I knew what it was I would remain on edge.

Placing my drink on the table, rather than sitting down herself, Maria headed back to the worktop and propped herself up against it. 'You're a good liar, aren't you, Leah?' She almost spat the question at me and it seemed to come from nowhere.

I turned to her, frowning, but didn't know what to say. It seemed to take forever before I could get any words out. 'What…what are you talking about? Look, if this is about the promotion—'

'Oh, come on!' she continued. 'Do you really think I care about that? I'm happy with the job I've got.'

Stifling the panic that was rising in my chest, I tried to keep my voice steady. 'Then what's this about?'

She started shaking her head. 'I wanted us to be friends, Leah, I really did. Even though you weren't very open, I understood that. I thought it would change the longer we worked together, so I tried to make our friendship work. But deep down, I knew.'

I had no idea where she was going with this, but I needed her to spit it out. I repeated my question. 'Knew what? What's this about, Maria? Are you going to tell me or not?'

She rolled her eyes. 'I knew that there was something off about you. It was that thing about your cousin that got me thinking. It just didn't add up. In fact, nothing about you added up. The thing is, while you've been distancing yourself from everyone at work, I've actually been forging friendships, and it's taken a while but I've come to really like Sam. I respect her. And she deserves to know who she's employed.'

Right at that moment my heart felt as if it had fallen to my stomach. My chest tightened and I could barely focus on what Maria was saying.

She knew.

She knew all about me.

'That man. Julian. He's not your cousin.' She delivered this statement then stared at me, her stern face challenging me to deny it. What was the point? She wouldn't have asked me here if she didn't already know everything.

I stood up. I had heard enough and it felt as if the walls were closing in on me.

'Sit down. Believe me, you'll want to hear what I have to say.'

As I watched her, it dawned on me that the woman I was staring at was my emailer. My tormentor. She had to be. But hadn't the messages started before Maria had seen Julian at the library? None of this made sense.

'How…how do you know that?'

Her eyes seemed to burn into me. 'You're really asking me that? That's the most important thing is it? Do you know what the worst of it is? That you made up a story about your grandmother dying. That's what you said the flowers were for, remember? How could you live with yourself?'

'I…'

'Save your bullshit, Leah. Just don't bother. Because the truth is, you've done far worse than that, haven't you?'

And then she came out with it. Told me things that for years I'd tried hard to hide from everyone, including myself. I closed my eyes while she spoke, reliving every moment, even though she was only providing an outline. When she'd finished, a heavy silence hung in the air and I felt empty. In a way, I was relieved. Whatever she wanted, at least this would soon be over.

'You know, I wondered why your flat was so soulless. But it all makes sense now. You're used to the bare, minimalistic look, aren't you?'

'Just tell me what you want.' My voice was shaky, matching exactly how my legs felt, and it was a miracle I had remained upright for this long.

She ignored me and continued her speech. 'Are you even sorry?'

I turned to her then, hoping she would see the truth in my eyes, if she didn't believe my words. 'Every day of my life.'

Seeming to consider this for a moment, she leaned her elbows on the table and rested her chin in her hands. 'Do you know, when I first called you, I had no intention of confronting you. I just wanted to see if you would do the right thing and come clean. But you wouldn't have, would you?'

Now was the time for honesty, so I shook my head. 'No. Probably not.'

'And you lied on your application form, didn't you? Left things out you were obliged to inform your employer.'

I nodded, a familiar wave of shame and guilt flooding through me.

'All those people. All those lives ruined. Why don't you put it right now?' Her voice was softer as she said this, filling me with hope that I would get out of there in one piece. 'You need to tell Sam that you're leaving. Tomorrow. I don't care if you tell her the truth, but you just need to leave.'

'What?' I had to get her to repeat what she'd just said, because I wasn't sure I'd heard right. After everything, could this really be all she wanted? Why was she letting me off so lightly?

She said it again, and there was no room for doubt when she finished her sentence by telling me to get out of her house.

I wasted no time rushing into the hall and pulling open the front door, stepping out into the cold, refreshing air. Taking in a lungful of it because I was seconds away from being sick.

Following behind me, Maria stood in the doorway, leaning against the doorframe. I turned back to her. 'So that's it? You're not going to do anything?'

Her forehead creased. 'Do anything? Like what? As long as you tell Sam you're leaving immediately and get the hell away from the library. I never want to see your face again.'

Facing the door once more, and the pavement outside, I could still feel her eyes on me.

'A similar thing happened to my sister, you know. That person got away with it too, and guess what? She has to work with him day in and day out. Now get the hell away from me.'

'How did you know?' I asked, once again turning to face her. 'Who are you?' It was a question I should have asked at the beginning, but had been too numb to think of.

'The email. It told me everything. More than I want to know. And what do you mean, who am I? You're even more messed up than I thought.'

The slam of the door reverberated in the silent night.

I should have called a taxi then. It was nearly eleven p.m. and the streets were quiet – no place for anyone, let alone me, to be walking alone – but I couldn't bear the thought of waiting around outside Maria's. I glanced back at the house and she was there in the window, a black shadow watching me and making no effort to hide the fact. That helped make my mind up. I would risk the walk.

It wasn't too bad to start with and the further I got from Maria's, the clearer my head felt. So she wasn't my tormentor, but whoever it actually was had told Maria everything, forcing me to give up my job. If I admitted the truth to Sam then she would have no choice but to let me go. Apart from what I had done, I had lied on my application form. That meant immediate dismissal. And if I kept quiet then Maria would tell her.

As I walked, the roads began to feel endless, as if daylight would arrive before I made it home. It was ironic that for years I had punished myself by barely living a life, yet the moment I wanted to set myself free, it was snatched away from me piece by piece. As much as it hurt, I could deal with not having Julian, but my job was the one secure thing in my life.

I couldn't let this continue. This person was winning; they had taken everything from me and I needed to find them before they found me. Because there was only one thing left for them to take.

Eventually I turned onto Garratt Lane. There were more people around now, but that was of little comfort; it was easier to be alert when there were fewer faces to scrutinise. I flinched every time someone passed me, my body tensing, preparing for an attack of some sort. But nothing happened. Nobody so much as glanced at me, although I continued to feel on edge.

Once I turned onto Allfarthing Road, I increased my pace, spurred on by the promise of safety only moments away. Making it to my road somehow felt like a victory.

Inside my flat, I changed into my nightshirt, throwing my thick towelling dressing gown over the top. But I couldn't get warm. Turning on the electric heater, I stood by the living room window waiting for the heat to kick in.

And that's when I saw him. Sitting on a low wall across the road, staring up at my window, his hands buried in his pockets. He was in the shadows, but it was unmistakably him. I recognised the navy jacket he'd worn when we first met up in Hammersmith.

Julian.

Rushing downstairs, an image of Adam outside my house, throwing stones at my window to get my attention, flickered in my head and I almost stumbled. I couldn't think of that. This was Julian, not Adam. I couldn't think about Adam. Throwing open the door, I ran out into the street, my eyes scanning the wall. But there was nobody there. He had gone.

Julian had disappeared again.

CHAPTER TWENTY-SEVEN
2014

I woke up and for a few seconds my mind was blank. It brought me a moment of peace, until I remembered everything that had happened. Jeremy. Maria. And Julian. Now that a few hours had passed, I wondered if I'd imagined him being there. That I was so desperate to see him, my mind had conjured him up. It was the only thing that made sense.

It was still dark and when I checked the alarm clock it was only three a.m. I closed my eyes but I was now too alert to fall asleep again.

Reaching across to the bedside table, I fumbled around for my book, but it wasn't there. I was sure I'd read in bed last night in an effort to forget I'd seen Julian, but I couldn't clearly remember. I'd had a bad headache, so it's likely I went straight to sleep. Why couldn't I remember? It had to be the anxiety getting to me. But whatever the case, I needed to read now, to help me relax so I could try to get a few more hours' sleep.

Climbing out of bed, I went through to the lounge and turned on the light.

Something wasn't right.

I couldn't immediately tell what was wrong, I just knew something was different. Looking around, it took me a moment to realise what that was. The sofa and coffee table appeared to be in their usual places, but when I looked more closely, each had been moved slightly so that the indents in the carpet where they had previously stood were showing. There was no more than a couple of inches difference and it made no sense. I hadn't moved the furniture. Which could only mean one thing: someone had been in my flat.

The bookcases hadn't been moved, but on every shelf the order of my books had been rearranged. I wasn't one of those people who ordered them alphabetically, but I knew roughly where each book was, depending on when I'd bought it, and what I was looking at was all wrong.

I stood still, not daring to move. It wasn't likely anyone was still in the flat – it was too small for hiding places – but I was petrified. Even though there was nobody there now, someone had been in my flat and they wanted me to know it.

The kitchen appeared to be undisturbed, but when I opened the cupboard to get a glass for some water, all my mugs and glasses had been swapped around and were now on the wrong shelves. If I'd had any doubts before, then this was firm evidence of an intruder. Perhaps I should have been, but I was no longer scared. Anger had replaced my fear and I just wanted an end to it.

My laptop was on the kitchen table and I switched it on, my stomach churning as I waited for Google to load. And then I did something I never thought I'd be able to: I wrote her name in the search box, each letter seeming to stare at me, accusing and sad at the same time.

Natalie Hollis.

The first few search suggestions clearly weren't the woman I was looking for, but when I got to the bottom of the page, there she was. Miss Hollis. It was a newspaper article from 2000 and I wondered if it was the same one my emailer had sent me. Taking a deep breath, I began to read, trying to pretend it was just another news story that had nothing to do with me.

And then halfway down the page I saw his name. Her boy-friend. Tim Fletcher. It seemed such an ordinary name, out of place in this story, as if it wasn't possible something so heinous could affect his life. But it had. And maybe he was making me pay for that now.

The article mentioned he was a business lecturer at West Herts College, but that had been fourteen years ago. I didn't think it likely he'd still work there but I could call in a few hours and find out. And if he was still there then I would go to the college and speak to him directly, just like I'd done with Adam's brother. I was sure with just a short conversation I would be able to tell whether or not he was the one doing this to me.

Once I had decided this I began to feel better. I still didn't want to be in my flat, it felt wrong and uncomfortable, like wearing a stranger's clothes. But there was nowhere else I could go. Instead of retreating to bed, I grabbed my duvet and sat on the floor by the window in the front room. I couldn't explain it, but somehow it felt safer being there, cocooned in my duvet.

My mind was too alert to sleep so I tried to read. I still hadn't finished rereading *The Color Purple*, when normally I got through a book in a couple of days, but instead of getting lost in Celie's story, every few lines my mind kept flitting back to Miss Hollis and who had been in my flat.

A few hours later I showered and ate some cornflakes, passing the time before I could call the college. There was also another call I had to make. To Sam. I would have to resign; Maria had left me no choice. But as much as I loved my job, I had to focus on finding my emailer before I could worry about work.

Reluctantly, I emailed Sam, explaining there had been a family emergency and I needed to resign with immediate effect. Once I'd sent it, I forced the sadness away and once more went over in my head what I needed to do.

I waited until nine-thirty to call West Herts College. When someone answered, I was surprised to be told that Tim Fletcher did still work there and that he would be in work all day. Hanging up, I wasn't sure whether I was relieved or disappointed. Now I would have to face him, and it would be even harder than it had been to look Imogen's mother and Adam's brother in the face.

But as I left the flat and headed to the train station, a sense of calm washed over me. I felt safer being outside, even after the mugging and other attack, because now I was alert, watching everyone, as prepared as I could be for whatever might happen next.

I hadn't told Mum I'd be back in Watford, and walking to the college, I prayed I wouldn't bump into her. How would I explain being here if she saw me? She would know I was up to something and that it had everything to do with Miss Hollis. I could never bring myself to call her Natalie, it was best if I always thought of her as our teacher, someone who hadn't exactly been human. I knew that made me seem cold-hearted, but it was just easier.

Reaching the college, I suddenly had second thoughts. If Tim Fletcher was my emailer then he would recognise me the second I appeared in front of him. But as was the case when I confronted Jeremy, we were in a public place so I had to tell myself there was nothing he could do to harm me here. And at least I would know. I hadn't thought what I would do beyond that, I could only take this one step at a time.

I found the reception desk and asked if I could see Tim Fletcher. The receptionist must have been in her late fifties and I wondered if, like him, she had been here all these years. She checked something on the computer then flashed a smile.

'You're in luck. He's finishing a lecture in about ten minutes and then he's got a free hour. You can catch him in room fifty-four in the new building out the back. Just follow the corridor round and it will lead you outside.' She pointed a manicured finger to her left.

It was too easy. I could be anyone and she was allowing me to walk around the college. Didn't this place care about safety? Although, right now, I was thankful for their lack of security.

'I'll just give you a pass,' she said, shoving a visitor's book in front of me. 'And sign this please.' It was something, but still didn't ensure safety.

I signed *Anna Proctor* and took my pass, turning it around as soon as I was out of her line of sight. It was unlikely anyone would recognise me, or the name around my neck, but I couldn't take any chances.

Following the directions the receptionist had given me, I found room fifty-four easily enough. There was a narrow window in the door and I peered through to see a classroom full of students, all engrossed in their lecture. And then I saw him. He had aged a lot but there was no mistaking he was the man Miss Hollis had been seeing.

Instinctively, I moved away from the window and leaned back against the wall, but it was pointless to hide when in a few minutes I would be face-to-face with him. It was five to twelve, which meant I had five minutes to prepare myself for whatever might happen.

Time moved excruciatingly slowly but eventually the first of the students shuffled out, not even glancing in my direction. I held my breath and waited, counting them all as they poured out of the room, their voices raised now that they were free to make noise. There were twenty-two of them and I found myself wondering whether Miss Hollis would have made a better college lecturer than secondary school teacher if things had been different. What had made her choose that age group when she clearly hadn't enjoyed a second of it?

'Can I help you?' a deep voice said, snapping me out of my reverie. I looked up and Tim Fletcher was standing in front of me, towering over me. He stood in the doorway, blocking the entrance with his wide body. I didn't remember him being so large, but then I hadn't been the most observant person back then. His tone was not unkind, but he did look as if he could do without having to talk to a stranger.

'I, um, sorry, I was looking for Tim Fletcher.' I didn't let on that I already knew I had found him.

'That would be me. Can I help you with something?' His eyes darted back and forth, as if he was taking me in and forming opinions before I'd even announced who I was.

I glanced behind him, checking his classroom was empty. 'Do you have time for a quick chat? Perhaps in there?'

Looking at his watch, he let out a small sigh. 'Yes, we can. But can I ask what this is about? Are you a student?'

I had to tell him now, I couldn't put it off any longer. 'No. I'm a…I knew… Natalie Hollis… years ago.' Her name jabbed at my throat like a knife. 'She taught me actually and I was passing by and just wanted to say…how sorry I am about…'

'You'd better come inside,' he said, his face suddenly as white as paper.

The classroom was cold and I wrapped my arms around my body, despite wearing my thick wool coat.

Tim Fletcher sat at his desk then turned to me. 'Sorry,' he said. 'I always keep the heating off in here. It stops the students falling asleep.' He gave a halfhearted chuckle then stared at me again, and I wondered if he expected me to laugh too. But that didn't seem appropriate given what I had told him I was doing there. 'Please, have a seat,' he said, gesturing to the table directly in front of his desk.

Sitting across from him, I felt like I was back in school again and it made me shudder. Those days were forever tainted. Tim

Fletcher looked away from me and stared at his hands. 'So you were a student of Nat's?' he asked.

I nodded. 'Yes. But I left the year before…you know. Before it happened.'

'What's your name? Perhaps she mentioned you?'

'Anna Proctor. But I doubt she would have mentioned me.' I studied his face, but there was no flicker of recognition.

'Well, I can't say your name's familiar, but then she did have a lot of students.'

'She was a great teacher,' I said, trying not to pull away from his gaze.

What he said next surprised me. 'Oh, I'm not sure that's true. I think she struggled. She never really enjoyed teaching but felt she had to stick it out. I think she would have retrained as a nurse. If she'd had the chance.'

'I'm so sorry about what happened to her.'

'Well, thanks for saying that.' He fell silent and I could tell he was revisiting his memories. Good or bad, both would be painful. 'But is that what you've tracked me down for? Because it's been a long, long time.'

My excuse was already in place. 'I know, it's just that I moved abroad with my parents soon after and have only just come back. And she left an impression on me so I just wanted to pay my respects to her.'

He fell quiet as he contemplated my words and I could see he was finding this difficult. 'I've got her mother's phone number, if that's any help? She was a friend of my mother's, actually, so I kept in touch with her for a long time afterward, but I haven't spoken to her for years now. Nat had such a small family and I don't even think any of them are still alive. The truth is, it took me a long time but I've moved on. I'm married with teenage kids now and, to be honest, the last thing I want to do is revisit the past. I loved Nat, of course I did, but I can't undo anything and it was so long ago.'

'I completely understand. Thank you for your time.' I stood up, by then convinced the man wasn't my emailer. Nothing about him screamed that he was lying and all I could do was trust my instincts.

'Let me get you that number.' He pulled out his mobile and began scrolling through it. I found it strange that he would have Miss Hollis's mother's number in his phone after all these years but shrugged it off. It's possible every time he bought a new phone he just copied all the numbers across without checking them.

'Here you go,' he said, scribbling on a piece of scrap paper. 'I have to say, though, she's quite elderly and the last time I spoke to her she wasn't very lucid, so if you call her I don't know how much sense you'll get out of her. That was years ago and I know Alzheimer's can progress rapidly.'

Reaching across for the paper, I thanked him and got out of there as quickly as I could. So that was that. The chances of Miss Hollis's family being involved were almost zero. Rushing past the reception desk, I didn't bother handing back my pass.

When I got home my flat felt even colder and emptier than usual. It hit me how bleak my surroundings were and how my attempt to have more had failed. How could I have ever thought I could have something with Julian? But it still bothered me that I had no explanation for his actions, and my heart fought against my head, determined not to let me move on.

Even though I knew he was no longer moderating Two Become One, I still checked the website, soaking up my disappointment when there was still no sign of him. And then, even though I knew it was terrible to think this way, it struck me how I had come out worse in all of this. Imogen, Corey and Adam had got off lightly. I was the one who was still being punished.

I took my laptop to bed with me and began looking at flats to rent. I would never be able to afford anything in Putney but I checked what was available anyway. And when I stared at the bright and modern flats, with their magnolia walls and sparkling white kitchens, I saw a glimpse of the life I could have had with Adam. I pictured us curled up on a leather sofa, drinking wine and chatting about what kind of day we'd had at work. And only then did the tears I'd kept trapped within me come flooding out, spilling onto my laptop like droplets of rain.

My eyes snapped open. I'd heard something. A bang? Someone thudding on the door? It was almost one a.m. and I'd managed to get some sleep, but now I'd definitely been woken by a noise. I froze, listening, but after a few moments of silence, convinced myself it had been part of a dream.

Until I heard it again.

This time there was no room for doubt: someone was pounding on my door. I tried to stay calm; the fact they were outside was a good thing, but I couldn't move. My mobile was on the bedside table and just as I grabbed it an email came through. My hands began to sweat as I checked it.

Would love to see your flat again, aren't you going to let me in?

He was outside my front door and there was nothing I could do. Everything had been leading up to this. Why hadn't I done more to try and prevent it? And then I heard glass smash and something thudding to the floor downstairs.

Grabbing my phone, I ran to the bathroom and slammed the door shut, locking it behind me. It wouldn't hold him off for long but at least it was another barrier between us. And I had my phone.

With shaking hands, I dialled Ben's mobile. He was probably asleep so the chances of him hearing it were slim, but there was nobody else I could call. I paced back and forth, willing him to pick up his phone quickly. After seconds that felt like hours, he did. 'Hello? Leah?' His voice was thick with sleep but I didn't have time to feel guilty.

I told him what was happening, while whoever was down-stairs continued banging, and suddenly he was alert.

'What? Are you sure? You need to call the police. Now. Give me your address, I'm coming there now.'

When I told him where I lived he said it would take him at least twenty minutes to get to me. 'But just call the police now, okay? And then call me back so I can stay on the line with you while I get there.'

I promised I would and ended the call. The noise downstairs continued, but I knew I had at least a bit of time; the sturdy front door wouldn't give in that easily. But instead of calling the police, I pulled up the email I'd just been sent and hit reply.

I've called the police.

I took a deep breath and waited, hoping my email would scare him off. It took a few moments but eventually the banging stopped. Five minutes of silence passed but I wouldn't leave the bathroom. Not until Ben got there.

Sitting on the floor by the bath, I was about to call him back but realised my phone battery had turned red. I couldn't let it die on me so texted him instead, asking him to call me when he got here.

It was too quiet while I sat there waiting for Ben. At least with the noise I knew where he was. Now I had no clue whether he ac-tually had gone, or if he'd been successful in getting into the flat.

Only when Ben's call came through, shattering the silence, did I dare to move. He said he was outside and assured me there was nobody there now and the only damage was smashed glass and a battered front door.

I went downstairs to let him in, stepping over the shards of glass that lay scattered on the floor. And when he stepped into the hallway, I grabbed him and hugged him tightly, knowing it was time I told him the truth.

CHAPTER TWENTY-EIGHT
2000

None of them are happy with me. They all want to go ahead with it and think I'm trying to stop them. But I can't, can I? I've objected enough and they're still going to do it. Tonight. Adam has planned it all as if it's a military operation, and the worst thing is that I've never seen him this excited. It should be me putting that smile on his face, not the thought of breaking into our old teacher's house.

I've been moping around again this afternoon and Dad keeps asking what's wrong. But I brush off his concern; if I let him think I'm just being a moody teenager he'll eventually give up. I've got to do something to take my mind off Adam and the others, but nothing works. I begged Dad for some money earlier so I could go into town and buy some books I'll need for September, and that worked for a bit, but now I'm home with nothing to distract me.

I don't want to admit it to myself, but what's also bothering me is that I don't feel part of the group any more. They are doing this without me and none of them seem bothered that I won't be there. Imogen called this morning and halfheartedly asked if I'd changed my mind, but her nonchalant attitude made me even more determined to say no. Perhaps I'm pushing my friendship with all of them to the limit, to test them all. Either it will explode in my face or we'll all be stronger together.

I'm so desperate to fill the time that I make Dad a cup of tea and take it up to his study. His eyes almost pop from his head when he sees what I've done, but I just shrug as if I do this on a regular basis; he doesn't need to know I'm going crazy and will remain this way until I know they are all back home and it's over and done with. Then none of us will ever have to think about Miss Hollis again.

Imogen has told me they've arranged to meet at midnight and that they'll all be sneaking out of their houses. Is it wrong that I hope they'll get caught? I don't like Miss Hollis but she doesn't deserve this. Adam's promised he won't take anything, but how can I trust anything he says when he's doing something so reckless in the first place?

For the next few hours I stare at the television, watching the flickering images but not taking in anything anyone's saying or doing. The only thing I'm thinking about is Adam and how he's slipping away from me by the second. I know I'm only sixteen but I want to be with him forever. There's no one else I want so I have to make this work. I have to fight for us.

As soon as I realise this, I rush to the hall to grab the phone, not bothering to shout up to Dad for permission to use it. Nobody answers at Adam's house so I try Imogen next, and when she picks up I tell her that they have to wait for me tonight.

I'm coming with them.

The night air is cool and I wish I'd worn a jacket. It had felt wrong sneaking out of the house, pulling the door shut slowly so that it didn't make that loud click it usually did. What if they'd caught me? I'd be grounded for the rest of the holiday for sure. But I have to admit there's also something exciting about walking down my road in the pitch black, knowing Adam will be waiting on the corner for me. I just hope he's not late like he normally is.

As soon as I turn onto the next street I see him, leaning against a fence with his hands in his pockets. He smiles when he spots me and it melts my insides. Everything's going to be all right now, I know it.

'I'm glad you came,' he says, pulling me into him and kissing the top of my head.

I lift my head so his mouth skims against mine. 'I'm here for you,' I say, looking around to check my parents haven't followed me.

'We're meeting the others there. Come on, or we'll be late.' He grabs my hand and practically pulls me along in his haste to get to Miss Hollis's house.

The walk seems to take longer than it has the other times I've been here, and as we get closer I begin to feel nervous.

'What if she comes back?' I ask. 'Or a neighbour sees us? What do we do then?' I am hoping Adam has a fallback plan for this eventuality.

But one look at his face tells me he doesn't. In fact, the shrug of his shoulders is proof he's not expecting anything to go wrong at all so hasn't bothered to consider alternatives.

'Just relax, will you? Everything will be fine.'

I want to believe him and I nod and squeeze his hand, but I can't lie to myself.

We turn onto Miss Hollis's road and I squint into the darkness, trying to make out whether Imogen and Corey are here yet.

'Don't worry, they'll be here,' Adam says, without even looking at me. It is just further evidence that we are connected.

I see Imogen first, sitting on the kerb opposite Miss Hollis's house, Corey hidden from view. Adam walks faster.

'I told them to wait by the tree,' he says.

When they see us they both stand up and we all hug, as if we are about to do something extraordinary like climb Mount Everest. I study Imogen's and Corey's faces and they both look excited, as does Adam. I must be the only one whose stomach is flipping.

'Right,' Adam says. 'I've checked out the house and there's a gate that leads to the back garden. Round the side there's a kitchen door and it's not double glazed or anything so we should be able to smash it. I've already hidden a brick in one of the bushes at the back.'

Imogen squeals and clings onto Corey's arm. 'You've got it all sorted, haven't you?' she says.

'Course he has,' Corey chimes in. 'He's been working on this for weeks. He's a bloody genius!'

I grow impatient with them. I agree Adam is a genius, but not for doing this. It doesn't matter how well planned tonight is, it's still a moronic thing to do. I just want to get it over with so we can start living our lives.

Ignoring Corey's praise, Adam flicks his head towards the house. 'Right, everyone ready?'

Imogen and Corey both nod, their faces too eager. Adam turns to me and I try my best to smile, but I'm so nervous it must be more of a grimace. He doesn't notice though, but heads towards the house, the three of us following like soldiers marching into battle.

I let them walk ahead of me and stare straight ahead at the back of Corey's jeans. They are too loose and I wonder if he's borrowed them from someone because Adam has instructed us all to wear black. He says it's so there's less chance of being seen, but this just makes me feel worse. A spur of the moment thing would have been bad enough, but the fact he has put so much thought into it makes me feel nauseous. But it is too late to turn back now.

Time seems to move slowly as we cross the road, but then we are on her property, crossing a physical and metaphorical line.

I look around but there are no lights on in any of the houses nearby. I desperately hope someone will spot us and shout out to scare us off, but there's little chance of that. It's as if Adam is meant to get his way.

He opens the gate and we all file into Miss Hollis's back garden. Although I can't see much in the darkness, I can tell she takes care of it: the grass is mown and the flowerbeds are crammed full of colourful plants. I imagine her out here gardening and a lump forms in my throat, threatening to choke me. She is a human being and we shouldn't be here.

'I'll get the brick,' Adam whispers, disappearing into the back garden while we hover by the door.

There are several plant pots on the ground and Corey begins scrambling around in them. 'I thought so!' he says, too loudly. 'She's left a spare key here!'

Rushing back to us, Adam grabs the key from Corey. 'What a dumb bitch!' He steps forward to the back door and pushes the key in the lock. There is a click as it turns, and we all stare at each other in disbelief.

'I won't be needing this, then,' Adam says, holding up the brick. He rushes back to the lawn and drops it on the ground. 'Although I was looking forward to smashing up her door.'

I cringe when he says this; he is enjoying this too much. If anything he's supposed to be angry, not excited.

'Come on,' he says, and once again we do as he tells us.

Once we're inside we can't turn any lights on, but of course Adam has thought of this. He reaches into his pocket and pulls out a small torch, shedding a circle of light around the room as he waves it back and forth.

'We should still whisper,' he says. 'Just in case any neighbours hear.'

But this is unlikely as the house is detached and the nearest neighbour is metres away. I wonder if Adam is nervous now that we're actually here.

'Come on,' he continues. 'Let's start in the front room.'

That answers my question.

He throws open the nearest door and shines the torch into the darkness. We all peer in and immediately my stomach sinks, bile rising to my throat. This is not the living room. What we are staring at is Miss Hollis's bedroom.

And she is in it, lying in her bed, staring at us with wide, horrified eyes.

'Fuck, fuck, fuck!' Corey says, his voice shattering the silence. 'What the fuck, Adam?'

None of us move. I don't know what Adam is doing or thinking but the torchlight is still shining on Miss Hollis. She shifts up in her bed and I see her eyes and nose are red and a mass of scrunched up tissues lies next to her on the bed.

'Who is that?' she says. 'What are you doing?' Her voice is croaky and barely audible.

We need to leave now, run for our lives, because she hasn't been able to see our faces in the dark. I nudge Adam and try to drag him back but he shrugs me off. Beside me, neither Corey nor Imogen makes any movement.

And then Adam steps forward and it is too late to run. 'Hello, Miss Hollis,' he says. His voice is deep and unfamiliar, and just for a second I fool myself into thinking this is a bad dream, that any moment now I'll wake up in my own bed.

But then she speaks, shattering my hope. 'Adam Bowden? What are you doing? Why are you here?'

She's saying all the wrong things. Why isn't she ordering us out, telling us she's calling the police? Shouting or screaming?

But I have heard shock does strange things to people, and perhaps that's why I am frozen to the spot.

'Because you're a fucking bitch,' Adam says. 'And you don't deserve this nice life you've got.'

She sits further up in bed. 'What do you want? Just take anything and get out, please!' Her voice is still too quiet and I wonder where her courage is. Why isn't she the woman who put Adam in his place on his first day at school? Squinting into the darkness, a frown appears on her forehead. 'Imogen? Corey? What are you…' But then she sees me and her mouth gapes open. 'Leah?'

I want to scream that this is all a mistake, that we're sorry and shouldn't be here. I want to run. But then Adam pushes me forward.

'We're all here because you need to be taught a lesson,' he says. He is too calm, as if he's known all along Miss Hollis would be here. He isn't thrown at all by his plan going awry.

She stares at him and then back to me. Why am I the one she's fixing on? 'Leah, what's he talking about? Please, you all need to leave now.'

I know immediately she has made a huge mistake by ignoring Adam. His face is a grotesque mask, fuelled by his hatred. 'What the fuck are you talking to Leah for? I'm the one you should be begging forgiveness from.'

She starts to get out of bed then but Adam rushes towards her, towering over her so that she shrinks back against her pillow. 'Look, Adam, I'm not well, please just go. What have I done?'

'Just get up. Get out of bed. We can't talk in your bedroom, it's making me feel sick. Go in the front room.'

Miss Hollis shakes her head but one look at Adam's face tells her she should do as he asks. Slowly, she climbs out of bed. She's wearing a short strapless nightie that looks like it's made of silk. It's pretty. Then on shaky legs she heads out to the hall. We all stand aside to let her pass, but Adam follows behind her.

'What's he doing?' I whisper to Corey. 'We need to get out of here.'

Corey chuckles. 'Oh, he's only having a bit of fun. He won't do anything.'

I want to yell at him that this has already gone way too far, but the words lodge in my throat.

'Come on, Leah,' Imogen says. 'We can't miss this.'

I don't reply. I can't even bear to look at her.

We follow Adam through a door and find Miss Hollis cowering on the sofa. One of them has turned on the light and Adam stands inches away from her.

'You've made my life hell for years,' he says. 'Why are you such a bitch?'

She's crying now and shaking her head. 'I haven't done anything to you. It's all in your head, Adam. Please, just—'

'All in my head?' he shouts, no longer caring if anyone hears. He reels off a list of all the things she has done over the years but her eyes show no signs of apology, or even recognition. It is only then I realise she was just trying to be a good teacher, disciplining him when she thought he needed it. This was never a personal vendetta.

'You did pick on him,' Imogen says, sounding like a petulant child. 'Why don't you just apologise?'

'Then will you go?' Miss Hollis says, wiping at her leaking nose. She really doesn't look well.

'Try it and let's see,' Adam says, and I no longer recognise him. I need to do something. Stop him. But now I'm too scared. He leans across to her so his face is only millimetres from hers. 'I've never hated anyone as much as I hate you,' he says, spitting the words at her so she reels back.

'Just leave me alone. Get out. My boyfriend's coming back soon…' Her voice trails off. She knows there is no way Adam will believe this.

And then she drops a bombshell.

'I'm pregnant! Please…I'm pregnant.' She rubs her stomach, which isn't that big so she can't be that far along.

The room falls silent, as if everyone has stopped breathing now that she's said this. All eyes turn to Adam because we know it will incense him to think that Miss Hollis is having such a great life, oblivious to what she has done to him.

His face flushes red, and for the first time tonight he appears to be thrown, no longer in control. 'What did you say?' His eyes flick to her stomach, just as mine did moments ago and I wonder if he'll think she's lying.

'I'm four months pregnant.'

Adam shakes his head. 'So you're happy about this, are you? Planning to keep it?'

'Of course! We want this baby. Please, will you just go. I won't tell anyone you've been here, I promise. Just go.'

And then calmness returns to his face and with relief I think he will let this go now. He is realising we need to get out of here. But I am wrong.

'Stand up,' he says to her, his voice measured.

'What? Why? Please—'

'Just stand up.'

She looks at me and I try to plead silently with my eyes to do as he says. It will be better for her.

Slowly she rises from the sofa, folding her arms across her body. She must be embarrassed that we're seeing her in such skimpy nightclothes. Adam stares at her for a moment and then bringing his knee up, he thrusts it into her stomach, sending her lurching backwards onto the sofa.

At first I think the scream has come from her, but then I realise it is me. I am the one shrieking, while Miss Hollis groans quietly. 'What have you done?' I shout. 'What have you done?'

But Adam ignores me. He hasn't finished with Miss Hollis and rams his foot into her stomach again and again until she's coughing and spluttering, begging him to stop.

I rush towards him and try to drag him off but Corey stops me. 'She deserves it,' he says.

Turning to Imogen, I see her eyes are wide with disbelief, but she only says that Corey is right.

Now a sound does erupt from Miss Hollis's mouth: a high-pitched shriek as she yells something about her baby. I scream at Adam to stop but he doesn't. Instead, he tugs at Miss Hollis's nightie, pulling it down so that her breasts are exposed.

Gasping, I look away, trying to spare her humiliation. But then her scream gets louder, forcing me to turn back to her.

And that's when I see Adam climbing on top of her, tugging at his jeans.

I run then. Faster than I've ever run before, crashing into things because the rest of the house is still shrouded in darkness. I hurl myself through the kitchen door and out into the garden, gasping for breath because I feel as if I'm suffocating.

And then, in Miss Hollis's immaculate garden, I throw up more violently than I ever have before, even the time I got food poisoning when I was twelve.

As soon as I'm off her property, I cross the road and wait for Imogen and Corey. Surely they won't be a part of this? They'll be here any second.

But nobody comes.

CHAPTER TWENTY-NINE
2014

Ben gripped my hand as we sat on the stairs. It helped me calm down, enabling me to tell my story. I had never had to do this before; the only people who knew – apart from Maria now – had been there at the time, so didn't need my narration. But somehow telling it to Ben felt right. It was time I faced the fact that I could no longer deal with this, could no longer expect him to help me, unless I was honest.

I avoided his eyes while I talked. My mind was too busy picturing that night: Miss Hollis's terror and Adam's menace. But I also didn't want to see the disappointment on his face once he discovered who I really was. What I was. I was surprised to find his warm hand still comforted me as I told him what we had done to our teacher.

Only when I finished did I dare to look at him, but his face was etched with concern. 'It wasn't your fault,' he said. 'You were just a kid. You were as scared as she was. That's why you didn't help her. You were just scared.'

I shook my head. Had I been scared of Adam? I didn't think it was as simple as that. The side I saw of him that night had terrified me, but not in the same way Miss Hollis would have felt it. Nowhere near. If I had been scared it was more because of what I'd lost. Because he wasn't the person I thought he'd been, that I'd wanted him to be. I explained this to Ben. He had to know there had only been one victim that night.

'It was the shock then,' he said. 'Shock does weird things to people. You never know how you'll react in a situation.'

Again I shook my head. 'But it doesn't matter anyway, does it? It still happened and I was part of it. I did nothing to stop it.'

He stood up. 'Look, let's not think about that now. Someone's clearly trying to hurt you and who knows what they'll do next? We have to go to the police.'

At least now I could explain why I could never do that. I told him I couldn't. That I'd had my share of police interrogations and that it nearly broke me. Surely now he would understand?

'So what happened?' he said. 'Did they arrest you?'

'That's the worst part of it. Nothing happened. We were questioned for days, kept away from our parents and each other, but then suddenly they dropped the charges.'

'See. They wouldn't have done that if they'd thought you were responsible in any way.'

'You don't get it. They didn't charge any of us.'

Ben frowned. 'Oh...I...why?'

'That's just it, nobody ever told us. Maybe there was just no evidence.'

Ben reached forward to pull me up from the stairs. 'Look, we at least need to get you out of here. Why don't you come back to my place and try to get a bit of sleep?'

'But won't Pippa mind? How will you explain it?'

'She'll be fine. And I'll think of something.'

I couldn't go back to Ben's. It was bad enough that he now knew about me, but I couldn't have his girlfriend being dragged into it too. 'I can't, I'm sorry. And I don't want to cause you any problems.'

He thought about this for a moment, seeming to weigh up options. 'Okay then, I'll book you into a hotel. We might not be able to check in for a few hours but at least you'll be safe while we work out what to do. How does that sound?'

I wanted to hug him then. Despite everything falling down around me, he was there for me. I didn't deserve his kindness, he should have been walking away from me instead of helping me. I checked my watch; it was only three a.m. That meant we would have to hang around here for a few hours.

'Okay, thanks.'

Ben made us both some coffee and while I headed to the bedroom to pack some things, I heard him on the phone booking me a room for the night. Would I need more than that? How could I ever come back here? I couldn't worry about that now, I just had to find out who was doing this, and now that I had Ben with me, and he knew everything, there was more chance of success.

After he'd made the call, he joined me in the bedroom while I finished shoving things I didn't even need in the biggest bag I could find. He told me he'd booked the Premier Inn in Putney, adding that it was far enough away from the flat, but close enough to him and the library. I hadn't even told him about Maria knowing or my resignation email to Sam. But that could wait.

The hotel had told Ben that the usual check-in time was two p.m., but when he explained my flat had been flooded and I had nowhere else to go they said they would make an exception. There was an empty room and they just needed to get it ready, so we could check in at seven a.m.

We went downstairs to the hallway to study the damage to the front door.

'We'll find out who's doing this,' Ben said, as he taped a bin liner to the empty space the smashed glass had left.

And then we both sat on the stairs once more, staring at my wrecked front door, neither of us suggesting the sofa might be more comfortable.

Finally, at half past six, Ben suggested we should leave. Neither of us had slept and black shadows circled his eyes. I didn't even want to know what I might look like. But what did it matter anyway? I had more important things to worry about. I thought about Imogen then, and how vain she had become once she'd got together with Corey.

It felt strange being in an RSPCA van with my large travel bag tucked in between my feet, but my anxiety began to fade the further we got from the flat.

As Ben negotiated the fairly quiet streets, his windscreen wipers scraping against the glass because rain was pelting down around us, I told him what had happened with Julian. And then, recounting the details, but sparing him descriptions of the night we had slept together, I suddenly felt empty. I shouldn't have cared so quickly about him, but it had happened, and just like my feelings for Adam, I'd had no control over them. I'd fought against them but the battle had been futile. What was it Dad had said once? The heart wants what it wants.

'You really liked him,' Ben said, briefly turning to me before focusing on the road again.

And I couldn't answer.

It was just after seven a.m. when we got to the hotel. Ben parked up and insisted on accompanying me inside. 'I want to make sure you're settled in the room,' he said, offering me his arm to cling to. With any other man I would have wondered at his motives for doing this, but I felt safe with Ben.

As we walked, my phone beeped in my pocket. Another email. It had to be him. I still hadn't charged it so I would have to read it quickly before the screen went black.

This is far from over.

I should have known it wouldn't stop. Just because Ben was with me, this person was not going to give up. Without a word, I showed the email to Ben, my phone dying just as he handed it back.

'Don't worry, we'll sort this,' he said, walking faster to the entrance.

At the front desk, I handed my debit card to the receptionist but Ben grabbed it from me, replacing it with his own. I hugged him, right there in the hotel lobby, clinging to him as if he could evaporate all my sadness. And it was only then I realised that's what I was feeling. That's what I'd felt all these years. I had so cleverly masked it with my determination to be cold and distant, to protect myself, but now that had been scraped away, the pain was exposed like a raw wound.

I don't know what Ben was thinking, but he let me hold him and made no move to extract himself until the receptionist handed back his card.

'Thanks,' I said, and we headed towards the lift. Every limb in my body felt heavy, and I was grateful to have Ben with me.

Inside the room, I sat on the bed while Ben called his work to tell them he'd be late. He wasn't due in until nine but said he didn't want to rush off and leave me. 'Plus the traffic will be bad by now,' he added, before I had a chance to object.

Pointing to a kettle and two cups in the corner of the room, Ben asked if I wanted a drink. I shook my head and watched as he made himself a coffee and sat on a chair by the window, gazing out across Putney Bridge. I'd walked past this hotel a hundred times before but never imagined I'd be sitting in a room here. Especially not in these circumstances.

'My friend's still trying to work on tracing that email,' he said, taking a sip of his coffee. 'But do you have you any idea at all who could be doing this?'

I told him everything I'd found out recently and the people I'd been able to rule out, and he stared into his cup, probably trying to make sense of it all. But if I couldn't do that myself then how could I expect him to?

Eventually he offered a suggestion. 'What if it's not someone you know of? I mean, your teacher, she must have had other family, or friends. Any one of them could be doing this to you.'

'I know, but how can I even begin to find out who she was connected to?'

'Well, that won't be easy. Which is why I really think you should tell the police. They'll be able to investigate and sort this out, won't they? That's their job.'

I fell silent. I didn't want Ben pressuring me to report this. I wanted him to help me find out who was doing it. He must have sensed my discomfort because he didn't push it any further. Instead, he asked me about Miss Hollis. 'Perhaps talking about her might spark something?' he suggested.

'I don't know. Lately I've done little else but think about her and it hasn't helped.'

'Did you like her? I mean, I know what happened…what he did, but did you really hate her that much?'

Surprised by his question, I wasn't sure how to answer. If I'd been asked the same thing during my school years I would have announced adamantly that I detested her. But had I really? A teenage idea of hate – and love – was far removed from my adult view.

'I thought I did then,' I said. 'But maybe that was more to do with Adam projecting his feelings about her so voraciously. Maybe I just thought I hated her, but that just makes it worse, doesn't it?'

'You make it sound like it's contagious or something,' Ben said, once again glancing out of the window.

'Oh, no, no, I didn't mean it like that. I just can't trust what I felt.'

'You mean you can't remember?'

I frowned at Ben, confused by his questioning. What was he hoping to find out from all this? Then it occurred to me that the atrocity of what I had done was only just sinking in. He'd had more time now to reflect on it so how long before he told me he couldn't help me?

I didn't reply, and tried to change the subject. 'I really appreciate all your help. For this.' I gestured at the room. 'I should be okay in a few hours. Ready to do something. I just need to know what.'

He stood up. 'Well, I'm here to help. To put all this right, okay?'

I let out a deep sigh. So he hadn't changed his mind. At least not yet.

'But I'll have to get to work now. I'll come straight back, though.'

I knew I couldn't keep him there with me, but I wasn't ready to be alone again yet. I needed just a few more minutes; everything seemed clearer when he was with me. I opened my mouth to ask him not to leave but nothing came out. I couldn't expect that of him.

'You know, there's just one thing I don't understand,' Ben said. He was by the door now and turned back to me.

Somehow I didn't mind him wanting to know more, needing clarification. I was just grateful he was still helping me after everything I'd told him. 'What's that?'

'How could you not have known what Adam was capable of?' It was strange to hear him saying Adam's name. It didn't seem right somehow.

'I don't…I—'

Ben walked back towards me. 'That's the problem isn't it? You just don't know how to work people out.'

But then I did know. Too late, of course, but I knew. I knew as his fist hurtled towards me, ramming so hard into me that it felt as if my nose had become detached from my face.

Ben was the emailer.

CHAPTER THIRTY
2014

I opened my eyes and had no idea where I was. Then Ben's face appeared, leaning over me, his eyes black and cold. I'd never noticed how dark they were; I could have sworn they were blue. I lay sprawled on the floor, my body twisted in a knot. This must be how I had fallen when he'd punched the life out of me. Every part of me ached, even my feet, but how was that possible when I only remember him smashing into my face? I could feel the blood, warm and heavy on my skin, without having to see it.

'About time you came around,' he said. His grimace seemed wrong on his face; it changed everything. Before there had been nothing but kindness.

'Why?' I managed to say. The blood left a metallic taste in my mouth.

He crouched down so that his face was even closer to mine, and I could smell coffee on his breath. 'I think you already know that, Leah. Don't you?'

He was right. I knew I was there to be held accountable for my actions, that Ben – whoever he was – would make sure I paid for my crime.

'Who are you?' I asked, ignoring his question.

He in turn chose to ignore mine. 'So, let's talk about Natalie Hollis.' He straightened up and dragged the chair he'd sat on earlier from the corner of the room, placing it directly in front of me. I was forced to look up at him then; he held all the power. It crossed my mind that this must be how Miss Hollis had felt when Adam was towering over her. But I couldn't let myself picture what Adam did to her after I had run from her house. What they all did. I found out later, of course. Every last detail of the torture inflicted upon her, then the three of them leaving her on the floor of her living room, the life draining out of her.

'She was a good teacher,' Ben said, forcing me back to the present. 'Young too. Younger than we are now. Did you know that? She had a future. She could have done anything. Gone as far as she wanted. And she was beautiful.' Although his eyes were fixed on me, he seemed to be staring through me. I was confused. Was he a relative of hers? Who else would do this? But he had spoken of her as a lover might, not a family member.

'Who are you?' I tried again, knowing it was futile. He was the one in control here.

He shook his head. 'You don't get to ask questions, Leah.' He was too calm. He had a plan for me and knew there was nothing I could do about it. 'Did you know she was pregnant? I think you did, didn't you? You all did. But that didn't stop you, did it?'

'I didn't —'

'Shut up! Shut your fucking mouth!' His serenity evaporated and I noticed a thick vein had appeared on his forehead. 'Did you know?' And just like that he was calm again.

I nodded, not daring to open my mouth.

'And you still stood by and watched while your boyfriend... raped her.'

Hearing him say this choked me up. I'd seen the word in print, but neither Mum nor Dad had ever spoken it aloud. Didn't he know just saying this was enough punishment for me?

Ben was silent for a moment and I wondered if he would let me speak.

'I…didn't know what Adam was planning. He told us all she'd be away, and that we were just breaking in to scare her a bit for when she came back. And I left, I ran away as soon as I realised—'

He seemed to consider what I'd said, rubbing his chin, while his eyes stayed fixed on me. 'But you didn't call the police, did you? So explain to me exactly how you're not just as guilty as the rest of them?'

But I couldn't. Because I was.

When I didn't reply, Ben leaned forward and slammed his fist into my stomach, forcing me back against the foot of the bed. 'Hurts, doesn't it? Now imagine how that would feel if you were four months pregnant.' He shook out his hand.

Despite the excruciating pain Ben had inflicted on me, I hadn't cried up until then. Perhaps it was the shock, I wasn't sure. But hearing those words again, with a timescale this time, making the baby real, I was powerless to hold them back.

Of course, it made no difference to Ben. In fact, he seemed to lap it up, enjoying the fact he was breaking me. 'So, Leah. If you take a life from someone, don't you think it's only right you should pay with your own?'

And then the shock evaporated and my whole body began to shake. Ben, if that really was his name, intended to kill me. There had been many times over the years when I'd wanted nothing more than to curl up and die. I'd even come close once. But now it was staring me in the face I was determined to fight for my life. Whatever existence I'd had, it was better than the alternative. But what could I do? If I moved even the slightest bit then he would pound me again, and next time the blow could be fatal. No, I had to keep him calm, go along with it, while I thought of how to get the hell out of there.

'You must be thirsty?' he said, suddenly, beaming a grotesque smile at me. 'Let me get you some water from the bathroom.'

He stood up and glanced at the bathroom door. That was my chance. The second he turned his back I would fly to the door. If I could trust my legs to get me there.

And to start with it worked. As soon as he reached the bathroom I took my chance, forcing myself up and hurling my body towards the door. But my injuries slowed me down and within seconds he had seen me and was dragging me by my hair, back to the floor by the bottom of the bed.

'Nice try,' he said, mocking me with his clown's smile. 'I think we'll need this.' He held up some thick rope, shoving me down so my head smacked against the floor. It wouldn't be long, I thought. I wouldn't be able to survive much more of his battering.

He forced me up, thrusting my arms behind my back and twisting the rope around my hands, pulling so hard it felt as if he'd wrench my arms from their sockets. And then he spat in my face, adding humiliation to the pain.

Once he was happy I wouldn't be able to use my arms, he wrapped another length of rope around my legs and secured it to the bedpost. There was no way I'd be able to go anywhere now. There was no escape.

Sitting back on the chair, he stared at me for a while but didn't speak. I found this worse, the silence deafening me, taunting me with the thought of what would come next. Would he rape me before he killed me? Would he see that as a just punishment for what Miss Hollis had suffered?

But whatever it was he had planned, he clearly wanted to torment me first. 'Would you say you had a good life, Leah?'

I didn't answer and looked away from him, focusing on the carpet. I wouldn't give him the pleasure of hearing desperation in my voice. I wouldn't beg him to let me go.

'I'll answer for you then, shall I? I'd say it's pretty crap. You live in a dingy flat, you have no friends and you've settled for a job you could do with your eyes closed. Well, actually, you don't even have that any more, do you? Am I about right?' He didn't wait for a reply. 'The only person in your life is your mother and you hardly even see her. There's no boyfriend, hasn't been since Adam, has there? Oh, unless you count Julian.'

I looked at him then. There was a reason he was bringing him up.

'You really liked him, didn't you? It must have really upset you when he wanted nothing more to do with you. The rejection. The humiliation. But all a drop in the ocean really.'

'What did you do?' I said, still tasting blood as I spoke.

Ben laughed. 'Oh, it was easy. I just told him the truth about you. That's all it took to scare him off. He was disgusted, but I suppose that's because he really liked you. You two could have really had something.'

'But I saw him…he was outside my house. On Thursday night.'

Once more his cackle filled the room. 'I seriously doubt that. But I can see why you thought you saw him. That navy jacket he always wears is quite distinctive, isn't it? But easy enough to buy. I mean, in the dark, anyone around his height might pass for him.'

My insides felt like they were folding in on themselves, but I wouldn't let Ben see what he was doing to me.

'Don't you get it yet, Leah? I've taken away everything that made your miserable life even remotely worth living. Your promotion and then your job. Your one friend, Maria. All of it, wiped out with so little effort on my part. What does that say about you?'

I still couldn't speak. So much made sense now. All those inexplicable things that had happened lately had been down to him. In a way it helped to know this, and I wondered what he'd think if he knew he was doing me a favour, giving me closure before he put an end to it all. I would have shouted it at him but I didn't want him to stop. I wanted him to admit everything he had done to me.

For a while neither of us spoke, but I could feel his eyes on me. Who was he? I had to know and although it was risky, I decided to ask him.

'I didn't think you'd recognise me,' he said, surprising me by answering. 'I mean, who pays attention to the younger kids in school, eh? It was hard enough keeping track of who was in your own year, wasn't it. Except for Adam, of course. Everyone knew him.'

I looked up at him, confused. 'You went to my school? But—'

'Like I said, you wouldn't have known me. Year below. But I knew you. I knew all about your boyfriend bullying Natalie.'

'Is she? Are you—'

'She was my teacher. And a good one. Until you...' His voice trailed off and he looked away from me. 'What the fuck gave you the right?'

None of this made sense. 'But why are you doing this? If she was just your teacher?'

'She wasn't *just* a teacher,' he said, mimicking my voice. 'She was an amazing person. If you'd just given her a chance. All of you.' He leaned forward. 'Do you know what it was like for me in my last year? Without her? She was my biggest defender, the only person who kept the other kids from beating me to a pulp. Without her I was nothing. She believed in me when no one else did.'

He looked down, staring at the floor, but not before I noticed the wildness in his eyes. If I hadn't known before how unhinged he was, I did now. 'Do you believe in karma?' he asked, abruptly changing the subject, staring at me once more.

I managed to nod.

'That's good. Then you'll understand why I'm doing this. A life for a life.'

I needed to get him onto a different subject. 'So it was all lies then? You don't work for the RSPCA?'

'Yes, I do. That's the truth. I'm not the liar here, Leah.'

'And your girlfriend? Pippa? Does she even exist?' If I could just keep him talking I could stall the inevitable.

He threw his head back and laughed. 'Good old Pippa. Course she exists! She's my pet Labrador.' He grimaced. 'How dumb do you feel now, you fucked up bitch?'

'A lie then.'

He leaned even further forward. 'No, I didn't lie. You made an assumption so I went along with it. Like I said, this has all been too easy.'

Then something occurred to me. The emails. At least three of them had been sent while I was with Ben. Was there someone else involved? I fired the question at him and cowered at his laugh.

'I put a time delay on those emails. Easy to do. I had to have your complete trust, so needed you to be sure I couldn't be involved.'

He needn't have bothered. I had trusted Ben from the very beginning; it had never crossed my mind that he could be involved.

'And breaking into my flat? I was on the phone to you when someone was pounding on my door. How did you do that?'

'Oh, Leah, it's really not hard to pay some delinquent kids to cause a bit of trouble.'

I risked smiling then. What did I have to lose? 'Aren't you overlooking something?'

'Really? What's that?'

'Karma. Who gets to punish you for doing this to me?'

They were the last words to leave my mouth before I was knocked senseless and blackness enveloped me.

When I came around I was alone. There was no sign of Ben, and no noise anywhere. I shifted myself up, wincing at the pain throbbing through my whole body. I needed to get out of there.

But then he appeared, a silhouette in the bathroom doorway, gradually coming into focus. 'Miss me?' he asked, pulling on his coat. 'I'm afraid I have to go out for a bit, but you'll be fine, won't you? Actually, tell you what. Don't answer that. Don't even speak. This will help.' He walked towards me and leaned over, pressing masking tape I hadn't seen in his hand across my mouth. I struggled for breath. 'Relax,' he said. 'Breathe through your nose.'

At the door, he turned back to me. 'By the way, don't get any ideas, I've got this.' He waved my mobile phone at me. 'Oh, I charged your phone for you and you've had a few missed calls. Dr Redfield. Shame you won't get to speak to her, I'm guessing if she's a doctor it's probably important.'

And then he left, closing the door and shrouding the room in darkness. It must have still been daylight outside but the curtains were so thick that no light could pass through them.

Letting my head flop back to the floor, I thought about Mum and how I would never see her again.

CHAPTER THIRTY-ONE
2003

It's November but the sun is shining brightly and I'm sweating underneath four layers of clothes.

I'm in the university bookshop and I spot Becky by the counter, talking to the cashier. She's okay. I don't really talk to her that much, but we're doing the same degree and have chosen most of the same modules. I like the fact that she's quiet and doesn't ask me loads of personal questions. When we do talk, it's only about our studies or lecturers.

She turns around and sees me looking at her, waving before turning back to the cashier, embarrassed. I stay where I am and make no move to head over to her. As nice as she is, I don't feel like talking. I just want to buy my books, go to my room and read.

I pull out my book list, which already has half the titles crossed off because I'm buying each one as soon as I can, even if I don't need all of them now. We're starting *The Handmaid's Tale* tomorrow and although I read it at the beginning of summer, I need to buy the recommended criticism on it.

'Hey!' Someone taps me on the shoulder. I look up and see Becky, clutching her pile of books. 'Did you have a good weekend?' she asks.

Nodding, I force myself to smile. There is no way I'll tell her every second of it was hell being back in Watford, in that house with Mum but no Dad.

'How about you?' I ask.

She shrugs and says it was okay, she was just busy studying.

She waits for me to say something else, but when I stay silent she gives up, hastily telling me she'll see me tomorrow. I take a deep breath. That wasn't so bad.

Back in my room it is freezing, so I turn on the radiator. I'm on the fifth floor of the student block so it's warmer than the lower floors, but I'm still convinced they regulate the heating to keep it as low as possible without having us freeze to death. I keep on the layers that only moments ago were making me sweat, then settle down onto the bed to read.

I must drift off because the next thing I know my mobile is ringing and vibrating next to me. It must be Mum; nobody else has my number. But when I pick it up and look at the screen it says caller unknown. Strange. Perhaps Mum's calling from a different phone? One of her book club friends or someone like that.

'Hello?' I let out a deep sigh; I'm in no mood for a lecture from Mum about how unsociable I'm being when uni days are meant to be about meeting new friends and living a bit. I don't ever ask her what she means by *living a bit.* Surely she's not advocating that I shag around like a lot of the students here seem to do? I shudder at the thought of being touched.

'Leah? Finally I've tracked you down.' The voice is both familiar and unfamiliar. It's not Mum.

'Who…who is this?' I say, barely able to get the words out because I already know. I pull the phone from my ear and stare at the screen, my finger hovering over the end call button.

'Leah, are you there? Is that you?'

For some reason I'm compelled to raise it to my ear again.

'I know this is a shock. But we really need to talk. Please?'

Finally I find my voice. 'There's nothing to say, Imogen. What do you want?' I try to make my voice sound strong, brave, everything I'm not feeling at this moment.

'Can you meet me tonight? In Watford? Please, it's really important that we talk.'

I want to scream at her. Why is she doing this now when we haven't spoken for three years? Not a word has passed between us since the night I fled from Miss Hollis's house. I have done so well to avoid her, and the other two, but now here she is, invading my head.

'No,' I say. 'No.'

'Look, Leah, I wouldn't ask if it wasn't so important. I know we haven't spoken for years, but we're nineteen now and I know I've grown up.'

She does sound different. More mature somehow. Perhaps what happened has changed her as fundamentally as it has me.

'Look, I'll be at The White Lion pub at eight o'clock. Please come. Please.'

And then she hangs up. It should be me disconnecting the call. I shouldn't have given her a chance to speak. I look at my watch and see it's only two p.m. Allowing for traffic, the drive from Cambridge to Watford would take less than two hours so I could easily make it. I wish I couldn't, but the option is there.

I spend the next few hours trying not to think about Imogen and The White Lion pub. But it's there in the back of my head, taunting me. Whatever it is must be important for her to beg to see me. Then, when I can no longer put it off, I finally make a decision and grab my car keys from the desk. Leaving my room, I tell myself I'll be okay as long as I don't think too hard about what I'm doing.

My car is a four-year-old VW Polo. Mum bought it for me with some of the money Dad left us and, although it's far from perfect, it has never let me down on the trips to Watford and back. I don't really use it for anything else because there is nowhere other than uni I need to go, and I'm right on campus so that negates the need for a car. The main thing is it keeps Mum happy, and I'm grateful for it now.

I drive in silence, thinking about Imogen the whole time, remembering our friendship. Before. Will she look different? What if I don't recognise her? The thought of walking into the pub and scrutinising strangers' faces sets my heart pounding.

When I get there I park up, the pub looming in front of me as I sit in the car, watching people entering and leaving. I'm early – it's only seven-fifteen – and I'm hoping to glimpse Imogen arriving. Somehow, to see her first will make me feel better. I will have the advantage.

But there is nobody who even remotely looks like her, so I sit and wait for the dashboard clock to tell me it's eight o'clock.

Walking into the pub is harder than I imagined. It's crowded and the air smells stale: a mixture of cigarettes, sweat and alcohol. I scan people's faces but there is no sign of Imogen. Taking a deep breath, I prepare myself to walk through the throng to the back of the room. But then someone tugs at my sleeve.

Imogen.

She looks the same, only more beautiful and slimmer. Much slimmer. As if she's shed the puppy fat she'd always had like an old pair of jeans.

'Leah! I'm so happy you came!' She leans forward, as if she is expecting a hug, but I back away, bumping into someone in my desperation not to be touched by her. 'Watch out!' she says. 'Are you okay?'

I shouldn't have come here. I regret it already and it can only get worse.

'Say something. Please.'

So I do. 'I shouldn't have come,' I tell her, turning towards the door.

'No, wait! Now you're here just let me buy you a drink.'

Without a word I follow her to the bar, staring at her skinny legs. She's wearing a short knitted dress but she doesn't look tarty. It suits her. It suits our age. It's what I should be wearing instead of my jeans and frumpy jumper.

'What would you like?' she asks, when we reach the bar.

'A Coke please.'

She frowns at me until I jingle my car keys in front of me.

'Oh, that's great that you drive. I haven't gotten around to having lessons yet, but I will.'

She orders my drink and a vodka and orange for her. It should come as no surprise that she's drinking already while I have never tasted alcohol. Nothing she does should come as a surprise.

'Let's just sit here.' She drags a barstool out and gestures for me to do the same. 'So how have you been? How's life treating you?' she asks, sipping her vodka.

This is unbelievable. She's acting like we're the best of friends just catching up. As if nothing happened. A scenario plays through my head: I grab her by the throat and scream at her. Scream that I don't want to make small talk with her. Not after what she did. Not after betraying me. And then I walk out, leaving her staring, open-mouthed, knowing she won't dare contact me again.

But I don't do this. Instead, I reach for her hand and tell her it's good to see her.

She looks surprised. 'Really? I'm so glad you've said that. I've been so nervous about this.'

But she seems far from that. Her eyes are sparkling so there is no way she feels the way I do.

'Do you know I'm studying to be a veterinary nurse?' she continues. 'How great is that? I should be qualified soon. And

Corey and I are engaged.' She thrusts out her hand and a small diamond glitters on her finger.

I stare at her, unable to comprehend anything she's saying.

'He's doing great too. He's training to be a motor mechanic and then he's going to set up his own business. And Adam…' She stops herself. Even though I haven't said a word, or shown any emotion on my face. I'm good at that.

'Well, anyway. We're all doing great.'

Taking a sip of my Coke, I try to keep my hands steady. 'I'm so glad,' I say. The relief on her face is visible.

'So how about you? Your mum said you're at uni. I knew you'd get a place. That's amazing. You always were the clever one.'

I blush at her compliment. 'I'm enjoying it. It's hard work, though.'

She nods, but isn't really listening. 'Let's grab a table round the corner,' she says, looking around. 'It's more private.'

She doesn't wait for me to agree, but lifts herself from her stool, picking up her half-empty glass. And I follow the girl who used to be my best friend, who somewhere deep inside her must still be the Imogen I loved.

We round the corner and suddenly time stands still. I rub at my eyes to make sure I'm not hallucinating, but they're still there. Sitting at a table for four, pints in their hands, laughing at something one of them has said. I stare at them, but I'm not shocked. They came as a three then so why should it be any different now?

Imogen turns to face me. 'Don't be angry. Just hear him out. Please.'

Adam and Corey look up and I feel as if the floor will collapse beneath my feet. They look the same. Nothing has changed, yet everything has, and it's too much.

We all freeze and it is then I realise they are just as shocked as I am. Imogen has arranged this secretly and kept all of us in the dark. Adam stares at me, as if I have come back from the dead. Without taking his eyes off me he addresses Imogen.

'What's going on?'

'I just thought it was about time. I don't know, call me sentimental or something. But anyway, we're all here now so let's just make the best of it.' She squeezes in next to Corey, who leans in to whisper to her. Patting his knee, in a loud voice she tells him it's fine.

I still have a choice now. I can turn around and walk away without a word. My exit would need no explanation. But I cannot leave. Adam is here and it's been three years and his pull is just as strong as ever. So I sit down, trying to ignore the fact that as I do, he edges closer to the window and further away from me.

'So, Leah, tell us what you've been up to,' Imogen says from behind her glass. 'We've got a lot of catching up to do.'

'Just studying,' I say, shifting in my seat. 'Not much time for anything else.' This is a lie. There are plenty of hours that I choose to fill only with a book in my hand.

'I bet you've made loads of friends, haven't you?' Corey says, suddenly getting in the spirit of this surprise reunion. 'Living it up at uni. What a life!'

He couldn't be more wrong. I study and then I go home to my empty room and sometimes I visit Mum when I have no choice. That is my life. But I only nod my head and agree that, yes, what a life I'm leading.

'You know, Adam's at uni too,' Imogen says. 'Studying law. Aren't you, Adam?'

He shrugs and continues staring out of the window. I'm furious with the injustice of it. He is acting as if I have done something wrong, when he is the monster. I force myself to be calm. Everything will be okay.

When I don't say anything, Imogen continues. 'And he's met someone great. Her name's Mione.'

Adam turns to her, glaring, and Corey slaps her arm, whispering again in her ear. But I don't care what they're saying because I'm too busy staring at Adam. Although I feel as if my insides have been ripped out, I'm not jealous. It is more the fact that this isn't right. It's not fair that Adam is enjoying his life, guilt-free, after what he did. And Imogen and Corey. I look around the table and anger wells up inside me. Why am I the only one who is paying for what happened? It should be all of us suffering.

'Look, Leah,' Corey is saying. 'Can we just all make peace? It's been years and…well, I think we've all grown up. We all made a mistake, it doesn't have to ruin the friendship we had.' He kicks Adam under the table, forcing him to look away from the window. He throws me the briefest of glances and a half-smile. I suppose this is the most I will get.

Corey has mentioned friendship, but it was never that, was it? We were just Adam's followers, letting him dictate what we did and how we felt. That's no friendship.

I weigh up what he has said against my gut feeling, and know that I have to make a decision. I can walk out of here without a glance back, or I can show them I forgive them. Mum is always talking about how important it is not to hold grudges. *They eat you up*, she says. Maybe she's right. The four of us have a history, good and bad, but a history nonetheless. For old times' sake, I need to let go. For all of us.

'You're right,' I say, leaning forward. They all turn to me. 'Enough time has passed. We need to put all this behind us. I'm not saying it will be easy, but I'm willing to try.'

Imogen's face explodes into a smile. 'Oh, Leah, I'm so glad to hear that. I've missed you. We all have.' She glances at Adam but he doesn't speak.

For the next two hours we talk as if nothing's happened, and I hear all about how well they are doing. Even Adam eventually joins in the conversation, but he speaks mostly to the others. Still, it doesn't matter. It is probably best this way. I don't want to feel anything for him again.

Despite how the evening has turned out, I am relieved when the bar staff head to our table to urge us out. It's past eleven o'clock and I'm tired. I'm ready to sleep.

Outside, the air is cold against my skin, making me grateful for my jumper and two t-shirts. 'Well, that's me,' I say, pointing at my car. 'How are you all getting home?'

Imogen flashes a look at Corey. 'Probably walking. Last bus will have gone now.' Her eyes plead with me and I know what she wants. She will take it as proof I am back in their lives. Sighing, I offer them all a lift – even though I know I will regret it – and am almost deafened by Imogen's squeals. 'Thanks, Leah, you're a star.'

Even Adam doesn't object and they all pile in, Imogen electing to sit in front with me. This is fine; I don't want Adam next to me, just being in the car with him is painful enough.

'Where am I going first?' I say, to no one in particular.

'My place is closest from here, I reckon,' Corey says. 'Do you remember it?'

'Course,' I say, pulling out of the car park.

I focus on the road but I'm not taking anything in. Just keep staring ahead, I tell myself. Ignore the loud chatter filling the car. Ignore the fact that you're nearly on High Elms Lane and will soon be passing the school. Breathe deeply. That isn't where it happened. Everything's fine.

CHAPTER THIRTY-TWO
2014

There was no way of telling how long I had lain there, my hands and feet bound, my mouth covered with tape. It felt like hours, but could just have easily been minutes. Or days. Everything was distorted and my throat was painfully dry.

It was almost a relief when Ben appeared. I watched him come in and click the door shut, not daring to take my eyes off him for even a second.

Half of me wanted to give up. Just let him do what he wanted and get it over with. But then I thought of Julian. I hadn't hurt Miss Hollis, after all, and we could have had a chance to work out if Ben hadn't twisted things. Who knew how he had portrayed the events to Julian? Whatever he said wouldn't have been the raw truth. He would have made me more culpable. Perhaps even suggested it was my idea. Maybe there was a chance, if I made it out of there, that I could try and salvage things.

But making it out of there was not looking like a possibility.

Ben walked towards me and crouched down by my head. He lifted my chin, forcing me to look at him. 'Listen to me carefully. In a minute we're leaving this room. There's a fire escape at the back of the building and we're going through it. Don't worry, there won't be any alarms going off, that's all been taken care of. You're going to walk with me to the car, without so much as the slightest fuss, okay? And then I've got a surprise for you. Nod if you understand me.'

I didn't move but then he grabbed my arm, twisting it forward so that behind the tape I let out a muffled scream. I had no choice then but to nod, anything to stop more pain.

At least we were leaving this room; there might be more chance to escape once we were out in the open. I pictured hurling myself out of the car while Ben was driving and it gave me hope.

'Right, I'm taking off your tape now. And the rope. But just so you know, I've got this.' He undid his jacket, revealing a knife that was sticking out of his jeans pocket.

We didn't pass a single person as we left the building and the whole time Ben clung to my arm, his grip tight enough to leave more bruising. No doubt that was what he intended. But I could barely walk, so wasn't about to complain about the extra support he was providing. Neither of us spoke, and as he pushed through the fire door, I was surprised to stumble outside into darkness. So I had been left in the room for the whole day. I shuddered to think what he had been up to. I didn't want to believe that he'd been searching for a place to bury my body, but that was all I could focus on.

At his van, he guided me round to the back doors, fumbling in his pocket for his keys. I turned to face him. 'But—'

'What? You thought you'd get to sit in front with me again? Not this time, Leah.' I hated the way he kept saying my name. It felt even more of a violation than anything else he'd done.

He opened the back doors and inside was a large metal cage. Large enough for a dog perhaps but surely he didn't intend me to fit inside it?

'Get in,' he said, shoving me forwards.

'But, I can't fit—'

'Make yourself. Or I will. Which would you prefer?'

I stumbled into the van and crawled forward, trying to scrunch my already aching body into the tiny space, but it wasn't working.

'For fuck's sake,' Ben said, climbing up and shoving me further in, forcing my limbs to contort so that eventually I was crammed inside. I wanted to cry then. At the pain. The humiliation. All of it. But I wouldn't let him see any tears.

He locked the cage and slammed the van doors shut, pulling the handles to make sure they were secure. And then everything was dark and silent.

I waited for the engine to start but nothing happened. Deciding he must have gone back inside the hotel to check out, I wondered how the hell I would get out of there. It was impossible. All I could do was hope I'd get a chance to escape once he let me out.

When the engine started, the vibration juddering through my aching body, I sucked in my breath, telling myself I was ready for whatever would happen.

Once again, there was no way to tell how much time passed as he drove, but I could tell it was long enough that we couldn't be in London any more. The speed increased, suggesting we were on a motorway. I tried to make myself sleep, because at least that would offer some respite, but all I managed was to drift in and out.

Eventually the van stopped and I heard Ben's door slam. Seconds later he pulled open the back doors and peered in at me.

'Comfortable trip?' he said, laughing to himself. He unlocked the cage and told me to get out, but I couldn't move. It felt as if my bones would snap if I tried so I stayed where I was. All my hopes of escape had evaporated; how could I hope to run when I could barely lift my arms?

Ben grew impatient. 'I said, get the fuck out!' he hissed, and I wondered why he was keeping his voice down. But when I still didn't move, he grabbed my legs, untwisting them, and dragged me out of the cage towards him, dropping me to the ground when he'd got me over the edge.

And then I did scream, piercing the silence until Ben rammed his boot into my face and I had no more sound left within me.

Forcing me up, he grabbed my arm again and pulled me away from the van. It was then I noticed where we were. It wasn't some remote field or wooded area where nobody would discover my body. This was a residential street. With houses on either side of the road. That meant people. Lots of people.

I tried to ask him where we were but the sound was muffled and he ignored my question.

'Just keep your mouth shut,' he said, leading me around the van and into the front garden of one of the houses. This must be his house. It would be easier for him to torture and kill me here than in a hotel room. He had lied about living in London.

He dragged me up the path to the front door. It was dark blue, my favourite colour, but after this, if by some miracle I survived, I knew I wouldn't be able to look at the colour again without remembering.

I waited to hear the jangle of his keys, but instead he leaned forward and pressed the doorbell. A chime echoed out and, confused, I waited to see what would happen.

For almost a minute we stood in silence, Ben's hand gripping my arm. I thought about trying to make a run for it but his hold was too tight. Even if I did manage to break his grip, given the state I was in, I wouldn't get very far before he caught me. And then what? He was clearly unstable so I couldn't risk angering him further.

I turned my attention back to who he was expecting to answer the door. Until now I hadn't given the possibility that he was in this with someone else much thought. I was just about to risk asking him when a shadow appeared at the glass and a featureless face peered through it. It was impossible to tell who it was, or even whether the person was male or female. Until the door opened.

And then I knew exactly who it was.

Everything about her had changed: her once blonde hair was now dark, almost black, and she was thinner. Too thin. As if the life had been sucked out of her. My heart began palpitating and my throat constricted. There was no need for Ben to kill me, I was sure I would drop dead right there on Miss Hollis's doorstep.

She didn't notice me at first and stared at Ben, her eyes wide. 'Ben? What are you—'

And then she saw me, somehow her eyes growing even wider. She grabbed the door for support. 'What's going on? What is this?' She looked back and forth between us, but it was me her eyes lingered on the longest.

Ben stepped forward. 'Natalie, I told you I'd sort everything for you, didn't I? You better let us in, I can't trust her out here.'

Frowning, she didn't move at first, but clung to the door, continuing to stare at me. And I was doing the same to her. She was the last person I had expected to see. Even though she was the most important. So many questions raced through my head and none of them made any sense.

'You shouldn't be here, Ben. And not with *her.* What am I supposed to do now?' She made no move to let us in.

'Can you let us in? It's better if we're inside.' His voice was soft and kind, like I'd never heard it before. Even when he was pretending to be a friend.

'I don't think...' Her eyes dropped and she seemed to be staring at Ben's hand encircling my arm. Without another word she stepped back and pulled the door wider, letting him drag me inside.

Once we were in the hallway and the door clicked shut, Miss Hollis – I just couldn't think of her as Natalie – turned to Ben.

'Why have you brought her here? I don't want her in my house. And what's happened to her?' I looked down at my arms, and in the harsh hall light was shocked by how much of my skin was a mixture of purple and black.

Ben reached out his other arm and placed it on her shoulder. 'Please, Natalie, just trust me. I'm doing this for you. I need to get her secured. Can we use the front room?' His eyes flicked to a door on the right.

Miss Hollis pulled away from him. 'No, no, no, Ben. This is all wrong. Take her away.'

But he shook his head. 'I can't do that. Do you know how hard I've worked to get her here? Do you have any idea? All the planning and risks. I did it all for you, Natalie.'

She studied his face and there was no way to tell what conclusion she was reaching. Until she spoke. 'Just go in there,' she said, her voice quiet.

Ben opened the door and pushed me through, finally letting go of his vice-like grip. I tried to rub my arm but he pushed me to the floor. There was no carpet this time, just exposed floorboards, and I landed with a thud that made my whole body vibrate.

She had been standing in the doorway but she came forward then, moving slowly before perching on the side of the sofa. I couldn't look at her. I didn't want to see her expression as Ben once again yanked rope around my wrists and ankles. It must have been in his pockets; I hadn't noticed him carrying it.

'That's better,' he said, leaving me on the floor while he joined Miss Hollis on the sofa.

I stared at the wooden floor, mentally tracing out the patterns in the wood, anything to avoid both of them as much as possible. But I couldn't shut out the sound of Ben's voice as he recounted everything he'd done to me. I wasn't surprised to learn it was all him. The break-in, the water attack, the mugging. All of it had been down to Ben. And I listened as he told Miss Hollis how he ruined the promotion for me at work.

'All it took was a word in her boss's ear,' he said.

I could tell without looking at him that he was smiling. He was proud of it, as if he'd achieved a great feat by destroying my life. But I could tell he was the most pleased about Julian.

'You know, she actually thought she had a chance at happiness with him. But I took it away from her, just like she did to you. Are you pleased, Natalie? Tell me you're pleased.'

And then I did look across at them. I needed to see her reaction. She placed her hand on his knee, stroking it gently. 'You did great, Ben. Thank you.'

His smile stretched across the whole of his face, but then quickly disappeared as he turned to me. 'I think it's about time you apologised, Leah, don't you? All these years and you've not once tried to put things right with Natalie. That's not right, is it? So go on, what are you waiting for?'

No matter what he was doing to me, he was right about that. I did need to apologise and I needed to do it now. I didn't know how much longer I had left but I couldn't let this chance go by. I turned to her and for a second the blonde teacher she had been flashed before me.

'I am sorry,' I said, my voice as shaky as my body. 'I know that's not enough, it will never be enough, but...please believe me. I had no idea what Adam was planning. He told us—'

'I don't want to hear what he told you,' she said, fixing her eyes on me. 'It's bad enough I've had to live with what he did all these years, I don't need to hear more about it now. Do you know he killed my baby?'

I got choked up then because it felt different hearing it from her rather than Ben. More real.

'Look around you,' she said. 'Listen. What do you hear?'

When I didn't say anything, she shouted her question at me, forcing me to respond.

'Nothing. There's nothing.'

'Exactly. No children. No husband. Nothing. This is my life. Tim and I didn't last after that, how could we when I couldn't even let him touch me? It wasn't his fault, he tried to make it work but I pushed him away and there's been no one since. I couldn't even teach any more. But you didn't care about that, did you?'

'I'm sorry,' I repeated, knowing any words I said would be futile.

Ben snorted. 'We talked about karma earlier, didn't we, Leah?' He turned back to Miss Hollis. 'So she knows she has to pay for what she did. She's clear about that.'

'Good,' Miss Hollis said, staring straight at me. 'Good.'

Ben leaned forward and whispered into her ear, so I could only make out a few words. *Bridge. River. Suicide.* Each word was like a bomb exploding in my chest, but at least I had a sense now of what he was planning. What *they* were planning.

Ben walked over to me. 'I suppose you think this is unfair, don't you, Leah? That you're not responsible because you left the house? That it was all Adam and Corey and Imogen? But you see, things have already been put straight with them because they're already dead, aren't they?'

'It…it was an accident…a terrible—'

'Yes, such a shame. Road accidents are just so heartbreaking, aren't they? No wonder you never got behind the wheel again. Anyway, my point is they've paid for what they did, and now it's your turn.' He stood up then and leaned down by my feet, pulling out his knife and waving it in front of me.

I flinched, squeezing my eyes shut tightly as if it would prevent me feeling pain. This wasn't what they had planned. Why was he changing things? But then I felt the ropes around my ankles loosen. I opened my eyes again, just to check I wasn't already dead.

'We'd better get going soon,' Miss Hollis said.

Ben stood up and walked over to her. 'I just need the bathroom. I've been holding it in since we left London and my bladder's about to burst.'

Miss Hollis stood up. 'Hurry, though. First door on the left at the top of the stairs. Hurry.'

He glanced at me. 'Watch her. Actually, take this.' He held the knife out towards Miss Hollis. At first she didn't move, but then she slowly reached for it. 'You'll be fine if you have to use it,' he said, squeezing her shoulder. And then he rushed out, leaving the two of us alone.

As soon as the door had closed, Miss Hollis stepped towards me, holding the knife out in front of her, pointing it straight at me.

'I'm sorry, please, I'm sorry.'

'Leah, shut up.' Her voice was a whisper. 'We've got about sixty seconds before he gets back down here so just keep quiet.'

Before I could interpret what she was saying, she bent down and sliced through the rope around my wrists, pulling me up and guiding me towards the door.

'Come on, you can do it, just try to move quickly. Lean on me.' She helped me out and then we were in the hall. Stopping for a second, she looked upstairs, but then nodded. 'It's okay, he's still in there. Come on.'

Outside, the night air hit me like another punch, making the wounds I already had throb. But I didn't care. She was helping me. Miss Hollis was getting me away from Ben.

'My car's across the road,' she said, pulling the front door but not closing it. 'We have to try and run, Leah.' And then she was tugging me along, neither of us daring to look back at the house.

She pressed her key fob and the lights of her car flashed, then guiding me into the passenger seat, she slammed the door and rushed round to her side.

With my heart feeling as if it would explode, I turned to look at the house and there he was. Standing in the doorway, shouting words I couldn't make out. He ran down the path but at the same time Miss Hollis was slamming and locking her door. She turned her key in the ignition and fired up the engine, just as Ben reached us, pounding on her window with his fists.

'Natalie!' he cried. 'What are you doing? Open the door!'

But then we were screeching away, and I watched in the side mirror as Ben became a small dot in the distance.

Neither of us spoke until we were a safe distance from Miss Hollis's road. We'd been driving for almost ten minutes when she pulled into a petrol station and fished her mobile from her pocket.

'Police, please,' she said, and for a moment I wondered if she was calling them to take me away. That was the problem with a guilty conscience. But when she gave them Ben's details and told them what he'd done, my breathing slowed.

'I'm sorry, Leah,' she said, once she'd finished the call. 'I can't believe what he did to you.'

'But why? How?'

'I used to teach Ben. He was in the year below you and, well, he was always attached to me. Always used to spend break and lunchtimes in my classroom, just chatting. I shouldn't have let him, I know that now. But I was young and I couldn't see that he was becoming obsessed. I guess I thought of us both as outcasts at the school and I wanted to help him, stop him being bullied. Anyway, after…you know… he kept in contact. I thought it was harmless at first, but then he was so overprotective and it just got weird. He never tried anything inappropriate, but would always call or email to see how I was. I guess I believed he was only being kind. I had no idea what he was doing to you. That he was so fixated on punishing you, so disturbed. I should have seen it, Leah. But I suppose it was nice after the way most of the kids treated me. Again, I'm so sorry.'

I listened to her words but didn't want, or need, her to apologise. She was the last person who should ever say sorry to me.

'Why do you think he waited so long to do this? It's been years.'

She shook her head. 'I'm not sure. But a few months ago I told him we shouldn't speak any more, and I used the excuse that our friendship just reminded me of the past. Perhaps that set him off.'

We stayed silent for a while, both of us watching the cashier in the petrol station. I couldn't believe I was sitting in a car with Miss Hollis. After all these years. And even more shocking than that was the fact she had saved me from Ben.

'But…don't you think I should be punished for what happened?' I said. I needed to know how she felt about me.

She tapped her fingers on the steering wheel. 'I think you already have. Double. Triple. Plus, you lost your best friends in that horrible accident. I heard all about that. It can't be easy having to live with knowing…' She didn't need to finish the sentence.

'Can I ask you something else? It's something I never understood. Why did the police drop the charges?'

'I asked them to. I withdrew my statement.'

Shocked, I struggled to form my next question. 'But…why didn't you want Adam to go to prison for what he did? Or Imogen and Corey for…watching it all? Or me?'

Natalie takes a deep breath. 'At first I did. But then I realised I'd be reliving it over and over if it went to court. I couldn't handle that. It wasn't an easy decision, though.'

She turned to me and I saw the glimmer of tears in her eyes.

'I'm sorry. I'm so sorry.'

'I hated you, Leah. For a long time. All this time, really. But… I know you were the only one who cooperated with the police. Your statement would have made all the difference if I'd seen it through. You told the truth while the others stuck together with their lie. That means something.'

'I'm so sorry,' I said again.

'Anyway, you'll be all right now, Leah, I promise. Make a life for yourself. Don't waste it. Don't do what I've done. Neither of us should have to suffer any more than we already have.'

I wanted to speak, to say something that would show her how grateful I was, but no words would form. Instead, I nodded, and hoped she could see the gratitude in my eyes.

'Let's get you home,' she said. 'You live in London, don't you? It will take us about three hours from here. Have you got someone you can stay with, just in case. I mean, I don't know how long it will take them to find him so you shouldn't be alone.'

I was choked up by her kindness. 'Where are we?' I managed to say.

'Dudley. West Midlands. That's my mum's house. She died a few years ago and I moved in.'

She started up the engine and began our long drive. It was only when we reached the motorway that I turned to her. 'If you don't mind, I mean, if it's okay, could you drop me at my mum's? In Watford?' As soon as I asked it I regretted being so selfish. How could I expect her to go back there when it was bound to cause her pain?

'No problem,' she said, offering me a sad smile.

The next morning was creeping in by the time we got to Mum's, but it was still dark.

'If you don't mind, I won't wait around,' Miss Hollis said, helping me out of the car. 'But here's my number if you need anything. And the police will want a statement from you. Just tell them everything. You should go to the local station as soon as you can.'

'Thank you,' I said, my words not enough for what she had done.

'So what will you do now?' she asked.

'Well, I no longer have my job at the library, but I'll spend more time volunteering at the care home until I can find something else.'

She nodded. 'Well, good luck, Leah. Just try to put this behind you, okay?'

I watched her drive off, knowing I would face my fear and make that statement to the police. Then perhaps I would finally be free.

Walking up the path to Mum's front door, I wondered if karma really was a possibility. And then I decided right then that I wouldn't, couldn't allow myself to believe it. Not any more.

CHAPTER THIRTY-THREE
2003

High Elms Lane. It has a nice ring to it. It sounds like the kind of road wealthy people live, where there is a sense of community, of people sticking together. I've never thought of that before.

I keep my eyes fixed on the road, ignoring Imogen's attempts to draw me into their conversation. I no longer hear what they're talking about. I'm too busy being overwhelmed. The past catching up with me. Any second now the school will appear to the right of us, and with it will come a thousand memories I want to cherish. They are not to be forgotten or dismissed. They won't be tainted because they are all from before. When it was just the four of us. And now, I can rewrite those memories and pretend Adam wasn't obsessed with Miss Hollis. That makes for a much better memory.

In the back seat, the others don't seem to notice where we are; they are giggling and their chatter grows louder, no doubt fuelled by the alcohol they have consumed tonight. When did they start drinking? Were they all together the first time alcohol passed their lips? There are so many things I don't know about the nineteen-year-old Imogen, Corey and Adam. So much they don't know about me.

I think they want it back. Our friendship, I mean. That's what tonight has been about, hasn't it? It's only natural that Adam remains a bit distant; after all, he always was, even at the best of times. But perhaps in time that could change. I could never be his girlfriend again, and not just because he has someone else now. Mione. No, too much has happened for that to ever be a possibility.

I glance in the rear-view mirror and I notice Adam is relaxed now, the smile I rarely saw when we were together back on his face. I tell myself maybe I have something to do with that. Maybe.

Imogen has craned her head around so that she's facing the two of them in the back, and I notice she keeps reaching forward to touch Corey's arm. It is sweet that they are still so in love. They were always meant to be, I think. Nothing that happened affected their relationship.

We approach the school and I slow down to glance at the place we were last happy together. It hasn't changed, but it's different seeing it from behind a car window rather than from the pavement. Different knowing we have walked those paths for the last time. I will never sit on the art block steps waiting for Imogen or Adam again.

I can almost see the ice-cream truck that never failed to turn up, summer or winter. And I can hear the shrieks and yells of excitement that represented freedom to stuff our faces without parents telling us we're ruining our dinner, freedom from constraints for another evening.

Once more I look in the rear-view mirror; they still haven't noticed where we are. I switch off my thoughts as if I'm turning off a radio so I can listen to the others for a moment. The others. I have not thought of them as that for a long time.

They are talking about a party they're going to next week. Some girl called Karen, who is a friend of Imogen's, is throwing it, and they're expecting it to be wild. Corey is telling Imogen she shouldn't wear that denim skirt again, the one that is more like a belt, and Adam laughs his agreement.

'Anyone would think you're trying to pull someone else, Imogen,' he says, nudging Corey.

'Shut up!' Imogen says, but she is laughing too. 'You're right, though, it is a bit short.'

And then they are planning where to meet and what time they should get there.

'We don't want to be too early, let the losers turn up first!'

Living in the present and future is more important than reliving the past.

They are so engrossed in each other that nobody has noticed the car is practically at a standstill. Turning to the side window, I take one last look at our place.

I slam my foot down, with such force I think my ankle will snap, and we all lurch backwards. I press harder and the car gathers speed, the engine growling. Staring at the speedometer, I watch the hand creep up. Fifty. Sixty. Seventy. Ignoring the gasps and pleas to slow down – a mixture of voices, I can't tell who is saying what – I keep the weight of my foot on the accelerator. Eighty. Ninety. A hundred.

It's now or never.

I maintain this speed for a moment then swerve the car to the left, sending everyone slamming against the doors with heavy thuds.

My timing is perfect because now the tree is in front of us, it's huge trunk solid and thick, and it feels as if it is careering towards us, rather than the other way around. It is coming for us.

I close my eyes and wait for karma to take us all.

LETTER FROM KATHRYN

Thank you so much for choosing to read *The Girl With No Past*. Your support is much appreciated and I hope you enjoyed the book as much as I enjoyed writing it. I particularly hope you were taken by surprise by the twists and turns.

If you did enjoy the book, I would be extremely grateful if you could take a few moments to leave a quick review on Amazon. It is always great to hear what readers think and it can also help others discover my books. Any recommendations to friends and family are also very welcome!

I love hearing from readers so please feel free to let me know what you thought via Twitter or my Facebook page. You can even contact me directly through my website.

To make sure you don't miss out on my forthcoming releases you can sign up to my mailing list at my website link below.

Thank you again for all your support – it is greatly appreciated.

Kathryn x

www.bookouture.com

www.kathryncroft.com

twitter.com/katcroft

www.facebook.com/authorkathryncroft